THE CHOSEN

THE
CHOSEN

TARAN MATHARU

SQUARE
FISH

FEIWEL AND FRIENDS
NEW YORK

SQUARE
FISH

An imprint of Macmillan Publishing Group, LLC
120 Broadway, New York, NY 10271
fiercereads.com

THE CHOSEN. Copyright © 2019 by Taran Matharu Ltd.
All rights reserved. Printed in the United States of America.

Square Fish and the Square Fish logo are trademarks of Macmillan and
are used by Feiwel and Friends under license from Macmillan.

Our books may be purchased in bulk for promotional, educational, or
business use. Please contact your local bookseller or the Macmillan Corporate
and Premium Sales Department at (800) 221-7945 ext. 5442 or by email at
MacmillanSpecialMarkets@macmillan.com.

Library of Congress Control Number: 201855555

ISBN 978-1-250-25100-8 (paperback)   ISBN 978-1-250-13871-2 (ebook)

Originally published in the United States by Feiwel and Friends
First Square Fish edition, 2020
Book designed by Eileen Gilshian
Square Fish logo designed by Filomena Tuosto

1   3   5   7   9   10   8   6   4   2

To my readers, for all your support.
This book could not have been written without you.

THEY WATCHED FROM THE SHADOWS. Watched the people of the world going about their lives, unaware of the insidious gaze that followed.

So many candidates to choose from. Such potential.

But still, they hesitated. For this would likely be the last of their contenders, and it would not do to hurry. So, they waited. Brooded.

Until they were sure.

A boy. Unremarkable in so many ways, yet somehow ideal for the contest he would soon be doomed to enter. His mind held the knowledge to appreciate their game. Understand it. Perhaps even . . . win it.

He might very well die at the first hurdle. But he had the potential for greatness.

Yes. Him.

They chose: *Cade Carter.*

CHAPTER
1

Place:Unknown
Date:Unknown
Year:Unknown

THE CREATURE CIRCLED BELOW CADE LIKE A SHARK AROUND a sinking ship. It leaped for him, its jaws snapping just below the narrow ledge he stood on. He shuffled back, pressing his shoulders into the cold stone of the canyon wall. There was an eight-foot drop to the ground, and the bare earth had been churned to a thick sludge by the pacing of the monster beneath him.

It knuckled the ground with sinewy arms, growling at him like a dog fighting over a bone. The beast was already caked thickly in mud, and the rusty brown leather of its skin blended well with the rock formations Cade had woken among just a few hours ago. A slavering mouth gaped, the long needle points of its teeth glistening with saliva. But it was its eyes that scared him the most: twin spheres of obsidian that bulged from its sockets.

The opposite wall of the canyon was perhaps a stone's

throw away from him, stretching up into the sky and casting the ravine Cade occupied in shadow. He was perched on a rock shelf, just above a narrow corridor of earth that formed the canyon bottom. The gully continued to his left and right, stretching in both directions to form a rough passage that curved out of sight, though he doubted he'd manage to run far before the creature tore him to shreds.

As he watched, the monster began to claw at the rock face, perhaps hoping it would crumble and send Cade plummeting down. Maybe if he remained still, it would give up and move on in search of easier prey. He ignored it, trying to figure out how he had ended up in this sorry mess.

The last thing Cade remembered was lying in his bed at his new "school for troubled youths," staring out of the locked windows at the moonlit sky. His thoughts had been tinged with misery at the time.

The stash of stolen laptops his trust-fund roommate had hidden beneath his bed. The arrest, the police interrogation. His court-appointed lawyer, who could barely remember his name. His mother, crying, and the confusion and shame in his father's eyes.

The ultimatum the judge had given him. One year of "alternative" school, or Cade would be sent to a juvenile detention center. His parents had agreed, though it devastated them to know his chances of being accepted to a top university would be ruined. That was six months ago now. Six more to go.

And then he wasn't in the dorm anymore.

It had been too immediate for him to be dreaming. One moment he was looking at the moon, and the next he was standing on a ledge in the depths of a rocky canyon. Before he could give this surreal turn of events more thought, the creature had appeared, slinking out from behind the boulders in the narrow passage that ran along the bottom of the chasm.

He was pressed against a rock wall covered in a fine red powder, but beneath that there was little purchase for climbing. It was smooth like marble, with the orange glow of what he assumed was the setting sun visible in the swath of sky forty feet above him.

And it worried Cade that the sun was setting. He had never tried to sleep standing up before, and the ledge was too thin for him to lie down. But if he sat and dangled his feet over the edge, he would be within reach of the monster below. This situation didn't seem to have a happy ending.

It also didn't help that a jagged rock was pressed uncomfortably into his spine. Just his luck, the rock wall was smooth everywhere but the space he had to lean against. He decided that if these were to be his last moments, they might as well be comfortable. The ledge extended a few feet across, so he shuffled to his left.

He winced as his movement agitated the creature, its low growling turning to yelps of excitement as it jumped at him. Its thick black nails scrabbled at the rock, trying to find a toehold so it could reach the thin ledge.

Each time Cade looked below, he felt the bile rise in his throat. He was trying to think clearly despite the frantic pulse of his heart in his temples. It was all he could do to stop himself from hyperventilating.

Cade took a deep breath and turned his head to the side.

The protrusion was a black stone embedded in the wall, tapered to a rough point. It seemed out of place, a drop of sable in the sea of rust.

He slid his right hand up and took hold of it, if only to help anchor him to his perch. But the edges were so sharp that if he gripped it any harder it would likely slice into his palm. The stone wiggled slightly as he pulled, and the tiniest hint of hope entered Cade's mind, though he wasn't sure what he would do with it yet.

It only took him a few minutes to lever it from its root in the wall. It was almost relaxing to fixate his mind on such a simple task. When the rock came loose, a fine shower of dust settled on the creature's head, leaving it sneezing and coughing.

The rock seemed to be made from volcanic glass, shaped like a teardrop. The thicker end was caked in dust, allowing Cade a firm grip at the base. The tapered end was smooth with a chipped, rough-hewn edge. Stranger and stranger. It looked for all the world like a Stone Age axe.

Cade banged the rock against the wall, trying to make a dent, a handhold. More dust rained down on the monster, who pawed at its eyes, snorting. Cade smiled and continued, the crack of stone against stone echoing from wall to wall. The shower of dust became an avalanche of debris.

Cade laughed aloud, scraping his arms up and down as if he were making a snow angel, the gritty dust sticking to the sweat on his neck. Soon the marbled walls were bare and smooth, revealing a surface of light brown stone beneath.

His entertainment was short-lived. Beneath, the creature

rubbed itself back and forth in the mud and was soon rid of the irritant. A long, forked tongue slipped out of its mouth and licked at its eyes like a lizard, clearing away the film of dirt.

It was a disgusting monster, looking for all the world as if a mad scientist had spliced the skeletal structure of an ape into the body of a primordial deep-sea fish. Where this abomination had come from, Cade couldn't even begin to guess. But the question of what it was didn't matter at that moment. All he wanted was to get away from it.

His fun with the powder over, Cade considered throwing the rock at the creature. Perhaps the blow would send the beast scurrying away and he could make a break down the corridor in the opposite direction.

It was then that he noticed the pile of dust that had gathered on the ledge around his feet. And the shadows of a new idea formed in his mind.

But even as the plan formed, he cast it from his thoughts. It was a stupid idea; the monster would tear him to pieces.

An hour later, his legs began to cramp up. He tried standing on one leg at a time, but that just made it worse for the other. Crouching had helped, but it had forced him to lean precariously over the empty space, leaving him off-balance, much to the excitement of the creature below. It was sitting and staring like a starved hunting dog, only stirring when Cade moved himself.

He was exhausted, thirsty, and terrified, knowing eventually he would have to jump off and meet his fate. There was no rescue party coming, that seemed obvious.

But if he was going to die, it would be on his own terms.

He was going to give this monstrosity the most difficult meal of its life. Cade placed his foot behind the dust piled on the ledge, terror throbbing through his body with each pounding beat of his heart. He had no choice. No other options.

"I hope you choke on me!" he yelled. The creature looked up, startled by his voice. He kicked the dust, sending a spray of red into its eyes. Before he could even see what effect it had, he jumped.

He landed awkwardly, jarring his ankle on the ground, shooting pains flaring up his leg. So much for his hope of outrunning the beast.

It had covered its face with its clawed hands, and Cade swung his rock, letting out a garbled scream of fear and revulsion. His blow glanced off the monster's head, poorly aimed and with little weight behind it. Still, the creature rolled away from him, yowling in pain.

For a moment Cade stared at the rock, surprised at his own daring. Fear pulsed through him, the reality of life and death hitting home for what felt like the very first time.

Even as he prepared to run, the beast sprang, slamming headfirst into the wall next to him. Cade tumbled onto his back. The creature was still blinded by the dust, grasping for him as it hissed its displeasure.

He scrambled away, slipping and sliding in the mud, horror choking him. The monster heard the slap of his feet and lunged again, this time landing just beside him. Cade bellowed and flailed the rock, his vision filled with needle teeth.

The sharp tip of the stone sliced deep into the creature's foot, pinning it to the ground before the beast wrenched itself free with a squeal of pain. Its tongue darted over its face, and Cade readied himself, even as the inky black eyes fixed upon him once more. The creature took a tentative step forward, then yowled as it put pressure on its injured foot.

Slowly, ever so slowly, Cade backed away from it. When the creature turned its tongue to the bloody wound, he ran.

Ran through the agony of a twisted ankle, fueled by the adrenaline pumping through him in wave after wave of fear. On and on, down the gully, high walls looming on either side. It was only when he stumbled and fell that he stopped, waiting for the monster to give chase at any moment.

Cade shuddered, inhaling with deep sobbing breaths. Finally, when he had calmed, he was able to think once more.

The beast seemed to have given up on him, for now at least.

So he limped on, gripping his hand axe as if it was his lifeline.

Perhaps it was.

CHAPTER
2

6 months earlier

CADE SHUFFLED DOWN THE LINE OF BOYS IN THE CAFETERIA, careful not to meet anyone's eye. He could feel them watching him, their gazes sweeping up and down, seeking weakness.

What they would see was a skinny, light-skinned Indian kid, though they wouldn't know his father was white.

Not short, but not tall either, with amber eyes and wavy hair, cut in a tight-back-and-sides cut. A military cut, one that he hoped would make him look as tough as all the other "troubled youths" at the school with him.

Lucky for him, he had no glasses or smattering of acne to give away the inner nerd hiding just beneath the surface.

He tried to convince himself he looked no more vulnerable than the other teens he'd seen at intake that day. Yet, try as he might, he could not keep the cafeteria tray from shaking in his hands.

His blue uniform itched. It was the "therapeutic" boarding school uniform, though it felt more like a prisoner's to him. Looking at the high walls outside the facility, he couldn't see much difference.

"What you want?"

Cade looked up at the snaggle-toothed kid in front of him, a hairnet on his head, ladle in hand. Cade pointed at the mashed potatoes, peas, and what he assumed was meat loaf, and the kid dutifully slapped them onto his tray.

The cafeteria reminded him of the gymnasium at his old school, but there were no basketball hoops on the walls here. Only straight-backed drill sergeant–like counselors, their eyes scanning the tables.

Cade quickly realized he should have been planning where he was going to sit. Most of the tables were full, and the air filled with the loud banter of kids who knew each other well. How could he sit down in the midst of all that?

Cade hesitated, searching desperately for somewhere neutral to sit. There were no empty tables, but he spotted a kid he recognized from the intake. A gangly, pockmarked guy who had cried silently through it all as the counselors shouted at them to face the wall and shuffle sideways toward their rooms.

The kid was sitting alone on one end of his table, while a trio ignored him on the other. Cade realized he had taken too long to find a seat. He didn't want to look intimidated, even if he was.

Adrenaline coursing through him, he walked the gauntlet of tables, his ears filled with the shouts, laughs, and belches of the guys on either side. It felt like an eternity before he reached the other newcomer, who startled as Cade dropped his tray opposite him.

Cade nodded, then turned to his food. He soon realized yet another mistake. He'd left his cutlery behind.

"Damn," Cade muttered under his breath.

He had to go back. He went to stand, but suddenly a plastic spoon clattered onto his tray.

Cade looked up.

"Cade," he said.

"Jim." The kid gave him a tentative smile.

Cade felt himself relax, and he dug into his mashed potatoes with the spoon. They were watery and unseasoned, not to mention that Cade wasn't hungry. He ate regardless.

An awkward silence filled the space between the two.

"Why'd your parents put you here?" Cade blurted, the words spilling from his mouth before he could stop them. Was that rude to ask? It was too late now.

Jim looked up, surprised.

"I . . . a lot of things," he began. He paused, looking shamefacedly at his tray. "But the last one did it. I threw a party," he finally said. "Our place got wrecked. My parents didn't like *that.*"

Cade gulped. "Sorry," he muttered. He racked his brain, trying to think of something else to say. Instead, he filled his mouth with another spoonful of bland mush.

"Well, hello there." Cade felt a hand clasp his shoulder, and his heart sank.

Here we go.

"Making friends already?"

Cade looked up, taking in the new arrival. He had a shaved head, with cool blue eyes and a pout to his full lips.

Cade's heart sank even further as he took in a bruise on the boy's cheek and scabs on his knuckles. The kid had been fighting. Cade had never been in a fight in his life.

Fear seized his throat, even as he searched for an appropriate answer. Any words would come out in a croak, so he remained silent.

"Nothing to say?" the boy said, taking a seat beside Jim, as another kid plonked his tray down beside Cade.

Cade turned and felt his heart thundering in his chest. The other kid was heavyset, with small piggish eyes and the beginnings of patchy stubble on his ruddy cheeks.

It was only then that Cade realized that the first guy was talking to Jim, not him. This made him feel a bit better, but the relief dissipated in an instant as the ruddy kid beside him cleared his throat, then licked his spoon purposefully, making sure Cade was watching. Cade felt his stomach twist as the boy reached over and dug it into Cade's meat loaf.

"You were just making introductions, right?" the newcomer next to Jim said, shifting unnecessarily close to him. "You're Jim, he's Cade. Aren't you going to ask our names?"

"Wh-what's your name?" Jim stuttered.

"I'm Finch, and this here is Gobbler," the first guy replied. "We call him that on account of his appetite."

Gobbler stuck his spoon into Cade's mashed potatoes demonstratively before slopping them into his mouth. He chewed loudly before going in for more.

"You're new, and we didn't want you starting off on the wrong foot," Finch said, putting a conspiratorial arm around Jim. He had pitched his voice to a stage whisper so that Cade could hear.

"This guy, he's not right for you. Apu here can sell you a candy bar at his convenience store, but he's not your friend. Get what I'm saying?"

He tightened his grip around Jim's shoulders, and the boy stared down at his plate, avoiding Cade's eyes.

Cade felt the anger rise in him, like hot bile. Apu . . . from *The Simpsons*. He had been dismissed by this boy like some caricature, to be ignored. Avoided.

But the fear that had kept him silent before remained, and all he could do was grit his teeth.

"You should sit with us," Finch said, placing a hand on the back of Jim's neck. "Like, now."

Cade could see the wheels turning in Jim's head, calculating the risk of turning Finch down. Then he gave a nod, his shoulders hunched.

Finch looked up at Cade, his lip curling with disdain.

"Go find somewhere else to exist."

Cade stood, but when he went to pick up his tray, Gobbler slammed a palm down on top of it.

"Leave it," Finch snapped.

Cade felt the blood rush to his cheeks. Fear and anger twisted in his stomach like a coiled snake. His last school hadn't been like this.

Oh, he'd experienced racism before. The disapproving stares when his mother and father went out together. The "random" selections at airport security. But nothing like this.

For the briefest moment he wanted to stand up for himself. Wasn't that what people said you should do with bullies? But this was a new school. He wasn't that guy.

Finch placed his clenched fists on the table, then looked up at Cade with an anger in his eyes that Cade could hardly believe was possible.

"I think he wants to say something, Finch," Gobbler mumbled through a mouthful.

But Cade didn't.

Instead, he hurried away, even as shame at his cowardice sent blood rushing to his cheeks.

CHAPTER
3

Place:Unknown
Date:Unknown
Year:Unknown

IT HUNG IN THE AIR IN FRONT OF CADE LIKE A GLAZED SHEET of glowing glass. An opaque barrier bisected the chasm, disappearing into the red-dust walls on either side and extending up to their summits.

Cade had almost run into it, for it had appeared suddenly in front of him, stopping him in his tracks.

He had been staring at it for the past few minutes, steeling himself to touch its surface. There was no other way out—the creature lay in the other direction.

Cade tried not to ask himself what the barrier was, or who had created it and why. He just needed to get as far away from the injured creature as possible. It could be following him, even now.

He extended a trembling finger and prodded the sheet as if it were a sleeping giant. The barrier was smooth. Smooth and chilly, like wet-slicked ice; as soon as he put pressure on it, his finger slipped to the side. It was strange to the touch, and he pulled his hand away, inspecting his finger for frostbite. But his fingertip wasn't even cold.

Suddenly, as if it had never been there at all, the barrier was gone.

"What . . . the . . . hell?" Cade said slowly, waving his hand through where the wall had been.

This was too strange. He tried to stay calm, think logically, even as his heart raged in his chest. He had no choice but to follow the path; see where it led.

Cade rounded a shallow bend and saw that the passage widened ahead. He stopped, confused. Rubbed his eyes, looked again.

The chasm ahead of him appeared almost exactly like the area he had started in. The same ledge—the same rocky outcrop opposite.

Had he gone in a circle? But the path he had taken was relatively straight. There was no way this was possible.

Stranger still, the wall above the ledge was caked with dust, and the same kind of rock he'd used as a hand axe was there too, protruding like a black jewel. This was all the same . . . but somehow different. As if the entire area had been sculpted to the same exact design as where he had been before. But how was that even possible?

He heard a bellow. Loud and far off, like a wounded bull. Only—it sounded human.

Cade didn't think. Instead, he hurried in its direction, cursing the twisted ankle that sent shooting pains up his leg. The yelling only got more frantic as he neared it, but he didn't care.

Anything was better than being alone in this desolate hellscape.

Then he saw them. Another monster, crouched in front of a tall kid, his back against another slick barrier like the one Cade had seen before. He wore only his underwear, using his uniform as a matador's cape in one hand, his other in a balled fist.

Strangest of all, Cade recognized him, even in the shadows of the chasm. The pale blond hair was unmistakable, as were the broad, muscled shoulders. Eric. Another kid from his school.

If Eric had seen Cade, he gave no sign, instead punching at the beast's face as its claws tangled in the cloth. As he did so, the creature darted forward, and the boy barely managed to evade its snapping fangs.

Cade wanted to turn back, but he knew that once the monster was done with Eric, it'd be after him. His best chance at defeating it would be when it was distracted.

So he charged, his heart pounding as he held the hand axe high.

Ten steps away.

Five.

He slipped in the wet mud, slamming onto his back. Ahead of him, the monster spun with a screech, its black eyes narrowed. It leaped onto him, and Cade lashed out, yelling with fear and desperation.

His hand thrust into its open gullet, the length of the hand axe all that stopped the teeth from clamping on his wrist.

The creature choked and screeched, its claws sinking into

his chest, the points breaking the skin. Blood ran down his arm, the stone's tip slicing the roof of the beast's mouth. Desperate, Cade kicked out, and the creature reared up, wrenching the stone from its maw.

Cade swung blindly, screaming as the monster's head whipped toward him. But the bite never came. Instead, the beast was yanked back, blood-flecked saliva spattering his face as it choked, crooked claws grasping at its throat.

Eric had whipped his uniform's belt around the beast's scrawny neck, and now he heaved on it, falling to his knees.

Cade watched as Eric's knuckles whitened, tightening the loop of leather as he pulled back on both ends. The monster's black eyes bulged as if they might burst from their sockets. Then there was a snap, and the eyes glazed over in death.

For a moment they remained that way, Cade panting on the ground, Eric holding the creature upright, the belt still in his hands. Then he let it fall, and stood. He kicked the corpse derisively and looked at Cade.

"Thank you," Eric said.

Cade stared back. It was the first time he had ever heard Eric speak. Not in the entire six months he had known him.

Eric had kept to himself, back at school, and most of the other kids were too scared to approach him. There were even rumors that he had killed someone. Cade only knew his real name because a teacher had said it in class once.

"You're . . . you're welcome," Cade stuttered as Eric helped him to his feet.

Eric craned his neck to see the back of his shoulder. Cade saw furrows in his flesh where the monster had managed to catch him with its talons. The marks didn't seem too deep and had already started crusting over, leaving a trail of dried blood down his back. Eric winced as he prodded at them with a large finger.

"It was fast," he said, kicking his downed opponent again. "I didn't think I had a chance."

Cade nodded dumbly as Eric fished his uniform from the muddy ground and began to put it on.

It had been clever to use the uniform to tangle the monster's claws. As a result, the top half had been shredded, so Eric tied the arms in a knot around his waist, remaining bare chested.

For a moment they stood there awkwardly.

"You're from school too," Eric finally said.

"Yeah," Cade said, holding out his hand.

"Eric," Eric replied, smiling at the formality. "You're Cade, right?"

Cade nodded, and Eric's big hand enveloped Cade's as they shook.

It was strange only to introduce himself now. They'd been in the same classes and sat near each other for so long.

"You know what this place is?" Cade asked, hopeful.

Eric shook his head.

"Maybe we're dead," he mumbled.

"Like . . . there was a fire or something?" Cade asked. "We died in our sleep?"

"Yeah." Eric shrugged, bending down and unraveling the belt from around the monster's neck. "Maybe this is hell, and this is one of the devils. It looks like a demon to me."

Cade stared at it, his gaze skipping from its translucent needle teeth to the inky black eyes.

"Its head looks like one of those deep-sea fish, you know? Like a viperfish, I think they're called?"

Eric shook his head, as if he'd never heard of them. "A viper." He shrugged. "As good a name as any."

He looked down the chasm where Cade had come from and gave him an inquisitive look.

"Any vipers where you woke up?"

"I fought one off," Cade said. "I hope that was all of them."

Eric looked impressed, even a little disbelieving, but Cade felt no pride at what he had done. It had been a desperate, frantic affair. He didn't like remembering how close he had come to death.

"Glad you can hold your own," Eric said, patting Cade's shoulder. "I underestimated you."

Cade winced as he was knocked forward, knowing Eric was just being nice. The kid was as strong as a bear, and built like one too, in stark contrast to Cade's lean frame.

Yet Cade couldn't decide if he was lucky in finding Eric. He'd heard the rumors about Eric's past—and this kid would have no trouble overpowering Cade if he wanted to.

Still, he gave off more of a jock vibe than anything else, now that Cade had heard him speak for the first time. He had the build for football too.

Then, just like that, the barrier behind them winked out of existence.

Eric stared, then swiped his hand through where it had been before.

"Yeah," Cade said. "They do that."

For a moment he considered telling Eric about the hand axe, still embedded in the wall somewhere behind them—it could be useful after all. But even as he opened his mouth, he closed it again. Maybe giving a rumored killer a new weapon wasn't such a good idea.

Instead, he examined the canyon beyond. This time, the passage looked different, although he wasn't exactly sure if that was a good thing.

"I'm guessing there isn't a way out behind us?" Eric said, motioning the way Cade had come with his chin.

"I don't know," Cade said. "But there's a viper there."

"Then we head this way," Eric said, wrapping the belt around his fist. "Let's go."

CHAPTER
4

5 months earlier

CADE STARED AT THE LINED PAPER IN FRONT OF HIM WHILE the teacher's voice droned on. It was strange to be in class, in this place, but he supposed the school had to educate them beyond its constant exercises and marching drills.

They even had a uniform—the blue shirt and pants worn by most of the students. A far cry from the uniform he had worn at his old school: a striped tie, shirt, and blazer.

Still, Cade found it hard to concentrate. Life at this new school so far had been one that oscillated between moments of anxiety and mind-numbing, soul-crushing boredom.

This lesson was a prime example. With the teacher at the head of the small classroom, he felt safe enough. But he wasn't learning anything new. His expensive private school had been light-years ahead of what they were teaching here. The teacher was currently outlining the very basics of the American Civil War.

Cade wasn't going to let himself fall behind, though. They had each been provided with a shiny new textbook. The class hadn't even cracked it open that month—Cade was pretty sure many of his fellow classmates could barely read anyway.

He'd heard that the vast majority of juvenile delinquents were functionally illiterate, and knew that many of the kids here would classify as such, having been sent there by court order, like he had, or because they weren't a "good fit" in mainstream schools. It had seemed impossible when he'd first discovered that, but now he saw it in action, in front of his very eyes. The reality was startling.

The teacher rarely used the whiteboard, though Cade could see the faded remains of what looked like a half-dozen examples of the male anatomy someone had drawn there in permanent marker.

With nothing better to do, Cade was slowly reading the textbook from cover to cover, working through the exercises and questions inside. There was nobody to mark his work, but it distracted him from his boredom.

He made sure to sit at the back of the classroom so nobody would see what he was doing, and he always scrunched up his work and trashed it when the lesson ended. So far, he'd gone unnoticed. He was doing the same with his textbooks in other subjects, but in history, he was on the final pages.

History was his favorite subject, mostly because his father was a college history professor. In fact, it was Cade's high grades in history that had led to his being offered a scholarship to attend the private school.

Even with the grant, his parents struggled to make payments, but they always beamed with pride whenever Cade came home from the dorm each weekend. Of course, that had been before the incident.

Cade was finishing an essay on the Great Depression's impact on international politics when a throat was cleared in front of him. He looked up, and suddenly boredom was replaced with gut-wrenching panic.

Mr. Daniels was standing there, his hand outstretched. The teacher was a bearded giant of a man, with spectacles that seemed to have been stolen from a Harry Potter convention.

"This isn't personal time, Carter," Daniels said, tapping his foot. "You're supposed to be paying attention. Stop doodling and hand it over."

Cade hurriedly scrunched up his paper and handed it to him.

"Sorry, sir," he said, earning some laughter from the others. Nobody called the teachers "sir" here.

"Shall we have a look at Carter's artwork?" Daniels said, striding to the front of the class.

Cade felt sweat prickle his forehead.

"No," he whispered.

But Daniels was already flattening out the paper on his desk. He stared at it for a moment, and the guys in the front row craned their necks to see what it was.

"This is . . . ," Daniels began, his brows furrowed.

He glanced up at Cade with surprise, then swiftly swept it into the wastebasket.

"A letter home," Daniels said, shaking his head. "Maybe save that for rec time, Carter?"

"Yes . . . Mr. Daniels," Cade said, bowing his head.

He spent the next few minutes with his eyes fixed straight ahead, ignoring the curious stares of the other students around him.

It was pure, unadulterated relief when the bell rang, and Cade and the others lined up in the corridor outside the class-room. Teachers barked orders, but by now Cade knew the routine. He stepped into the tight, three-person-wide formation and began to march at their command.

That was how they always walked between classes, and soon they were left in the rec room, a crowded space full of noisy students and tables and chairs along with a television, foosball table, and several stacks of old comics.

Cade didn't spend much time here, though. It was a mine-field, where one wrong move could earn resentment from other kids and, by proxy, their friends. Usually he retreated to the library, a far quieter area. Given the choice between fear or boredom, he always chose the latter.

"All right, boys, let's have a look at Cade's letter home to Mommy," a voice called out.

Cade spun around in horror, only to see his essay being waved in the air by Finch. Gobbler swaggered beside him, his deep-set eyes daring Cade to provoke him.

Clearly, Finch had fished the paper out of the wastebasket in class. Already, a crowd had gathered around him.

Even as Cade made to leave, Finch unfolded the paper and cleared his throat as the others laughed and gathered to listen.

"Dear Mommy," he began in an exaggerated tone before turning his eyes to the writing at the top of the page. "The Black Friday stock market collapse of 1929 set off a global . . ."

He stopped, confused. The room fell silent, and Cade seethed with fear. This was far worse than Daniels reading it in class.

"Hold up," Finch said, scratching his head. "You were writing this . . . for fun?"

Cade snatched at the paper, but Finch held it out of reach.

"I'm just trying to learn," Cade replied. "Like everyone else."

"No, not like everyone else," Finch said, holding the paper higher as Cade jumped for it. "You don't see us writing this crap, rich boy."

The onlookers laughed, and Cade cringed. His parents had *never* been rich.

"I've seen you avoiding us, all high and mighty. You think you're better than us, Apu?"

Cade backed away with his palms raised.

"I'm just—I'm trying to get by, like everyone else," Cade said.

"Listen to him. 'Get by'?" Finch put on a pompous British accent, though Cade sounded nothing like it. "Why'd your parents send you here; you not clean your room?"

"Nah, man, he forgot to mow the lawn," Gobbler chimed in.

More laughter.

"I got done for grand theft," Cade snapped.

That shut them up. But even as he said it, he realized it was a mistake.

"Yo," another boy said, a pasty-faced boy. "Man thinks he's gangster."

"Watch out, boys." Finch laughed. "Apu here's a kingpin."

"King Apu," someone yelled.

"Bow to His Majesty," said another, bending in mock reverence.

Finch bowed too, letting the essay fall to the ground. Cade backed away, stuttering denials and shaking his head. Finally, Finch turned around, distracted by a shout from someone across the room. It was his turn on the foosball table. Just like that, the crowd began to disperse, the afternoon's entertainment seemingly over.

Cade fought back bitter tears and sought refuge somewhere else. He couldn't leave—most of the onlookers were now leaning against the wall by the door. But there was a line of ragged armchairs up against one wall. Usually these were occupied, but today they were mostly empty, perhaps because of the kid sitting among them, reading a magazine.

Eric. He ate alone, and spoke to nobody, not even during rec time. He simply glowered at anyone who came near him, and few did.

After all, he was a veritable giant, lifting weights in the gym and standing several inches above Cade's own five-foot-eight frame. No one wanted to mess with him.

At this point, Cade didn't care. He threw himself into the seat farthest away from the boy. Only, instead of glaring, Eric gave him a level look. Was that sympathy in his eyes? Before Cade could decide, Eric turned back to his reading.

Cade was glad to have not annoyed him, but even so, his hands shook with frustration. King Apu. His new nickname.

Someone tapped his shoulder. Cade looked up, preparing himself for another barrage of insults, but instead found himself face-to-face with a short, stout kid with glasses so thick they looked like the bottoms of soda bottles. Cade knew him by his nickname: Spex, though he knew from the teachers calling on him that his real name was Carlos. He held out Cade's essay.

Cade took it and stuffed it into his pocket.

"Thanks," he muttered.

Spex sat down next to him. Even the librarians called him that, and Cade often saw him reading the same book: *Guinness World Records.*

Cade wondered why he'd come to talk to him. After this, nobody would want to be caught dead with him. But then, he'd seen Finch haranguing Spex too.

"You're really here for grand theft?" Spex asked.

"Yeah," Cade said. "Doesn't mean I did it."

Spex nodded contemplatively. Cade hesitated, then finally found the courage to speak.

"My roommate stole a dozen laptops from my school. He must have kept them hidden under my bed, because the school found them during a room inspection. Called the police right away."

"Did you tell them it wasn't you?" Spex asked.

"I did. But my roommate's family was rich, you know? Donors to the school. Why would he steal the laptops? He didn't need the money. But me? A poor kid on a scholarship? I got expelled right away."

"That sucks, man," Spex said.

Cade had loved that school. Then the laptops had been found. Everyone had believed it so . . . easily. Nobody expressed surprise. Their assumptions about him had been lurking just beneath the surface.

"The police said they found my fingerprints all over them," Cade went on. "And stupid me, I believed them. You know the police can lie to get a confession?"

Spex shrugged.

"My parents tried to fight it, but they were in shock. Couldn't believe I might have done something like this. They told me to do whatever the lawyer said," Cade went on. "Only that crappy, overworked public defender couldn't be bothered to take it to court. He said if I pleaded guilty, the judge would take pity on me."

Cade cringed at the memory of it.

"The laptops were expensive—it was grand theft, a felony. So the judge said I had to come here for a year, or he'd send me to juvie."

Spex shook his head.

"Man, you got screwed. But hey, this place is better than juvie."

Cade nodded dully.

"What about you?"

"Forgot to clean my room." Spex winked, the gesture all the more noticeable behind his magnified glasses.

"Seriously?" Cade laughed.

It felt good to laugh. It felt like the first time he had done so in a long, long time.

"Nah," Spex sighed. "My parents are super religious, and I've been straying from"—he paused to crook his fingers into air quotes—"the path."

He shrugged.

"They'd been threatening sending me to this place for

years. If I missed church, it was, 'We're sending you to that boot camp.' Skip class—'boot camp.' Bad grades—'boot camp.' Never thought they'd do it. Then one night they catch me out with a girl, sneaking a beer in the park. And I thought it would be a good idea to run away for a few days after that."

Cade groaned in sympathy. "Worst. Idea. Ever."

Spex nodded. "I won't argue with you. Brazilian families, they can be judgmental, you know? I swear, half the time my parents were more worried about what my grandma would think than what *they* thought. And when I ran away, the whole family found out. Even back in Brazil."

He gave a long sigh and pushed his glasses up his nose.

"I went back home when I ran out of money, and that was the last straw."

Cade opened his mouth to speak again, but Spex was already on his feet.

"Maybe see you in the library sometime. Take care, Cade."

Then he was walking away, leaving Cade to his thoughts.

Cade didn't dare to hope Spex would hang out with him, at least not in public. But now Cade didn't feel quite so alone. Not a friend but . . . someone.

Someone who didn't hate him.

CHAPTER
5

```
Place:Unknown
Date:Unknown
Year:Unknown
```

THE PASSAGE WIDENED. ONE MINUTE THEY WERE SHUFFLING sideways through a tight corridor of rough-hewn rock, the next they found it falling away. Now they stood in a V-shaped opening, and beyond, an expansive plain of flat, white ground lay before them.

"Is this a salt flat?" Cade said, unable to take his eyes from the shimmering expanse. "I saw one in a documentary once."

It was almost identical to the one he had seen all those years ago, stretching endlessly into the horizon, the crystals that coated its surface glimmering in the dusk glow. The dry heat seemed to suck the very moisture from Cade's skin.

Cade turned as Eric grunted with surprise. They had walked out of one of three identical passages, all converging on the opening they now stood in.

"Look," Eric said, pointing at the wall on their left side.

To Cade's amazement there was a basin there, carved into

the rock itself, protruding from its wall like a shallow bathtub. As they approached, they saw the barest trickle of water seeping into the receptacle from the cliff above, and within, a still pool waited for them.

Both immediately began slurping cupped handfuls of the lukewarm liquid into their dry mouths, gulping it down until their bellies sloshed full to bursting, then drinking some more.

It was heavenly, and, for the briefest moment, Cade could think of nothing else. He hadn't realized just how thirsty he had been.

"Save some for us, would you?" a voice called from behind.

Cade spun, only to find himself looking at the gap-toothed grin of a scrawny ginger kid. He wore the same uniform, and he held a hand axe.

"I'm as thirsty as a hungover camel," the kid continued.

Beyond, Cade spotted a second kid peering at him from the shadows of the passage they had emerged from, another bloodied hand axe in his hand.

"Scott," the first kid said, giving Cade's hand a cursory shake before scooping up a handful of water for himself. "And this is Yoshi."

He leaned in conspiratorially and mumbled through a mouthful.

"But don't mention *Mario Kart*, okay? He doesn't like that."

Cade backed away as Scott dipped his head into the basin like a horse at a trough. He watched as the water level fell with each heave of his shoulders.

Yoshi approached, his face dark with foreboding—a grim contrast to the smiling Scott. Yoshi was new to the school, and

Cade knew little about him. His hair was thick, styled in a sweeping wave, with sharp cheekbones and a thin mouth beneath.

The boy sidled out of the shadows.

"'Sup," he said, giving Cade a curt nod before joining Scott at the water basin. By now, Eric had stepped aside too, and the large boy looked bemused at the new pair. Somehow, everyone seemed a whole lot calmer than Cade felt.

By the time the two were done, there was barely any water left, and Scott groaned and clutched his distended belly with mock exaggeration.

"So," he said, wiping his face with the back of his hand. "Any ideas how we got here?"

Cade looked at Eric, who shrugged, and said, "I think we're dead."

Scott slapped the hulking boy's back and laughed.

"The big dude speaks at last."

Cade remembered Scott now. Like Yoshi, Scott was new at the school. He'd been sent there for joyriding, or so Cade had heard. The kid was obsessed with cars.

But Cade didn't have time to search his memory for long. A bloodcurdling scream drifted from the third passageway, tearing Cade from his thoughts and setting his teeth on edge. A human scream.

Then, before he could even consider heading toward it, the same glowing wall that he had seen before appeared, blocking the three passages.

"Sounds like someone didn't make it," Eric growled, striding to the wall and pressing his fists against its surface. "The vipers got them."

Silence.

"You see the monsters too?" Scott finally said.

Eric gave him a slow nod.

"So, what's the verdict?" Scott asked. "Mutants? Monsters that go bump in the night?"

"Hell," Eric muttered, scooping up a handful of the reddish sand from the ground and letting it trickle through his fingers.

"He's a cheerful one." Scott winked. "Yoshi, any thoughts to add?"

Yoshi gave Scott a level look.

"No," he said, taking another sip of water.

Scott chuckled and turned to Cade, who shrugged and looked out at the salt flats again.

"Someone put us here," Cade said. "And someone built this place—the layout is the same down each passage, like identical movie sets. I think they're watching us. Why else go to all this effort?"

"A military exercise?" Eric asked.

"Maybe," Cade said, squinting at the horizon. "Maybe we're guinea pigs in some kind of experiment."

"So they knocked us out with gas or something in the dorm rooms," Yoshi said.

"I don't think so. I wasn't sleeping, I just . . . appeared here," Scott said. "And why this? A glowing force field, some creatures straight from a lunatic's nightmares, and putting us in a weird canyon they built to look real. Then giving us nothing but a rock to fight them with? What the hell kind of experiment is that?"

Cade shook his head. "The real question is, what do we do

now? There's water here, but it won't last us, even with that trickle refilling it."

"We'll go hungry too," Yoshi agreed. "We can't stay here."

"Oh right, let's go wandering around the desert," Scott said sarcastically. "Sure to be plenty of water and food there."

Cade gritted his teeth, glaring at the endless flats in front of him, as if he could force the answer of where to go next. And then . . . he saw it.

At first he thought he was imagining things, but then it happened again. A glimmer. Flashing, like a polished piece of glass spinning in the wind.

"There's something out there," he said, pointing at the horizon. If he squinted, he could just make out a few specs of black. Objects of some kind, or a trick of the light.

Eric walked to his side and peered into the distance.

"I see it," he grunted. "Something shining."

"Whatever it is, it's miles away," Scott grumbled.

"Well, we should finish the water and head for that," Eric said. "It's metal, maybe glass. That means civilization."

"Or a sniper scope," Scott said airily.

"Or a camera, filming us," Yoshi added.

"Whatever it is, we leave at sunrise tomorrow," Eric said. "Soon it'll be too dark to see where we're going."

"It's already night," Yoshi said. His voice was quiet, but the fear in his voice cut through Cade's thoughts like a hot knife. "We can leave now."

Cade turned, confused. Yoshi was staring into the sky.

"We need the light to see where that reflection is coming from," Cade said. "After sunset, we won't be able to see it."

Yoshi didn't respond, only continued to gaze upward and pointed with a trembling finger.

Cade looked up, and suddenly his knees seemed to buckle as he saw what was there.

A red-orange moon hung in the sky, casting the wan light that Cade had taken for the dim light of a sunset. A second, smaller moon floated in front of it, like a white baseball orbiting a basketball.

"That's . . . it's not—" Cade began, but his mind couldn't begin to form a reasonable explanation. He had to be dreaming. This was impossible.

"Yoshi . . . ," Scott said. "I've got a feeling we're not in Kansas anymore."

CHAPTER
6

3 months earlier

"Turn."

Cade turned sideways, and the counselor leaned closer with his flashlight. They were doing body checks on all the boys, making sure there were no unusual bruises. If they found injury or markings, it was a sign that they'd been in a fight. That meant punishments—if you didn't rat out who'd done it.

Cade couldn't believe that the adults didn't differentiate between fighting and a beatdown. How was it fair that if some boys jumped Cade, the counselors would punish *him* for getting beaten up?

Luckily, his strategy of keeping to himself had kept him mostly safe so far. He got bullied in passing, which had never happened at his old school, but here nobody hated him enough to risk being punished for attacking him.

It wasn't much of an existence, but it would be over eventually.

The counselor grunted with approval before moving on. They were in a barracks-style room, among wall-to-wall bunk beds. The place was cramped and smelled like a locker room, and he'd even seen mice scampering about. And the counselors only seemed to care about getting through the day and keeping the boys in check. Even the therapy sessions often devolved into sports talk.

He knew not all therapeutic schools were like this. In fact, he knew many of them were good places that helped troubled kids learn leadership and discipline.

He just didn't think this was one of them. Not to mention the fact that he knew he didn't belong here.

Cade had almost told his parents about the conditions at the school. But he didn't want to worry them, especially since they couldn't change anything. He didn't mention it on his weekly calls, or the few times they visited.

His dad hadn't visited him for two months. His mom said it was too painful for him, so she came alone the last time. Cade had asked her to stop coming so often. After all, when he had been at the private boarding school, he had seen his parents only a few times a year.

But now Cade couldn't forget the distrust in his father's eyes. The suspicion. The doubt. Before, they had been thick as thieves. Now . . . he didn't want to think about it.

"Nice chicken legs," said a kid standing behind Cade. "You got some spaghetti arms too, damn. Yo, guys . . ."

Cade swiftly tugged his uniform back on, and the kid gave up, his friends uninterested in mocking Cade's body. He'd always been thin and had already lost weight at the school, in part because Gobbler stole his food several times a week—and what he didn't steal, Cade rarely finished. The food here tasted terrible.

This was compounded by the exercises they did, seemingly endless push-ups, jumping jacks, and interval courses. Despite the exercise, he felt himself weakening. Drifting through the corridors like a ghost, careful not to be seen, not to be heard. He never spoke at their group therapy sessions—but then, few did.

A shout snapped Cade out of his reverie, and he suddenly saw two kids wrestling further down the room. The counselor had moved on to the rec room to check on the others.

It was typical. Scores were always settled directly after the body checks; it gave the best chance of any bruises to heal before the next inspection.

But this was more than a tussle, he realized. It was two on one, and Cade recognized all of them. Gobbler had pinned someone to the ground, and Jim was helping him, if somewhat reluctantly. And he'd know those glasses anywhere. They had jumped Spex.

"Get him up," Finch said, striding into view, a few of his cronies following.

Cade could see the reluctance on Jim's face, and in his body language. It was like he was trying to hold Spex without actually touching him.

"Heard you've been talking shit about me, Spex," Finch said as Gobbler hauled the boy to his feet.

"I didn't say anything, man. You got the wrong guy." Spex's chest heaved with fear, and his words were choked by Gobbler's thick forearm around his neck.

Finch tapped his chin. "Maybe."

He stared contemplatively at Spex, then his fist whipped forward, thudding into the boy's stomach. Spex doubled over as the breath whooshed out of him, followed by a mouthful of vomit.

For the briefest moment, Spex caught Cade's eye and, despite the pain, he motioned with his head, almost imperceptibly.

"Just in case," Finch said.

Cade knew what Spex wanted. He wanted Cade to get an adult. But that was taking a side. That was making a choice.

"Jim, get over here," Finch said.

Jim went to stand beside him, and Cade could see the terror on Jim's face.

"Hit him," Finch said.

Cade stayed hidden in the shadow of the doorway. The corridor was so close—the rec room just a few dozen feet away. He could do it. And yet he was frozen by indecision. By fear. He felt sickened with himself.

"He l-looks like he's had enough," Jim stuttered.

Finch laughed.

"He's faking," he said, lifting Spex's chin, drool dribbling from the boy's mouth. Spex was gasping like a beached fish, taking small, shallow breaths.

"Come on. Do you have my back or not?"

Jim hung his head, and Spex turned his face to Cade once more. Pleading with his eyes.

Cade knew why they'd picked Spex: he had no real friends to protect him. There would be no retaliation, only a small risk of intervention if a teacher came in. Finch was a cold, calculating bastard.

Now that Cade thought about it, it could easily have been him. They'd just spotted Spex first.

"You're with us, or you're with him," Finch said, moving closer and forcing Jim to meet his gaze. Now, Finch's face was an inch from Jim's, and Cade saw the boy's resolve waver.

Again, Cade glanced at the door, only to see another member of Finch's crew standing outside. A lookout. Cade doubted they would stop him from leaving, but they'd know who'd gone for help. Cade willed himself to move, but he stayed rooted to the spot.

"Come on," Cade urged himself under his breath. "Do it."

There was a slap. Cade saw the imprint of Jim's palm blazing red across Spex's cheek, and heard glasses clatter to the ground. Then a crunch as Finch stomped down, shattering them. Jim had made his choice. And Cade his.

"Good man," Finch said, clapping Jim on the back.

Gobbler left Spex to collapse to his knees, and the group filed out of the room, congratulating Jim.

"Oh, and Spex?" Finch called over his shoulder. "If you tell anyone about this, I will hunt you down. Blind you permanent."

Then they were gone, their laughter receding down the corridor.

Spex cradled the broken pieces of his glasses in his hands, blood bubbling on the corner of his mouth. Cade hurried over, picking up the pieces and placing them in Spex's hands.

"Cade?" Spex said, looking blearily up at him.

"I'm so sorry, Spex. There was a guy at the door . . . I couldn't."

"Yeah. Whatever," Spex said, touching the side of his

mouth. His lip was swollen. There was no hiding that. Serious punishments were meted out for fighting, and it would only be worse if Spex didn't tell them who else had been involved.

"You gonna tell?" Cade whispered.

"Nah," Spex said.

Cade hovered uncertainly. Spex wiped his chin and staggered to the nearest bunk.

"Can I . . . can I get you anything?"

Spex shook his head, staring at his broken glasses.

"Just leave me alone," he whispered.

Cade opened his mouth. Closed it.

Then he went back to his bed, staring at the names scratched into the metal slats of the bunk above him. There was nothing he could have done . . . right?

So why did he feel so guilty?

CHAPTER
7

Place:Unknown
Date:Unknown
Year:Unknown

HEAT. IT WAS ALMOST ALL CADE COULD THINK ABOUT. THE red moon and its smaller pale satellite had sunk below the horizon hours ago. But a sun, white and hot as Earth's own, had risen to replace them, turning the flat plane of white into a glaring, dry desert, and leaving the horizon shimmering with heat.

They were traveling blind, trudging endlessly in what Cade hoped was the right direction, aided only by the glimmering thing he might have seen, but what could well have been a mirage or his own desperate imagination. Their only bearings were their footprints trailing in a straight line, pointing away from the outcrop of rocks.

Stranger still was the sight of two outcrops, identical in size and shape, beside their own. Cade assumed there could be other people there, facing the exact same situation that they had.

It had been too hot to discuss investigating it. Only to acknowledge it and continue on.

"Is something out there, or am I seeing things?" Eric croaked, pointing with his uninjured arm. "The gleam?"

Cade looked up and squinted at the horizon once more. The view danced and shifted in front of his eyes, and before long, he had to close them and shade his face.

"I don't see anything," Cade replied, forcing each word through his parched throat.

"Maybe we should turn back?" Scott rasped. "Get one last drink in before we die. I'd prefer a Coke, but beggars can't be choosers."

"No," Eric said, stumbling past Cade. "It's there. I know it's there."

Cade didn't look up. He followed Eric's footsteps, concentrating on putting one foot in front of the other. It was more than likely a mirage, but there was no turning back. He'd rather die fast in the heat and have had a chance than slowly waste away in the shade.

Left. Right. Over and over, he stumbled forward, refusing to let his gaze stray to where they were headed. Not even when Scott let out a hoarse cry, and Eric turned his walk into a run. If he didn't look, it still might be real.

But something strange happened. The crystal-white ground had suddenly ended, and now he was walking on soil. Soil and dried grass.

Left.

Right.

Then a shout of surprise from Eric. Cade finally looked up, wincing at the self-inflicted crick in his neck. And gaped.

A corpse sat on the ground, hunched over like a monk in prayer.

It was practically a skeleton, though the skin still clung to its bones. It was a desiccated mummy, preserved by the arid heat of the desert. Scraps of red cloth hung from its body in a shroud, and a metal disk dangled from its neck on a leather braid, twisting in the faint breeze. It barely shone now, for the sun was behind it, but it was the only reflective surface he could see.

Cade had never seen a dead body before, and he choked back a gasp of horror. Bile rose in his throat, but he swallowed it back with some difficulty. He didn't want the others to see him puke his guts out.

"Who the hell is that?" Scott groaned.

"That's a good question," a voice called out.

Cade spun, elated to hear a new voice. The smile died on his lips before it had even begun.

Three new arrivals were toiling across the salt flats behind them, and they were the last people he wanted to see. Finch, Jim, and Gobbler.

Overheated and fatigued, Cade couldn't think, could only watch as the boys trudged closer. Of the three, only Finch appeared injured, with blood staining his uniform. Had they survived the same trials with the vipers?

"We followed you," Finch rasped, stopping a few feet away. "If you know what's going on, you'd better tell us."

Cade swallowed, trying to moisten his throat, but Finch continued before he could reply.

"Eric, Scott," Finch said, nodding his head at Eric with a modicum of respect. He ignored Cade and Yoshi and walked over to the corpse.

"Wait—" Cade began, but Finch snatched the metal disk from the fraying leather thong and peered at it.

"Gibberish," he growled, closing his fingers.

Cade's curiosity almost outweighed his fear of the boy. Almost.

"Well, now that we're all here, we'd better make a plan," Scott said loudly. "Unless we want to end up like our new friend here."

"We need to keep going," Yoshi said.

"Great idea," Finch said, clapping his hands slowly. "Think of that one all by yourself?"

Gobbler sniggered, but Yoshi didn't seem fazed. He simply stared at them with his dark eyes.

"So, you know what's going on?" Finch asked, directing his question to Eric.

Eric ignored him.

"Maybe these men did," Yoshi said, pointing ahead. More bodies, these ones half covered in salt and sand. Cade had almost missed them.

Cade took a few steps closer, giving Finch and his crew a wide berth. Jim may have been a party boy, but Finch and Gobbler were prone to unprovoked acts of violence.

Now that he looked around him, he could see that there were many more corpses, at least a dozen. But these looked different from the previous one. They wore faded, patterned pants and had been better preserved, perhaps due to the sand that half covered them. Cade felt his gorge rise at the sight of them for a second time, and once more he resisted the urge to throw up.

They were all emaciated, bearded, and hollow-eyed, but he could still see the dried blood from the wounds that had killed them. Not claw marks, at least not as far as he could tell, but instead what looked like stab wounds to their torsos. In fact, he saw what might have been an arrow sticking from one's shoulder, but he didn't want to get closer to check.

Still, even taking in all these details, the strangest part was their skin. They were pale, with a hint of yellowing from desiccation, but all were tattooed with strange whorls of blue, seemingly from their faces to their toes.

"Weird-looking bunch," Finch said, stepping over the body. "Come on, boys."

He swaggered on with a confidence that Cade thought had to be an act. Cade fell back with Eric, Scott, and Yoshi.

"You have a better plan?" Scott asked Eric with genuine interest. "You got us this far."

Eric gazed after the trio ahead of them.

"Better to stick together."

They caught up with the others, and as they moved away from the corpses, Cade took note of the ground. The area surrounding them was uneven, and made entirely of soil, scattered only with sand and salt. There were the remains of what had once been grass beneath his feet, roasted to a yellow crisp by the hot sun. Nothing like that should be able to grow here.

Stranger still, the area seemed to be formed in a perfect square, as if someone had built a giant soccer field in the middle of the desert. Had someone teleported a giant hunk of earth and dropped it on top of the salt flat? Just like he had been dropped on the ledge?

As they walked back onto the salt, more bodies appeared, these ones lined up in a row. They resembled the first—dressed in ragged red cloth and with no beards. If anything, it would appear that two opposing forces had done battle here—the blue-skins against the red-cloths. And the red-cloths had won.

"Well, that's not a good sign," Scott groaned.

"Somebody put all those bodies there," Cade said. "Laid them out. And look at the ground—it's all torn up." He could see footprints in the salt, like a cheap sandal might leave. "There were people here, a lot of them."

"Hey, check this out," Eric called

Cade walked around the bodies, and his heart leaped at the sight ahead. Among what looked like a pile of trash—bits of wood, scraps of cloth, and other detritus—were pots. Or vases. Whatever they were, they could be a sign of the one thing they needed most. Water.

They stumbled toward the pile like zombies, mesmerized by the sight. Cade lifted one of the vases by the handles on both sides and heard the slosh of liquid within.

"It's a freaking miracle," Scott yelled hoarsely, picking up one for himself. The top had been plugged by a cork, but Scott tore it out with his teeth and tipped the pot back, drinking its contents without so much as a sniff to check it.

He gulped for a few more seconds, then came up for air with a gasp.

"Too good to be true," he said, bringing it back up to his lips. The others rushed to collect their own, and Cade was thankful that there were more than enough to go around.

The next few minutes were spent in silence but for the

groans of relief and the guzzling of water. Cade could feel the life returning to his body with every mouthful. But with each sip, he couldn't help feeling uneasy.

It *was* too good to be true. Who would leave water here, in the middle of this desert, among rows of bodies?

This had been planned. The water, certainly. Maybe even the disk around that corpse's neck. It was like a test . . . a puzzle. And they were the guinea pigs.

If this *was* a puzzle, then Cade knew that every detail mattered.

He looked at the jug in his hands. It was a faded rust color, like the terra-cotta pots his mother used for plants. But older, like the containers he'd seen in museum trips his historian father had dragged him on. He'd learned there that they were called amphorae. The drinking vessels of the ancient world.

"What did the disk say?" Cade asked, his curiosity finally outweighing his fear of Finch. It could be a key piece to this puzzle, and he needed to see it.

Finch held his gaze for a moment, then shrugged. He tossed it over, smiling as it fell short and Cade had to scramble in the salt to get it.

Cade picked it up and stared down at the markings there. It was rough, the letters and numbers made up of holes punched through rather than genuine engraving. But the alphanumerics were clear as day, and they shocked Cade to his core. He stared, his mouth flapping open. It was the last thing he had expected to see.

"Maybe not so useless after all," Finch said, his piercing blue eyes boring into Cade's face. "Spit it out."

Cade let the token fall to the ground, trying to wrap his head around it. It had to be a trick. This all had to be a trick.

"I said spit it out," Finch snapped.

"It says . . . *Legio I X*," Cade said, spelling out the last two letters. "Then *Hispana*."

Finch stared at him blankly. Only Scott had any reaction at all, furrowing his brows as if trying to remember something.

"So?" he asked.

"It says he was a Roman soldier," Cade said, hardly able to believe his own words. "From the Ninth Legion."

CHAPTER
8

1 month earlier

CADE GASPED AND STAGGERED TO HIS FEET, NAUSEA ROILING through his stomach like a coiled snake.

"Again!" the counselor shouted. "Three more."

Down he went, flat on his belly, then up into the push-up position, an awkward hop into a crouch, and finally the jump straight into the air, his hands pointed at the sky.

Burpees, they called them, a terrible, full-body exercise that used his own weight against him. Cade had thought the name funny at first. It wasn't funny anymore.

"Down," the counselor barked. "Faster."

Cade went down.

It had been so stupid. Gobbler had tripped him up in the canteen, sticking out his leg when Cade walked past. Cade hadn't been looking, too focused on finding a table among the crowd.

Usually, he sat with Eric. Not beside him, but at the same

table. Even though Eric pointedly ignored Cade, he was safer territory than the others. Having somewhere to sit made Cade's life a little easier.

In any case, when Cade had fallen, he'd smacked his face on the floor. Just a minor bruise on his cheek, but the wardens had seen it later that day and threatened him with punishment if he didn't tell them who else had been involved in the "fight."

But the kids here didn't rat on one another—the code of silence was ubiquitous, and those who broke it were duly treated with contempt, even violence, by all if they were found out. Cade kept his mouth shut, and he was given a month on "punishment duty."

For the past four weeks, each lunch break and evening, he was put through his paces: push-ups, star jumps, and of course the dreaded burpees.

He'd do the interval courses at full tilt, only to be told to run back to the start and do it all over again.

The red-faced counselors would scream in his face for minutes at a time, daring him to do anything other than stare straight ahead, his body rigid and at attention.

One had bellowed their job was to break him down so they could build him back up again. But Cade didn't think he needed breaking, or fixing for that matter. Most of the students didn't.

A garbled voice came from the counselor's pocket radio, jarring Cade from his thoughts. The blood was pounding too hard in his ears for him to hear it.

"Two four," the man replied. "Sending him now."

Cade, suddenly able to stand still, swayed on the grass. Then, in a sudden bout of nausea, he puked.

"You're done," the counselor said, wrinkling his nose. "Now run back to your room, and I better not see you slow down."

Cade stumbled away, forcing himself into a half jog as he wiped his mouth. He watched the other boys, tossing around a ball out in the yard. Though he wouldn't have had the courage to ask to join in before, he still felt a pang of jealousy.

The counselors there had separated him from the others, just as they had done to Spex a few months earlier. It was a strange mix of detention and solitary confinement, with his meals brought to his tiny new room, and his evenings spent alone there too. The only time he shared with the other students was in class.

At the time, he'd scoffed at the punishment. Hell, he'd even wondered if he'd prefer it in there. Time to himself, away from Finch and the others.

Now, staggering back into his room, he hated being there. The drip, drip of condensation from the air vent was almost intolerable, yet it broke the heavy silence that had been his downtime for the past month.

Cade had thought he would be able to meditate. Write letters. Plan his life. But instead, his mind raced, endlessly. He couldn't calm it, even when he did his homework, such as it was. He could hardly sleep.

The regret over what had happened seemed to bounce around his skull, while anxiety squeezed his chest like a vise. His parents, loving though they were, had believed the school. The police. That it had been *him*.

That, in many ways, was the most painful part of all. The injustice of being falsely accused still hurt. It made him rage, at least in private. Scream into his pillow.

But though the judge had practically forced his parents to send him here, the way they had acted after the incident had not changed. Disappointment and resentment, as if he had let them down. When none of it had been his fault.

Still, he missed them. Punishment duty also meant no contact with parents. No calls, visits; even letters had to wait until after.

Cade's belly rumbled despite his recent vomiting, and he pushed away the angry thoughts. Food would be arriving soon. He ate later than the others, and the food was always cold when it was delivered.

The portions were at least generous—likely they scraped up the surplus of what was left in the cafeteria after the main meal. And there was no Gobbler to steal his meals.

In the midst of such misery, he had made a decision. That he would not let himself waste away. That he would stay healthy. They had taken his freedom, his joy. But they would not take away his body.

So, each day he ate all his food. His workouts, as he tried to think of them now, at least now served some purpose beyond punishment.

Already he was seeing results. He was filling out, and this time without that paunch around his middle. He had been in terrible shape before, in part due to the jalebis and other Indian sweets his mother used to send to him at boarding school.

Now, his stomach was flat and his chest wasn't. His arms

now had definition and didn't hang like a scarecrow's from the sleeves of his blue uniform. Even in that moment, he admired his new shape in the room's small mirror. No Hercules, but no scrawny beanpole either.

The door rattled, and Cade looked up, startled from his reverie. It swung open, creaking on its hinges. A teacher stood there.

"Come on," the man said.

"Am I going back to the dorm?" Cade asked, glad that punishment duty might be over with but sad to lose his private room.

"I said, come on," the man snapped. "I won't ask again."

Cade shrugged and hurried after him. It took a few more minutes of walking to see where he was going. Visitation. The small room where parents could see their kids.

Cursing the timing, Cade licked his hands and tried to fix his hair into some semblance of decency for his parents.

He was sweaty from the workout, and he knew he likely stank.

The teacher stood at the window in the visitation room, and Cade sat down on the ragged old sofa, his parents opposite. A coffee table scattered with leaflets of smiling kids lay between them.

He felt a mixture of joy and sadness fill him when he saw them. His father gave him a thin smile as he entered the room, but neither spoke until he had sat down.

"How are you, Cade?" his mother asked, putting a hand on his knee.

She seemed so tired. There were fresh lines on her face.

"I'm fine," Cade said, putting on a brave face. "I've been exercising. Want to see my guns?"

He lifted his arms and tweaked his bicep. She forced a smile at his cheesy joke, but Cade knew her heart wasn't in it. His father was no better—he looked haggard. Why didn't he say something? He just wanted to hear his dad's voice.

"We understand you've been fighting," his mother said.

"I tripped, that's all," Cade said quickly, hearing the worry in her voice.

She shook her head. "You don't need to lie, Cade."

Cade felt a flash of anger. The same anger he'd felt when his father had first spoken to him after he'd been arrested. Asked him if he'd done it.

"I'm not lying," Cade said, trying to keep his voice calm.

She sighed and looked away, as if holding back tears.

"How have you guys been?" Cade asked after a moment of awkward silence.

His father paused, and he saw his parents exchange a glance. It was only then that he noticed the distance between them. His father sitting behind her rather than beside her. The way she leaned away while he was speaking. They'd been arguing. He knew it.

"We're hanging in there," his father said, giving Cade a tight-lipped smile. "Talking to your old school, seeing if they'll take you back."

Cade took a deep breath, resisting the urge to let his temper run away with him.

"Don't waste your time," he said. "They think I did it."

"They said they might consider letting you go back, if we pay full price."

"Don't," Cade pleaded. "We can't afford it. And everyone there will treat me like a thief."

"Cade, we can't just give up on your education!" his father snapped. His mother flinched at the noise.

"What's done is done. Don't let it cost us any more," Cade said, ignoring the pain in his father's eyes.

"If you don't go back, what does your future look like?" his father asked. "You'd be lucky to get into a community college, let alone a top university. This isn't another few months, this is your whole life!"

"Shut up about that, all right?" Cade snapped back. "You think I don't know, you think I don't—"

Cade forced himself to calm, taking several slow breaths. He hadn't realized how angry he had become. He'd worked so hard at keeping his emotions hidden from the others, but now it was all spilling out on the people he loved.

Shame heated his cheeks, and he wiped the moisture from the corners of his eyes. What was he becoming?

"We're doing it," Cade's father said. "Soon as you get out."

"It's not like I can stop you," Cade muttered.

He sat there, staring at his hands, until his father cleared his throat.

"So," his dad said, avoiding Cade's eyes. "You must know why we're here."

Cade stared at him blankly. "Because you heard I was fighting?"

He saw his father take his mother's hand, and her pull it

from his grip. The sight was like a knife in Cade's heart. They wouldn't be arguing if it wasn't for him.

"No, Cade. It's about me," his mother said. "I'm not going to be visiting as often."

"You're not?" Cade's heart quickened.

"Didn't you get my letter?" his mother asked, and now he could see her anger too as she glared at the counselor behind them.

"I've been on 'punishment,'" Cade whispered. "Remember?"

His mother took in a sharp breath.

"What's happening?" Cade said quickly before she could ask about it.

"Money's been tight lately," she said. "What with the fine for the laptops, the fees for this place, I'm going back to work. It's full-time, and with the drive up here being so long . . ."

Cade felt his heart quicken in his chest. The visits were painful for him, true, but they were the only thing that reminded him of the outside world. That there was a life waiting for him, if he could only get through this.

And his mother, having to go back to work? She loved being retired. Had worked hard her whole life just so she could.

This was all his fault.

"We'll still call every week, okay?" Cade's mother said. "We love you."

Cade closed his eyes, trying to fight back the black wave of despair. This wasn't fair. None of this was.

Tears sprang up in the corners of his eyes, and he turned his face away. He couldn't let them see him cry.

"Love you guys," he whispered.

They had driven a long way to see him, but he couldn't bear it a moment longer. He stood and nodded to the counselor.

"Cade," his father called, his voice almost pleading.

He didn't look back.

CHAPTER
9

Place:Unknown
Date:Unknown
Year:Unknown

"IT'S A PRANK," CADE SAID. "IT HAS TO BE."

"What do you mean?" Finch growled.

Cade closed his eyes, trying to remember.

"The Ninth Legion supposedly went missing in the early second century, probably somewhere in modern-day Scotland," he said, thinking back to the long discussions he'd had with his father on the matter. "The theory goes that most of them were slaughtered in an ambush by the ancient Picts . . . who must be our tattooed friends in the ditch over there. It's one of the most famous historical mysteries ever."

"I've never heard of it," Scott said.

The others grunted in agreement.

"So you're saying this dead guy was a Roman soldier?" Eric asked.

"That's right," Cade replied. "Thousands of men, struck from the admittedly sketchy Roman record, but nobody could ever figure out why."

"And then they ended up here? Like us?" Jim wondered aloud. He earned himself a glare from Finch, as if even talking to Cade was a sin.

"Or that's what they want us to think . . . whoever *they* are," Cade muttered. "But it couldn't be. For one thing, this was almost two *thousand* years ago. Jesus was crucified less than a century before these guys were around—even a perfectly mummified body would be in way worse shape than those corpses are."

"So, what? This all some sort of joke?" Finch asked.

"I can't think of any other reason they'd put this here."

"Just to see how we'd react?" Finch said with a sneer. "You're saying someone's gonna pop up with a TV camera and shout 'surprise, we kidnapped you and flew you to a desert, and pitted you against some monsters that tore a bunch of you to ribbons, then we put some obscure historical prank here after you almost died of heat stroke, isn't that hilarious?' That's what you're saying?"

Cade shook his head.

"Maybe they were reenactors? Like they do with the Civil War?" he ventured. It seemed thin, but it was the best explanation he had.

"I don't give a crap what that thing says," Gobbler said. "All I know is I'm starving and there's nothing to eat but two-year-old, or two-thousand-year-old, dead dudes. We need to move on."

Finch stood and picked up an amphora, and his two sidekicks did the same.

"I say we keep heading in the same direction," Finch said. "You can follow us if you want."

He glanced at Eric as he spoke, ignoring Cade, Scott, and Yoshi. Then the trio left, lugging the water behind them.

Again, the others looked to Eric.

"He's right," Eric said grudgingly. "We should take as much water as we can carry—hopefully we'll come across more soon enough. I don't think whoever brought us here wants us to die of thirst in the middle of the desert. They have other plans."

"Sure," Scott said, picking up one of the containers. "They'd much rather watch us get eaten by a mutant. Makes for better entertainment."

They saw the clouds before they saw the mountains. The white mantle stood out in the empty sky, hanging above a dark stain on the horizon. That stain soon became a jagged sierra of the same brown rock as before, but these seemed to stretch for miles and miles around.

As they neared, the oppressive heat from the sun began to dampen, helped along by a gentle breeze. But what was strange was that the clouds did not move from their position above the mountains despite the wind, as if held there by some invisible force. Cade didn't mention this to the others, who seemed oblivious. Things were weird enough as it was.

The four of them approached what appeared to be a broad natural entrance, with two cliffs jutting on either side. They let out a collective sigh of relief as they stumbled into the shade, but there was little time for respite.

Because there were bones there, littered all through the canyon.

Finch and the others were standing just ahead of them, staring at the ossuary that was scattered across the dark soil. It looked for all the world like an elephants' graveyard, but there was no rhyme or reason to their sizes and shapes. A rib cage that looked like it might have come from a whale rested nearby, while closer still, the basketball-sized skull of an unidentifiable fanged creature lay half-buried in the ground. And there were human skulls too, interspersed among the rest like dice on a game-room table.

How long these had been there, Cade could not tell, but it sent an icy chill up his spine despite the muggy heat. The air was suddenly moist here, as if it had rained recently, and the scent of decomposition fouled his nostrils.

"Well, this is just great," Yoshi said, crouching to examine one of the yellowed human skulls. "Do you think this is what happened to whoever came before us?"

"Maybe," Cade answered, biting his lip. "But it's not like we can go back."

The canyon was as wide as two football stadiums end to end, with sheer cliffs on either side, stretching as high as office buildings. Yet, as Cade scanned their surroundings, he saw Finch's trio hurrying toward a structure directly opposite them, hundreds of yards into the valley. His eyes widened as he saw it. A wall.

"Come on," Eric grunted, leading the way.

It felt like a long walk, their feet squelching through the rain-damp mud, crunching over bones with every other step. As they neared, Cade saw the wall was at least twenty feet high. It was built in a haphazard fashion—some parts red brick, others stone and mortar, with various sections plastered over with a rough cement.

The entire structure was crumbling, with cratered holes and scorch marks along its surface. And worse still . . . furrowed scratches, large enough to be seen even from a distance. No animals Cade knew of had claws as large as whatever had made those markings, and he found himself avoiding looking at the ground for fear of seeing the remains of the creatures that had.

Now he could see a ramp of cobbled stone going up its center, where a set of double doors were built deep into the structure. Already, Finch was banging his fists against it, yelling hoarse pleas to be let in. But there was no response. Only the susurration of the breeze.

"It's locked," Finch said, kicking the door with frustration.

Cade sat on the edge of the ramp and groaned with relief. His feet were sore from the day's endless walking, and the amphora clutched beneath his arm had chafed his side raw. Somehow, even in all this chaos, he wanted to sleep. Sleep for days, if he could.

"I know I'd rather be on the other side of the wall than this one," Eric said, approaching the wall and running his hand along it. "More vipers could come soon. Maybe that's what this is. Another test?"

"Yeah," Yoshi said. "And looks like some of those skeletons back there didn't pass it."

Cade uncorked his amphora and took a deep swig, steadying his nerves as the lukewarm liquid pooled in his stomach.

"We should get a move on," Eric murmured, moving closer to Cade. "Night is coming."

Cade glanced up and saw the sun had already made its slow descent behind the mountains, and a chill had begun to fall around them. Light was fading fast. As his eyes dropped, they took in the wall once more—damaged but intact.

"We climb," Eric said. "That's the only option."

"And break our necks?" Finch snapped. "We'd never make it up that thing."

Already Cade's eyes were scanning the structure's surface, mapping a path to the top. It was possible. Just. He knew his reputation among these boys. Knew what they thought of him. A spoiled, geeky kid who didn't belong.

Now was his chance to show he was useful. To earn their respect.

Cade took off his boots and socks, flexing his toes. After a moment's thought, he tied the laces together and hung the heavy boots around his neck, not wanting to leave them behind.

"You're gonna climb?" Finch asked with raised eyebrows.

Cade nodded.

"Better you than me."

"Eric, can you give me a leg up?" Cade asked, ignoring him.

He approached the wall and pushed his hands into a crack between two bricks. Even as he did so, the edge crumbled, and he was forced to dig his fingers in deeper to get a decent grip.

"Leaving us so soon?" Finch called. "What a shame."

"I'll see if I can unlock the door from the other side," Cade replied through gritted teeth, scraping his feet against the wall. He found a toehold and pushed, before feeling Eric's shoulder against his backside, heaving him upward.

He dug his nails into a claw mark and pulled, even as another shoulder found its way beneath his free foot. He pushed off and found a crevice for his hand, and now the exhaustion of the day surged over him as he held himself by his finger-tips, standing on tiptoes on the shoulder beneath.

"You're heavier than you look," Scott called breathlessly from below. "Up you go."

Cade looked down as Scott pushed his foot up with an arm, and Cade made a desperate grab above, his fingers scrabbling against the concrete before digging into the gap between some bricks. He was halfway up the wall now, but no longer had the support of the others beneath him. He found a new toehold and held himself there for a moment, coughing dust from the mortar he had dislodged. For once, he was glad of the weight he had lost.

"We'll catch you if you fall," Scott called helpfully, giving Cade the courage to push up once again. He latched onto a loose brick and heaved upward.

On he went, focusing on one hold after another. With each move upward, his arms were forced to take the strain as his toes searched in vain for purchase. But each time he managed it, with some helpful shouts about where to put his feet from below. Even Jim called out, though a hiss from Finch swiftly silenced him.

Finally, muscles twitching and limbs trembling, Cade reached the parapet. With a herculean effort, he hauled himself over the top and, seeing a platform of rock built just beneath the crenulations, collapsed on his back, taking deep lungfuls of air. After a full minute, and with some trepidation, he rolled onto his side and looked out at what lay behind the wall.

Relief flooded over him like a cool balm as he took in the view. Because there in front of him were buildings.

CHAPTER
10

THE IRON BAR THAT SECURED THE DOORS WAS DIFFICULT FOR Cade to lift, as it had rusted into the iron brackets that kept it in place. But eventually it clattered onto the floor with a clang, and Finch barged him aside, eager to get away from the bone fields.

"Now, this is more like it," Finch called out, throwing his arms wide. "Looks like someone survived long enough to build this place."

Cade couldn't help but agree with him. The main building looked more like a medieval keep than anything, though built from the same materials the wall had been and only three stories high. They stood in a courtyard of cobbled ground, overgrown with weeds, just in front of a looming entrance. The front doors there were missing, with the inside dark and foreboding.

To the left, Cade could see what looked like stables, though many of the tiles from the roof had fallen in. On the right, though half-blocked by the building's edge, there was a dark cave that seemed to disappear into the mountain beyond. Unsurprisingly, that seemed far less tempting to explore than the building's interior.

But none of these discoveries were what excited him the most. No, it was the stone well that stood in the center of the courtyard, complete with an iron bucket, a rope, and a circular trough that surrounded the well—clearly used for watering horses or some other animal. Maybe they wouldn't die of thirst here after all.

Eric handed him his amphora and Cade drank long and deep. The others did the same, and Finch finished his off with a burp before tossing the pot to shatter on the floor.

"There could be food in there," Finch said, wiping his mouth and nodding at the building.

Nobody wanted to go first. Finch turned to Cade and shooed him toward the entrance with a grunt.

"Hurry up."

Sighing, Cade edged inside.

The only source of light came from the few windows, devoid of glass and with rough, slatted shutters hanging from the apertures. It took a few moments for his eyes to adjust to the gloom, but what was immediately apparent was that he was in a hall of sorts, a large empty space of cobbled floor and high wooden ceiling, with two passageways leading left and right. Twin staircases of stone were also built beside these ill-lit passages, leading to the second floor.

The mountain's rock face made up the back wall directly

opposite him, with a broad, rough-hewn tunnel in it showing stairs going downward. He padded across the deep atrium and heard the sound of rushing water at the bottom of the stairs. It seemed to go down only one story, but it was too dark to see much more than the stone floor at the bottom.

"Love what the decorator did with the place," Scott announced, and Cade turned to see the others had followed him in. "It's got a real *Blair Witch* vibe, you know?"

There was little furniture to speak of—just two dozen wooden benches and tables pushed up against the walls of the chamber, as if a school cafeteria had cleared a space for a dance recital. However, Cade was pleased to see medieval-styled torches ensconced in the walls.

He approached one and found flint and steel tied on a string at the base, and after a few tries succeeded in lighting it, the sparks catching the tarred fibers on the top. The flame was weak and spluttering, but better than nothing. He tugged it from its holder and carried it through to the short passageway left of the entrance. There, a new surprise awaited him.

Bunk beds. There were dozens of them, packed to the rafters, each three beds high and leaving barely any room to walk between them but for a single corridor of clear space down the middle. The chamber was as large as the atrium had been, and straw sacks filled most of them—rudimentary mattresses and pillows.

Here, there were more personal effects—mostly wooden bowls and cups, but no writing, symbols, or artifacts of any note. No clues as to who had built this place, or why they had disappeared, but at least there would be somewhere to lay their heads.

Cade heard raised voices and turned back. The others had gone into the other room across the hall. Cade walked over, just as he heard Finch say:

"... worthless, it's all worthless."

The room was almost empty. But it seemed that weapons had once been kept here, if the outlines in the dust were anything to go by. There were a few useless items scattered on the floor: the handle to a spear shaft, a broken piece of armor. The cheek guard to a helmet, a worn-through scabbard. There were also a few bent pickaxes that might be useful, though as Jim, Gobbler, and Finch brandished them, Cade saw the metal heads were hanging loose on their shafts.

The three boys were armed now, and Cade could see Finch assessing the rest of the group with cold, calculating eyes. But Scott, Eric, and Yoshi hadn't noticed.

If Finch wanted to make a power play, Cade was sure Finch would pick him to make an example of. He was the weakest.

"Here's something," Yoshi called from the corner. He'd lit a torch, and Cade saw him take something from a crate hidden in the gloom. Cade caught it as Yoshi tossed it over, and held it up to the light of his torch.

It was an oval-shaped piece of lead, if its weight was anything to go by, around the size of an egg. On it, Cade saw letters scratched into the surface. Despite himself, he chuckled.

"Something funny?" Finch asked.

"There's a Latin word on here: *prende*. It means catch."

"So?" Gobbler demanded.

"This is a sling stone, like what David used to kill Goliath in the Bible. You can't say the Romans didn't have a sense of humor."

Finch growled with frustration.

"I thought you said the people here couldn't be Romans."

Cade shrugged and threw the stone back to Yoshi.

"How the hell can you read Latin?" Finch demanded. "Seems a bit coincidental to me."

Cade considered his next words carefully, the suspicion in Finch's eyes mirrored in those of the others.

"I learned Latin in school. I was planning on majoring in . . ."

The memory of a life cut short hit Cade in the gut then. College. Like that was going to happen anymore.

"My father taught me, too. He teaches history. I'm more of a layman than anything—"

"You don't think it's weird?" Scott interrupted. "That all this Roman stuff is here and you happen to know about it?"

"Everything about this is weird," Cade replied, struggling to keep the panic from his voice. Now even Scott suspected him.

Finch's stare didn't waver. The distrust in his eyes was scary enough, even without the pickaxe in his hands.

"Lots of people learn Latin in school," Cade tried again. "I just happen to be one of them."

"Still seems too convenient," Finch said in a low voice.

"Maybe . . . maybe they picked me for a reason," Cade ventured. "Maybe we *all* got chosen for a reason."

It wasn't really an answer, but it was enough. The temperature in the room seemed to go up a few degrees.

"If you can read Latin, maybe you can read this," Eric said, pointing at the flat rock of the mountainside that formed the back wall.

Cade moved closer and held his torch up to where crude letters had been scratched.

Quis fortuna erit, vel bestiis devorari vel gladiatores fieri?

"Um, my Latin isn't *that* good," Cade muttered, half to himself. He was wary of revealing his knowledge now—but based on what he *thought* it meant, it seemed too important to keep to himself. And pretending he didn't understand it now could make it all worse.

He furrowed his brow, sounding out the words.

"I think it means, 'What is our fate, to be devoured by beasts or fight as gladiators?'"

He was met with blank stares.

"Devoured?" Yoshi asked.

"The Romans used to execute criminals in the arena by way of dangerous animals," Cade explained, wondering if any of the others had ever cracked a history book in school. "Ever heard of the term 'thrown to the lions'? That's what they used to do to people, while thousands of citizens watched for entertainment. Unlike gladiators, they usually didn't put up much of a fight, wearing nothing more than a loincloth, sometimes even placed there with broken limbs. I think the person who wrote this is wondering if they were put here with a fighting chance . . . or just to be slaughtered for the spectacle of it."

Silence followed.

"Well, that's reassuring," came a voice from behind them.

Cade turned and jumped in surprise. They weren't the only ones who had crossed the desert.

CHAPTER
11

"Y OU SHOULD'VE LOCKED THAT DOOR BEHIND YOU," SPEX SAID. "Those things could have followed you in."

"We *should* have," Finch said. "Would have kept you out too."

"Sad to see you, Spex," Gobbler said, earning himself a chuckle from Finch. Meanwhile, Jim stepped farther into the gloom, avoiding Spex's gaze. Guilt was stamped on his face, plain as day.

Spex's eyes widened at the sight of Finch. He glanced at the pickaxes in the trio's hands, and fear sparked in his eyes. There were no counselors here.

Spex switched his gaze to Eric. "Sounds like you don't know much more than we do."

Cade jumped in. "Someone wants us to think this place was built by the Romans," he explained. "But that's impossible—it was too long ago."

"The bodies were too fresh," Spex agreed, his gaze flicking to the writing on the wall.

He paused.

"So this is a game?" he asked.

Spex looked at Cade expectantly, but now Cade was reluctant to answer. It seemed showing off his intellect wasn't going to do him any favors.

"Whoever wrote those words on the mountainside wall seemed to think so," Cade said as the silence dragged on. "But who knows when they wrote it. It could be before this place was even built."

"Well, maybe there are more clues here, maybe not," Eric said. "But we won't find out standing around."

He walked on without waiting for the others to follow. Soon the group was trooping into the main chamber again.

Cade was glad to see Spex, even if they hadn't spoken since the incident with Finch. It was a small comfort to have another person there who wasn't allied with Finch's crew.

Eric headed down the stairs built into the rock face, stepping hesitantly into the gloom. Cade felt relieved at the break from being their guinea pig.

Below, they found a damp cavern, with water dripping from stalactites above. At its end, an underground river rushed from one side to the other before disappearing into the depths of the earth. A platform of wood had been built along its side, with holes carved into the tops to form a latrine. In fact, Cade knew it must be when he saw sponges on sticks lying on top—*spongia*, used by the ancient Romans in lieu of toilet paper.

Everyone in his history class had gotten a kick out of that detail in the textbook.

Of course, he didn't mention this. He was beginning to think that solving the puzzle was less important than his place in the pecking order among the others. Any reminder that he was a history buff made them suspicious.

Further inspection revealed that a wide pool had been carved into the cavern's center, with a channel leading to the river, where the water seemed to slosh back and forth. A bathing area, perhaps, though with little in the way of privacy. Then again, the school's showers had not been much better.

"Starting to look like home sweet home," Scott said as they made their way up the stairs. "Got our own spa and everything."

Even Finch gave a half smile at that one.

They moved to one of the stairways and emerged on the second floor. To Cade's surprise, they found private rooms there. Each was laid out identically, and many contained much the same: a wooden bed, fur blankets, a straw-filled mattress, a desk, a table, a chair, and rudimentary candles.

Cade assumed these were the officers' quarters, if this was indeed where a Roman army had once lodged. Again he kept that thought to himself.

The stairs on either side continued, leading to the final floor. Here, they had more luck, emerging into a room as wide as the atrium, though with lower ceilings. A large, circular stone table stood in the middle of it, surrounded by rough-hewn stone chairs.

And in the very center . . . sat a machine. There was no other word for it.

It was grapefruit sized and teardrop shaped, set on its side and facing their direction. The front looked for all the world like the shutter of a fancy camera, while around it, complex mechanical circuits and wires lay beneath a hard, transparent surface.

As they circled the room, Cade lowered his gaze in line with the tabletop, noticing something strange about the device. It was not on the table, but floating just above it.

Scott caught his expression and stooped down to look too.

"It's floating," Scott blurted.

"So . . . that's weird," Spex muttered.

"Looks like a camera," Eric said. "Do you think they've been watching us with this thing?"

"Must be," Finch said. He turned to Cade and furrowed his brow maliciously. "Apu, why don't you take a closer look."

Again, Cade seethed. But now was not the time to stand up for himself.

He paused, hoping someone else would step up, but none seemed willing.

He set his jaw, resisting the urge to huff with frustration. He wanted to prove himself, but did that mean always being the one they sent in first?

Cade handed his torch to Eric, then climbed onto the table and approached the object. He dropped to his knees as he took it in his hands. It was light—unnaturally so. In fact, it was almost weightless. He let go, and the machine hung there.

"Damn," Yoshi whispered.

Suddenly, a light flashed, and a flat male voice emanated from it.

"Identified—Cade Carter."

"Shit," Cade said, backing away.

"It knows who you are," Finch growled, raising his pick-axe. "You're one of them."

Even as he spoke, the object swiveled in the air, and a broad beam of light scanned across his face.

"Identified—Finch Hill."

Despite his shock, Cade couldn't help but smirk at that one.

It spun again and again. Yoshi Endo. Eric Larsen. Scott Moore. Jim Webster. Cade even learned that Gobbler's real name was Tom Andrews and Spex's was Carlos Silva. It knew all of them . . . and it knew their faces.

The voice paused. Then:

"Contenders identified. Qualifier round commences in one hundred and forty-four hours."

An image appeared, directly in front of its lens. A digital timer, made of blue light. Counting down from . . . six days.

```
05:23:59:59
05:23:59:58
05:23:59:57
```

The hologram hung in the air, so real and perfectly formed that Cade felt like he could reach out and touch it.

They stared at it, dumbfounded. Cade knew what they were all thinking. He was thinking the same thing.

What is the qualifier round?

Scott, unsurprisingly, was the first to break the silence.

"Well, that doesn't sound good."

"No, it doesn't," Eric agreed, waving a hand through the countdown clock. It flickered as he did so, but remained there.

"I recommend we move as far away from this thing as possible," Spex said, pushing his thick glasses up his nose.

"If the last 'games' were anything to go by, a qualifier sounds like a walk in the park," Scott said sarcastically. "And I was just warming to the place."

"More vipers?" Cade asked.

"Or something worse," Finch spat. "You saw the bones outside. That's probably what happens to people who stay for the 'qualifying round.'"

Finch paced back and forth, twirling the pickaxe in his hand. Cade took a furtive step back. He knew what Finch was capable of.

"The people who built this place left in a hurry," Eric said, oblivious to Cade's worries. "Armed people, and over a hundred of them at least. How many in a legion, Cade?"

Cade hesitated.

"Thousands," he said.

Spex had been staring into space, but now he looked up, the large eyes behind his glasses full of fear.

"They didn't leave long ago either, if the state of this place is anything to go by. Maybe a year or two?"

Cade was relieved he wasn't the only one with some common sense in the room. But at the same time, he wondered where else there was to go. His mind flashed to the cave he had glimpsed beside the Keep. Now, it seemed a whole lot more inviting.

"There's shelter here," Gobbler groaned. "A roof, even toilets and baths. The wall will protect us. Did you see any bones in here?"

"Maybe the people who built this place were those corpses

we saw," Cade muttered, half to himself. There was silence, until he noticed them all staring at him. He shuffled his feet.

"I mean, they were supposed to be Romans, right?" Cade plowed on. "And the people who lived here were supposed to be Romans too, or at least Latin speakers. The writing's on the wall, literally."

It made some sense . . . if it weren't for the fact that this place was far older than the corpses had been. Could there have been two sets of Romans: those who built this place and the Ninth Legion who had been found in the desert?

Whatever the answer, this story was getting stranger all the time.

"So . . . let's look at what we're *supposed* to think," Spex said, holding up his hands as he thought it through. "Romans were teleported to the desert, along with some dead bodies. They appeared there maybe two thousand years ago, maybe a few years ago. Then they came here and build this place, right?"

Finch grunted in reluctant agreement.

Cade suspected that the legion had been transported mid-battle with the Picts, along with the football field–sized hunk of grass they'd found them on, but he didn't want to complicate the issue.

"All the while, they were made to play this 'game,' whatever it is," Spex went on, his brow furrowed in thought. "Then one day they decided to leave, in a hurry."

"Maybe because the game got too hard," Jim said suddenly, earning himself another glare from Finch.

"It's where they went that I'm interested in," Finch said,

and Cade resisted the urge to snort derisively. Apparently *Jim* couldn't talk to Spex, but Finch could.

"So either we play this game or we leave," Eric said.

Scott laughed aloud.

"Well, as much as I'm enjoying the game so far, my vote is we take our collective balls and go home. Right?"

There were a series of nods and groans of assent. Nobody really wanted to leave the relative safety of the fort. And at the same time, everyone did.

"We have a few days yet," Eric said. "We'll sleep here tonight—it's as safe a place as any."

"Who put you in charge?" Finch demanded.

"You want to go now?" Eric asked, motioning out at the darkened sky. "Be my guest. We'll bury you in the morning."

Finch muttered something under his breath. Cade ignored him and looked to the doors on either side of the room—these were still on their hinges. Yoshi caught his eye and pushed open the door nearest to him.

"A bigger bedroom," he said. "More furs, that's all."

There was a gasp, and Cade spun to see Jim staring into the opposite room.

"Um . . . this one's a room too. But there's something else in here," Jim said.

CHAPTER
12

JUST AS YOSHI HAD SAID, THE ROOM LOOKED MUCH THE SAME as the others, only with a bigger bed and what seemed like better furnishings, including ragged curtains that cast the room in darkness.

But Jim was right, there was something different. A large, polished wooden box stood upon a table near the mountainside wall. Cade noticed something else too—a book, sitting open another table.

As the others crowded around the box, he took the opportunity to flick through the book's contents, squinting to see in the flickering light of Eric's torch. It looked like Latin, but he couldn't make head or tail of it. The letters were jumbled, though separated into what might have been words. A cipher maybe?

"Louis Le Prince," Finch said, distracting Cade from his thoughts. "Anyone know who that is?"

Cade abandoned the book and approached the wooden box. Upon its top, embossed in gold letters, was the name that Finch had read aloud, though he had butchered the pronunciation.

"A French king maybe?" Eric suggested.

"Maybe," Spex said. "There were eighteen kings called Louis."

The group stared at him in surprise.

"I'm a trivia nerd, sue me," Spex explained, looking suddenly as worried as Cade had been. "I watched a lot of *Jeopardy!* growing up, always wanted to be on it."

"Any ideas?" Gobbler asked, turning to Cade.

Cade examined the box more closely. On one side were two lenses, one above another, in a seeming separate compartment, while on the opposite, a handled crank was embedded. As for the side that faced the mountain wall, there was a single lens embedded in the center. Stranger still, the wall in front of it seemed to have been flattened and whitewashed in a square the size of a bedsheet.

The box looked old, but not ancient. He would have guessed at its being an oversized old-timey camera. Certainly not something that any Romans would have been using. It didn't make sense. But then, nothing did in this place.

"Doesn't seem like a Roman name," Eric ventured as Cade examined the box further.

For once, Cade didn't mind being the group's test subject, curiosity getting the better of him. There was a crank on the side of the box, as well as what appeared to be a switch.

Not much good had come from messing with the last piece

of technology they had come across, but he needed to know what it did. He flicked the switch. Immediately, a light came on somewhere inside the box. On the wall opposite, a square of light appeared.

"Dude, what are you doing?" Jim hissed.

But Cade knew what it was now. Carefully, he began to turn the crank. An image appeared on the wall, flickering in black and white.

"Madness!" Yoshi exclaimed.

The sight was beyond anything Cade could have imagined. There couldn't have been more than sixty-odd frames to the blurry black-and-white film, and they sped up and slowed in tandem with Cade's turning of the crank. It repeated over and over, cycling the short clip until the outline was seared into Cade's retinas. It was a battle scene.

There were Roman soldiers in the foreground, their shields aligned in a rough wall, while a centurion on horseback held his sword aloft, the crescent of horsehair on his helmet delineating his rank. A standard-bearer encroached on the image's right side, a long-fanged lion's pelt and head resting on his helmet.

But it was not these soldiers that drew Cade's eye. No, it was the creatures that were charging toward them in the background, smashing into the front ranks with unparalleled ferocity. Tentacled monsters, ripped straight from H. P. Lovecraft's nightmares.

One was as large as a horse on its hind legs, a bipedal behemoth that threw men aside like pinballs, its clawed arms slashing, its tentacled maw open and lined with razor teeth.

Others were the size of wolves, much the same as the giant but running on four legs. Still-smaller iterations seemed to lack any arms at all, running on two legs and as large as turkeys, swarming over the men as they stabbed and slashed with their short-swords.

And far in the back, too blurry to see in much detail, were veritable giants, lumbering toward the Roman lines. Larger than elephants. Much larger.

"What the . . . ," Cade whispered.

But there it was. The scene lasted no more than six seconds, and it was scratched and unfocused. Yet this looked as real as anything he had ever seen in a cinema. More so, even.

Most damning of all, Cade recognized the twin cliffs on either side and the desert beyond them. This had been filmed just outside the walls.

"What *are* those things?" Cade whispered.

They were like nothing he'd ever seen. Best guess, tentacled sea monsters pulled from ancient Roman myths. What else could they be?

"If they can fake everything else, they can fake this," Finch said, clenching Cade's arm and freezing the film.

"You call this fake?" Yoshi asked, motioning around them. "Feels pretty real to me."

Finch flicked the switch, and the room was cast in darkness once more.

"It might be fake," Cade said, half to himself. "But do you think they went to all that trouble just for a few seconds of film?"

"Why go to the trouble to make any of this?" Finch

snapped, motioning at the fort around them. "None of this is real. None of it."

Cade sighed and gently pulled his arm from Finch's grip. He hated to admit it, but the kid had a point.

"It looks like it's not just vipers we have to worry about," Eric said. "Whatever those things are."

"Never thought I'd say this, but I miss the vipers," Scott said. "At least we had a chance against those."

"Who cares?" Gobbler groaned. "I'm starving, and there's no food."

Cade's own stomach twisted at the mention of food. He was ravenous, and the copious amount of water he had drunk was no longer sating the feeling of emptiness in his belly.

But even as he considered it, the gloom seemed to deepen around them, lit only by the dying torch in Eric's hand. Looking through the ragged curtains, Cade could see the sun had set.

"Let's get some rest," Eric said. "Unless you want to go wandering in the dark alone."

CHAPTER
13

CADE WOKE TO YOSHI GENTLY SHAKING HIM. THE SNORES from Spex and Scott permeated the room, but he could see the morning light filtering through the window.

"Come on," Yoshi whispered, motioning for him to follow.

They were in what Cade had come to think of as the Commander's Room, where the box and book had been found. Finch, Jim, Gobbler, and a reluctant Eric had gone to sleep in the bed chamber opposite, since the two rooms were the only ones with doors on them—giving them a semblance of security in case of any vipers.

Cade had thought it would be hard to rest, knowing what he did now about the creatures that inhabited this world. Yet as soon as his head had hit the straw-filled pillow, he had fallen asleep. That had been small comfort though, for his dreams had been filled with flashes of teeth, tentacles, and blood. He had woken several times, only to see the ominous light of the timer, glowing beneath the door frame.

He groaned and rubbed the sleep from his eyes, and saw the tables and chairs they had piled up against the door had been moved. Beckoning with a finger to his lips, Yoshi led him through, back to the stone table. The drone—for that was what Cade had begun to call it in his head—still hung in the air, its countdown ticking away.

```
05:08:56:27
05:08:56:26
05:08:56:25
```

Yoshi pulled him closer, and they sat together, one on each stone chair. For a moment Yoshi stared at him, his dark eyes boring into Cade's own. Finally, he spoke.

"I heard you almost went to juvie," he said. "What happened?"

Cade shook his head. "I didn't do anything," he said. "They made a mistake."

Yoshi nodded slowly, his gaze never leaving Cade's face. It was quite disconcerting.

"I could ask you the same thing," Cade said.

Yoshi finally broke his stare. Cade could hardly read his expression. Was that regret? Or pride?

"I got done for fraud," Yoshi said. "So my mom shipped me off."

"Fraud?" Cade asked, surprised. That wasn't the most common crime for kids.

"Yeah. My mother sells antiques from Japan; it's how our family make a living. Mostly to rich American Japanophiles. So, I . . . took on the family business, so to speak."

Cade furrowed his brows in confusion.

"Basically, I started selling fake antique swords to neck-bearded anime obsessives," Yoshi said, catching Cade's expression. "Knew enough to get by. Then I got caught. Simple as that."

"Was it worth it?" Cade asked.

Yoshi looked down, twisting his hands.

"Nah," he said. "My mom can't even look at me now."

Cade nodded. He knew what that felt like.

"I think you're telling the truth," Yoshi said, looking back up at him.

Cade nodded, feeling pathetically grateful. He realized it was the first time someone had directly told him they thought he was innocent. Even his parents had never said it out loud.

Yoshi outstretched his fist and opened his palm. Cade saw he was holding three coins.

"You understand these, don't you?" Yoshi asked, pouring them into Cade's hand. "I found them in the baths."

Cade examined them one by one, his heart pounding. Each coin was in far better condition than he could have expected. Better than anything he had ever found metal detecting with his father while vacationing in Europe. But what they had stamped on them was stranger still.

"What's wrong?" Yoshi asked.

"See here, this one," Cade said, holding up a bronze-colored coin. "It's a copper *sestertius* with Emperor Hadrian's head on it, which puts it right around the time the Ninth Legion was in Scotland. But look at this."

He held up another one, a heavier, silver coin.

"A silver *sestertius*. It's too old; they stopped making them from silver long before the Ninth Legion disappeared. It's from the old Roman republic, before there were even emperors at all. And even if some legionary was holding on to an old coin for good luck, this one's the strangest."

Cade proffered the third coin.

"Emperor Constantine from the fourth century. Almost two hundred years after the Ninth Legion."

Yoshi frowned.

"What does this mean?" he asked.

"It means that if there *were* Romans here, they were from at least three different time periods, maybe more. Which doesn't make any sense."

But Cade wasn't so sure anymore. If they *had* been transported to another planet, would time travel be so out of the question? He didn't want to believe it. That this was all part of some cruel trick, or a vivid nightmare he could not wake up from. Perhaps this was what all dreams felt like, until you woke up from them.

Yoshi shrugged.

"Nothing here makes sense," he replied. "And I don't really get what you're talking about. But Finch and his cronies are dangerous . . . let's keep this a secret."

He motioned at Finch's door with his chin.

Cade nodded and slipped the coins into Yoshi's pocket.

The revelations, such as they were, came with new worries for Cade. It seemed now a mad coincidence that he, someone who knew about Roman coins, was now here among . . . well . . . Roman coins.

This wasn't a random selection. He, and perhaps even the

others, were here for a purpose. Though what purpose that was became less and less clear with each new discovery.

It wasn't long after that the others began to stir, emerging with yawns from their rooms. Few were in the mood for talking, and barely a word was exchanged as they gathered their paltry belongings.

"Time to leave," Finch announced, hefting his pickaxe on his shoulder. "Come on."

Cade took one last look at the drone, still hanging in the air with its ominous timer. He was glad to be seeing the back of it. Frankly, he wanted to smash it in with his rock.

As they trooped down the stairs, Cade regretted not going for a dip in the baths as Yoshi had. He was sure he smelled like a barnyard animal. Still, there was enough time to dunk a bucket of water over his head as they drank long and deep from the well outside, refilling their amphorae and their bellies. Cade caught Finch looking regretfully at the shards of the amphora he had smashed the day before, and Cade couldn't help but smirk.

"Well, looks like we know what the previous occupants were eating," Spex said.

"What do you mean?" Cade asked, turning around.

Spex pointed toward the shadow of the building, where what looked like a second pile of bones had been scattered haphazardly among the cobbles and weeds.

Cade approached, examining them. It was hard to tell what the creatures had once been, for the bones had been smashed open, likely to get at the nutritious marrow within. A few leering skulls stared at him, but they could have been anything from dogs to giant lizards as far as Cade could tell. Certainly no humans.

What he did recognize were the piles of shells. What looked like oyster shells, snail shells, even ostrich-sized eggshells. This was their trash pile. Somewhere in this place, there were animals. Edible ones.

His heart leaped at the thought. There was an ecosystem here. Maybe somewhere they could hide. Somewhere they could survive.

Even with that twinge of hope, Cade felt despair. To be thinking of staying here for good—he might never go back home. Never see his family again.

Cade looked around, but apart from the weeds that grew between the cobbles, the place seemed bereft of life. And somehow he doubted that the creatures came from the black tunnel in the mountain directly ahead of him.

"I don't like the look of that cave," Eric said. "There may be another way out of here."

"I second that motion," Spex said. "Lead the way."

There was only one place they hadn't explored—the left side of the building, beyond the derelict stables. Even as they rounded the corner, Cade saw what they were looking for, cut into the mountainside itself.

A stairway, one so broken and poorly carved that it looked more like a goat trail than anything else, but a stairway nonetheless. It twisted all the way up the steep cliff, and Cade found himself swallowing at the sight of it. He didn't like heights at the best of times.

But it was the only way out, other than the dark cave. And it would give them a better lay of the land.

"You want us to walk up there, don't you," Scott groaned.

"Would you rather go into that dark hole in the ground instead?" Eric asked, pointing in the direction of the yawning cave mouth.

Scott grumbled under his breath.

"It could give us a better look at our surroundings," Cade said. He didn't care anymore about being the guinea pig. It was more important to find a way out of this terrible place.

"I'm going," Cade said. "You guys can do whatever you want."

"Like you'd come back for us if you found anything," Finch spat. "I'm going too."

Cade shrugged and mounted the first steps. He thought for a moment, then placed his amphora carefully against a large rock. If this *was* a dead end, he'd be lugging the jar up and down for nothing. If it wasn't, he'd come back for it.

He didn't look behind him as he climbed, but he could hear the panting of at least one other as he pressed on, stones scattering as he pulled himself up toward the skyline.

He saw green vines dangling down the side at the top, and other vegetation growing in along the upper reaches. A good sign—where there were plants, there were likely animals. And both could mean food.

Cade quickly realized that with an empty belly and a half gallon of water inside him he was almost too weak to keep going. When he was halfway up, he collapsed onto a flat rock and surveyed the view behind him.

He was pleased to see that all the others had followed him

up, though Finch, Jim, and Gobbler had brought their pickaxes with them. This fact sent a twinge of fear through Cade's stomach. Were they for protection from potential vipers . . . or to keep the group under their control?

Letting his eyes drift upward, Cade saw the vast expanse of the salt flat stretched out to the horizon, broken only by the rock formations they had emerged from the day before. The desert surface shone glaringly bright, so much so that he could not look at it for too long. Beneath, twin spits of cliffs branched outward from the mountain on either side of the keep like extended arms, embracing the valley of bones. Whatever he found at the top, there was no going back the way they had come. There was only desert that way.

As Finch caught up to him, Cade pushed on, leaving Finch panting behind him. His legs screamed for rest, but a will to survive pulled him onward. What lay above would likely shape the rest of his life . . . however long that might last.

CHAPTER
14

CHEST POUNDING, CADE RESISTED THE URGE TO SLOW AS HE neared the crest of the mountaintop. Here, the steps were in better shape, and he mounted them two at a time. Then he was at the peak, buffeted by the breeze. The sweet smell of vegetation hit him.

He was standing on a mountain ridge, as wide as three football fields, stretching across in a flat plateau that was framed by two jagged spires on either side. The other end of the ridge was obscured by rows of trees, and the chirr and buzz of insects filled his ears.

Fruit trees. The scent of fallen fruit was unmistakable, and Cade hardly saw the purple figs that littered the ground before he was on his knees, sinking his teeth into the overripe fruit.

He gorged. There was no other word for it. Fig after fig disappeared down his throat, until his face was coated with their thick syrup. He barely registered the arrival of the others as he crawled on his knees in the shade of the orchard, tossing rotten figs over his shoulders before seizing a fresh specimen and reveling in its sweetness once more. There were other fruits here too, farther away than he wanted to move before the next fig was in his mouth. Apples, oranges, even grapes, they could all wait.

Finally, his hunger sated, Cade stood and took in more of his surroundings. The trees ended somewhere to his left, so he headed in that direction, clutching his distended belly, already churning at the sudden influx of food.

As he stumbled into the light, Cade found himself in a field of overgrown wheat swaying in the breeze. It came up to his chest, but beyond that, he could see vegetable gardens with broad leaves overflowing the wooden fencing that surrounded them.

Rodents scurried away underfoot, disturbed by his arrival. They looked for all the world like mice, or perhaps small rats. It was good to see familiar creatures here. Not everything was like the vipers.

What was obvious was that nobody had tended these crops for a long time. Nothing had been gathered, pruned, or replanted. Instead, the vegetation had run rampant, left to its own devices.

It was a relief to find so much food, but at the same time, Cade knew they would have to leave soon. They needed to gather all they could and move to the next area before the timer reached zero.

But where was the next area? Beyond the fields, he could

see the edge of their mountaintop, surmounted by a cloud-strewn sky. Curious to see what lay beyond, Cade waded through the wheat until he stood on the plateau's edge.

Green. He had never seen so much of it. A forest sprawled beneath him in a viridescent ocean, stretching as far as the eye could see, lost in a haze of fog before it met the horizon. To his left and right, the mountains stretched in a sierra that curved around, as if they stood on the edge of a giant meteor's crater. It was awe inspiring and terrifying all at the same time.

A few hundred feet beyond the steep cliffs that bordered their plateau, a waterfall blasted out over the mountainside, filling the air with moisture and forming a deep pool beside the forest below. If someone had indeed created this place, they had an artist's eye.

"It's a caldera," a muffled voice said.

Spex stepped beside him, his mouth half-full of fig.

"Wait, what?" Cade asked, pleased that Spex was talking to him. Spex hadn't quite ignored him since his beating, but he hadn't exactly been warm to him either.

"Like Yellowstone, or Crater Lake. The sinkhole of a giant, dormant volcano. We're standing on the rim; these mountains probably form a ring, hundreds of miles around." Spex stooped and scooped up a handful of the dark earth. "That's volcanic soil—black, fertile. No wonder it's so overgrown everywhere."

Spex leaned out over the mountainside and looked down.

"That's the basin; see how the jungle tilts downward the farther in it gets?" Spex said, waving a pulp-stained hand over the forest. "And the river, following the incline? There's prob-ably a body of water right in the center, miles that way."

Now Cade saw a river, offshooting from the waterfall pool and disappearing into the jungle's edge. It cut a furrow through the tree line, heading into the undergrowth.

"How do you know all this?" Cade asked. He tried not to sound surprised.

Spex shrugged.

"I have a good memory," he said. "Geography trivia."

For a moment the pair stared out at the expanse of vegetation, somewhat soothed by the breeze and the distant roar of the waterfall. It was an impossible place, Cade realized. An oasis of life, contained within a ring of impassable mountains and surrounded by endless dry desert. Was it safer out there, in the great green jungle?

As if reading Cade's mind, Spex spoke up.

"Do you think we're dead? Like in an afterlife?"

Cade sighed, watching as Spex chewed his bottom lip.

"If we are," Cade said, "I think we could die again. Maybe the next afterlife would be better?"

He was only half joking.

"Yeah," Spex said, forcing a grim smile. "Let's not test out that theory."

The boy lifted a fig and groaned with satisfaction as he took a bite from it.

"Speaking of which, what's your theory?" Spex asked, mumbling through his mouthful of fruit.

"Too weird and elaborate for a prank," Cade replied. "Too difficult and pointless for a government experiment. It's all too un*real*. Maybe we're hooked up to some sort of super-advanced virtual reality, playing a video game to rehabilitate us. Or we're being used by big pharma to test some hallucinogenic drugs. Maybe I lost my mind, and I'm in a psych ward with electrodes glued to my temples."

"Dunno," Spex said, scratching his chin. "This all feels pretty real. And I'm definitely not a figment of your imagination. I'm me."

"That's exactly what a figment of my imagination would say," Cade said, grinning.

Spex grinned back and shook his head.

"Well, wherever we are, let's just focus on surviving it," Spex said. "I mean, if it's a dream, let's make it a happy one, right?"

"Right," Cade said.

It can't be a dream. Maybe a nightmare.

Cade gazed out over the jungle once more. Even as he looked, he thought he could see the shape of something in the mists, a deeper gray that stretched above the trees. Then it was gone, obscured once more by the rolling mists. A building? Or another mountain.

Cade's mind turned to the timer, slowly ticking down. And the bones, scattered beyond their derelict wall.

"We should go," Cade said, motioning at the rain forest with his chin. "I think I know where that cave leads."

CHAPTER
15

THERE WAS A LIGHT AT THE END OF THE TUNNEL, IN BOTH senses. The cave was a wide, level tube of rock, with edges as smooth and round as a straw. This hadn't been dug by any Roman, or modern machine for that matter. It was practically laser cut, and this told Cade it was all part of the game, a passage designed to allow access both to and from the jungle. Constructed by whatever twisted people had brought them to this place.

If they were people at all.

"You think we're safer out there?" Scott asked, squinting at the circle of the light at the end. "That was a pretty nice stash of food we had up there."

"We've probably got enough to last us a week or two, if we're careful," Spex replied, hefting the heavy sack of fruit across his back. The sacking they had found had been half-rotting, and seemingly used to transport grains from the wheat field to the keep, but in a pinch they had served to be stuffed with fruit. Holding an amphora and a sack each was all they could carry.

"And after that?" Scott asked. "We need to figure out how to get home, not spend two weeks crouched in a hole, scrounging food."

"If you want to stay and see whatever that countdown is ticking to, be my guest," Eric said, his voice echoing down the tunnel. "I'd rather take my chances out there. Maybe there are more like us who made it this far."

"What if we can't find anyone?" Yoshi said. "Or find a safe place?"

"We lie low in the jungle, maybe come back and gather more in a week or so," Cade said, shading his eyes as they emerged into the light. "Whatever the qualifying round is, it will be over by then."

Or at least Cade hoped so.

They emerged from the tunnel, blinking in the late-morning light. It looked much as Cade had imagined, based on what he had seen from above.

The area surrounding the cave mouth was clear of trees, and it was easy to see why. Tree stumps were scattered as far as a hundred feet to the jungle edge—the occupants of the keep had needed lumber after all. To their left, the waterfall roared, and the mist from its crashing coated them all with a thin film of moisture. It was a blessed relief because by now the sun was beating down on them from high in the sky.

The forest ahead looked daunting from the ground. He hadn't realized the sheer scale of it earlier.

Once, Cade had visited the giant sequoias in Redwood National Park, even stopped by "Hyperion," the tallest one in the world. Now most of the trees that made up the top layer of the canopy looked to easily match Hyperion's height, with others exceeding it by a full third.

Worse still, the shadows they cast left the forest interior shrouded by gloom. There were no animals here—no birds, no deer. Only the soft whine of insects, hovering around his head. It was eerie, as if some giant predator had scared everything away.

"Let's take a breather," Eric announced, settling on one of the rotting tree stumps. The others followed his lead, though Finch wandered a ways farther before sitting with his two cronies.

Uneasy at the thought of entering the jungle, Cade busied himself by approaching the waterfall instead, weaving his way through the thick mat of vegetation that still grew in the clearing. Mosquitoes buzzed around his head, and he slapped at them, leaving his amphora and food sack on the ground.

Then he saw it, his eyes widening with shock. He hurried forward, tripping and stumbling to get to the plunge pool at the waterfall's base. Because sitting there, moored by a frayed rope and half-obscured by reeds . . . was a boat.

"Thank you," Cade whispered, though who he was thanking, he did not know.

Kneeling at the water's edge, he saw it was over twenty feet long, with a cabin and opposing benches inside. It bobbed uneasily in the stirring waters of the lake that had formed around the waterfall's torrent, tugged toward the broad river that cut into the jungle beyond. A ragged rope tied to a wooden stake was all that kept the cabin cruiser from drifting away.

"Damn," Yoshi panted, catching up behind him. "Jackpot."

But now that he was up close, Cade wasn't so sure. The boat's hull and cabin were covered in a thick layer of green lichen, so much that he could barely make out the letters emblazoned on its side. He hauled on the rope and ran his hand across the slimy coating as it drifted closer, revealing the stencil beneath.

"*Witchcraft*," he read, furrowing his brows.

A strange name for a boat.

"Yeah, that's *one* explanation," Yoshi said.

Cade blinked the sweat from his eyes. Could they survive on the boat, out there in the jungle? It was certainly better than a hut made of sticks and leaves.

"Hell yeah," Spex shouted, hurrying over with the others. "That's our ticket out of here."

"Ticket to where?" Scott huffed, collapsing onto a nearby tree stump.

"I don't care, but I'm not hauling this with me through *Jumanji* over there," Yoshi replied, nodding at the jungle and setting his food and water on the ground.

"We don't even know if it's working," Cade said. "It looks old."

But not so old as the Romans, clearly. What this modern machine was doing here was anyone's guess.

"One way to find out," Finch said, leaping aboard.

For once, Finch was going first . . . but it didn't seem like the boat would be dangerous.

Cade sighed and followed, stepping into the cabin.

The inside of the cruiser was as moldy as the outside, with two upholstered benches for sleeping on either side, along with a tiny latrine at the end. But what was strange was the long lengths of wood lying along the bottom, as well as rough, makeshift oars stacked like kindling in the corner.

"Looks like the owners didn't use the motor," Cade said. "Must have used punts and oars to get it up and down the river instead."

Even as he spoke, he noticed a set of keys hanging from a corkboard on the wall. He took them and stared incredulously.

"It won't work," Yoshi said, ducking in behind them. "Fuel'll have gone bad."

"Fuel doesn't go bad, jackass," Finch said, snatching the keys from Cade while he was distracted. "It's millions of years old."

"Whatever." Yoshi shrugged.

Finch stomped back to the exterior and jabbed the keys into the ignition. To Cade's surprise, the lights on the dashboard flickered, but there wasn't even a cough from the engine.

"Like I said, fuel's gone bad," Yoshi said, glaring at Finch. "You ever see *Mad Max*? That film was inaccurate as hell. You leave gas in a car's fuel tank for a year, it won't start. If the gas is stored in a tanker, or a barrel, maybe you got a decade, but after that, might as well take out the engine and hitch a horse to the front—it's back to the Stone Age. You're the jackass."

"So we'll row it, then," Cade interrupted, stepping between

the two, struggling to hide the fear in his voice. "The current will do half the work; we just need to guide it."

"And what if there's another waterfall?" Finch asked, distracted by the suggestion.

"We swim for it," Yoshi said.

Finch grinned, but there was no warmth to his smile.

"Maybe we take the boat, leave you here," he said. "Since you want to swim so much, seems like you don't need it."

"Nobody wants you here," Yoshi said, "Maybe we should leave *you*."

Instantly, Finch's face darkened, and Cade saw him shift his weight to his back foot. In a fair fight, Yoshi would have a shot. But he wasn't the one holding the pickaxe.

"Let's get one thing straight," Finch said, his fingers twisting around the pickaxe's haft. "If you want to leave, then leave. But the food, the weapons, this boat, the keep. That's mine. I own it."

Cade could see Finch's fury bubbling beneath the surface. Waiting to erupt. Yoshi's hands balled into fists.

"How do you figure?" he said.

"Because I say so," Finch replied. "Your betters say so."

And then, ever so slightly, the pickaxe lifted from the ground.

This was it. Cade predicted that in seconds there would be a bloodbath. He had to do something. Even if it meant putting himself at risk.

He was already at Finch's side, just out of view. Cade wasn't a threat to Finch. He was a nobody, a weakling. Not part of the equation.

So he made himself a threat, evening the odds. He took two quick steps, placing himself behind Finch. It was time to show he had some fight in him after all.

"You sure about that?" Cade said.

His hand strayed to his pocket, and he grasped the hand axe. He didn't know if he'd have the courage to use it, but it gave him a semblance of a chance if he had to defend himself.

Finch's head turned slightly to the left, but he dared not take his eyes off Yoshi. For a few heart-stopping moments, Finch hesitated. But it was Yoshi who moved first, stepping back and to the side, making room for Finch to go.

Finch walked by slowly, his back straight as a ramrod, ready to defend himself at any moment. Then the boy was gone, leaping from the boat's back end to join his cronies.

Cade breathed a sigh of relief.

"You got my back if things kick off later, yeah?" Yoshi muttered once Finch was out of earshot.

Cade hesitated. Would he? Or would he run away, take his chances on his own?

"I'd rather there were no problems," Cade said, feeling a twinge of guilt run down his back. "I'm a lover, not a fighter."

Yoshi shook his head.

"I thought I could count on you," Yoshi said, banging Cade's shoulder as he walked out. "Guess I was wrong."

He jumped back to shore, and Cade was alone on the *Witchcraft.*

Cade groaned, sitting on the mold-covered bench with a

squelch. When the food got low, things *would* kick off. Maybe even before. He imagined facing down Finch, Gobbler, and Jim, armed with nothing but a rock. Somehow, it filled him with more dread than the vipers had.

The sooner they found more people, the better.

CHAPTER
16

THE BOAT ROCKED IN THE WATER AS THEY SHOVED OFF USING the makeshift poles they had found inside. Cade sat at the front, with everyone but Finch's crew beside him. He had thought he would end up guiding the boat with his oar, yet as the current took them and they began to drift down the river, he found no use for it. Finch had commandeered the helm of the boat, while the others paddled at intervals to keep it in the center of the river.

They followed the main waterway, though there were several places where tributaries split to their left and right. Even if they had wanted to change course, they were at the mercy of the current, and Cade doubted they could redirect the boat easily with their oars.

The river had by now broadened to as wide as a tennis court was long, but even in the daylight it seemed somewhat gloomy, the canopy casting much of it in shadow. Still, among the rush of water and the chirping of birds, Cade began to feel at ease for the first time. He took off his boots and dangled his feet in the water, reveling as the cool liquid washed the blisters, sweat, and grime that had gathered there in their trek across the desert.

Then a dark shape passed beneath. It was deep down, murky among the green, trailing fronds that made up the river bottom. But the size alone made Cade jerk his feet from the water—it looked almost as long as the boat itself. Perhaps relaxing would have to wait.

"Good idea," Scott muttered, moving up to crouch behind him. "God knows what's down there."

"I don't think God had much to do with this place," Spex sighed, stretching out on the bow. "But it's nice to be out of that sun."

Cade shook his head and stood, peering into the jungle on either side for something, anything that would give them some clue as to where they were. But the trees at the water's edge were thick with leaves, stretching for the meager sunlight that filtered through the gap in the canopy along the river's center. It was as if twin halves of a leafy roof arched over the water, with a long strip of clear sky separating them.

Even as he looked up, something came down from the sky, plummeting toward him like a meteorite. Cade scrambled back with a yelp.

He landed on Scott in a tangle of limbs, eliciting a tirade of curses. But there was no splash, nor thud. Instead, the object hung there, hovering in the air, just as it had above the stone table at the keep.

The drone. It followed in tandem with the boat, as if perched above the stern upon an invisible pillar. Cade could only gape as it pivoted its lens-like front toward them, looking for all the world like a robotic teardrop floating on its side.

"What the hell," Scott groaned. "It's following us?"

As if to compound their misery, the drone projected the timer once more.

05:06:43:12
05:06:43:11
05:06:43:10

"So, no matter what we do, that timer's gonna end with us next to this thing," Spex said, scratching his head. "Kind of makes me think we should have stayed at the keep."

Eric let out a groan of frustration, then stood.

"Why are you following us?" Eric demanded, standing up and prodding at the drone with his oar. "Stupid damn thing."

Immediately, the drone moved closer . . . and answered.

"I must retain proximity to contenders at all times."

It was a dull, polite, robotic voice, but one that sent chills down Cade's spine.

He stared at it. All this time—it could understand them?

"What is this place?" Cade blurted, the question that had been bouncing around his head for the past two days rising unbidden to his lips.

"Answer prohibited."

Cade cursed. Of course, whoever they were, they wouldn't make it that easy.

"Are you allowed to tell us anything?" Cade demanded.

"Yes."

Scott chuckled.

"Well, at least he's honest."

"What can you tell us?" Eric asked, speaking slowly.

"The scope of your question is too broad. Please narrow parameters."

"It's useless," Scott groaned. "If they wanted us to know what's going on, we *would* already."

"What are you?" Spex tried.

"The primary function of a Codex is the collection and dissemination of cataloged earthbound knowledge. It is my pleasure to provide this service for you."

"Earthbound?" Yoshi muttered. "What does that mean?"

"Maybe it's mostly supposed to give us information that originates from Earth," Cade said, thinking aloud. "That's why it knew our names—we come from Earth. Is that right . . . Codex?"

"That is correct," the Codex answered.

Silence reigned for a few moments longer, and the boat continued to float down the river.

"Really helpful, isn't it?" Finch called sarcastically from behind the wheel.

"Sounds like one of those voice assistants," Scott said, grinning. "Hey, Codex, play 'Despacito.'"

Cade snorted as the Codex turned to the boy.

"I'm sorry, I don't understand. Can you be more specific?"

Cade sighed and resumed his scanning of the riverbanks, trying not to look at the timer that continued its ominous countdown just above his sight line.

And then, as the waterway began a slow curve, he saw it. A giant, rock-carved human head, half-submerged in the shallows.

"What the hell . . . ," he breathed.

It was enormous, larger than a pickup truck. The head had a flat-nosed face, and a square helmet on its brow. But other than that, there was no text, runes, hieroglyphs . . . nothing that might help him know where it came from.

"What is that?" Eric said. "Another Roman thing?"

The Codex moved. One moment it was hovering above Cade's head, the next it was beside the carved head. Blue light flashed along the statue as the Codex scanned it, then it darted back to its prior position.

"This remnant is an Olmec civilization colossal head from an area that is now called Mexico, 1023 BC."

Cade gaped at it. Perhaps the drone could be useful after all.

"Does that mean we've gone three thousand years into the past?" Jim gasped, poking his head out from the boat's cabin.

"Not necessarily," Cade replied. "This thing could've sat here since then."

The head seemed to stare at them as the boat floated by, and Cade felt a chill down his spine, despite the heat.

By now they had passed the statue, and Cade could see the

river was narrowing and picking up speed. But that was not what caught his eye. It was the wide, gray stone arch that curved across the river ahead, high above them. Only . . . it wasn't stone at all.

It was moving.

CHAPTER
17

A GREAT PILLAR OF KNOBBLED FLESH STRETCHED ACROSS THE river like a crane. At its tip, a hump-nosed, reptilian head munched softly on the waxy leaves of a tree, while at its base, an enormous, elephantine body stood in the dappled shadows. Its four great legs were planted like ancient tree trunks, and beyond, a tail even longer than its neck lashed back and forth. From end to end, it was as long as an airliner, and it looked just as heavy.

"Is that what I think it is?" Spex asked.

"*I'm afraid I do not know what you are thinking,*" the Codex intoned.

"Oh, shut up," Eric said. "He wasn't talking to you."

"This is some next-level madness," Yoshi groaned. "Either I'm tripping serious balls right now, or that's a goddamned dinosaur."

Cade couldn't believe his eyes. It was as if he were watching a film and any second the illusion would be shattered by some poorly rendered animation. Instead, the giant sauropod's head swiveled to look at them and watched them go by with dull, cow-like eyes.

"I'm ready to go back to the keep," Scott groaned.

The current pulled them out of sight in just a few minutes, leaving Cade stunned as the others argued around him. He couldn't help wondering if he had imagined the whole thing. Romans? Dinosaurs? Mutants? Maybe Yoshi was right. Maybe he *was* hallucinating.

Then, as if prompted by his thoughts, the jungle fell away on the boat's right, casting them in bright sunlight once more.

"You've got to be kidding me," Cade whispered.

The banks were awash with color, but these were no flowers that broke up the green grass of the wide plain to his right. Animals. Hundreds upon hundreds of them. From great behemoths to small, fast-moving critters.

Sleek, birdlike theropods with blue-black plumages strutted back and forth on two legs, snapping their teeth at one another's tails as they tumbled playfully on the muddy banks. These smaller, scrawnier creatures drank from the round footprints left by the herds of great, ponderous sauropods that dominated the skyline, matching the dinosaur they had seen at the river in shape, if not quite in size.

The long-necked sauropods were a sight to behold. With each gulp from their enormous gullets, a bowling ball of water traveled up their throats in an undulating wave, as the beasts sated their thirst in the cool waters of the river.

Duck-billed hadrosaurs lined the river farther down, their

strange, round-beaked mouths sucking up weeds and water alike. Some sat on their haunches, their shorter, clawed fore-feet in the air; others on all fours, walking through the shallows with a strange, lopsided gait that made them look as if they would fall forward at any minute.

Watching as the boat floated by, the hadrosaurs lowed mournfully, a strange cross between a moo and a honk that seemed to reverberate through Cade's chest as he stared across the water, keeping time with the frantic beating of his heart.

Among the herds, individual creatures slunk between the great beasts, each different, but no less fascinating: furred mammalian predators that looked like dogs, cats, even wart-hogs and hyenas, but larger and stranger than anything he had seen. There was so much to see, and yet he couldn't focus, his eyes skipping from one creature to the next with wonder.

Some of the dinosaurs had hoary, bumpy skin; others scales like those of a lizard. More still had plumages, and all sported some form of display—red wattles, bristled spines, balloon-like vocal sacs, vivid skin tones, and plumes of kaleido-scopic feathers more colorful than a peacock's and twice as flamboyant.

A far cry from the fossilized bones that had fascinated him so much in his childhood visits to the museum. Who would have known that coating their skeletal structures, there was so much more?

But just as he began to smile, a flood of fear coursed through him as a dinosaur that lived in the psyche of every prehistory lover emerged from the tree line. It moved through the gathered masses like a shark through a shoal, the crowd parting and closing as it stomped toward the water. A Tyrannosaurus rex—or a large bipedal theropod much like it—buried its head beneath the waters, oblivious to the creatures nearby. Its body was dusted in dark proto-plumage, spiny follicles that sat somewhere between fur and feathers.

Then the boat disappeared into the tunnel of the jungle once again, and the scene disappeared from sight.

"Dinosaurs?" Eric shouted, slapping the bow with his hands. "Is this a joke?"

Cade stared back the way they had come, the reality of their situation finally hitting home.

"This place is twisted," Scott muttered.

He paused.

"Maybe my mind's twisted."

Somewhere behind Cade, Spex began humming the *Jurassic Park* theme song.

"Will you shut up," Yoshi groaned.

Cade couldn't begin to explain what he had just witnessed. Certainly there was a common theme. History, even prehistory, was at play here. Creatures, people, and civilizations long dead were where they should not be. Had they traveled through time and space? A wormhole, perhaps, that they had unknowingly flown through, bringing them to this place.

It did not explain the vipers though. Not unless they too were some ancient Earth species, their fossils undiscovered beneath the sands of time. Nor did it tell him what the Codex was, or who had generated those strange force fields in the canyon, or placed him there.

But there was no time to contemplate, for the river had

changed. Now, the current was picking up speed, the once-placid surface swirling and cresting with white. And beyond, Cade could see rocks in the water, at first a few scattered boulders, then more and more. For a brief, terrifying moment, he and the others stared in terror.

He saw it then, half-beached on the muddy bank at the jungle edge. A red, wooden vessel, its hull splintered and holed, the back end half-submerged in the water. Cade spun to look at the boat's cabin in horror, panic finally unfreezing his throat.

"Row!" he yelled. "Get to the shore!"

Finch's face was pale behind the algae-stained window as he heaved on the wheel, while water sprayed as the boys around him paddled desperately. Their boat edged toward the shore. But it was slow . . . too slow. A rock swam into view, just beneath the surface ahead of them.

A thud shuddered through the boat, pitching Cade forward. For a second he flailed, grabbing for a railing that was not there.

Then he was in the water, plunged into cold darkness. He slammed against the river bottom, the long weed fronds grasping at him as they tangled about his body. For a moment he struggled, a silent scream bubbling from his lips, but seconds later he was tugged free by the current, surfacing and gasping for air. It was all he could do to breathe before he was snatched beneath once again, crashing into one immovable rock, then another, the pain blossoming across his ribs and back.

Again and again he was pulled beneath the surface, breathing when he could, gagging when he couldn't, and all the while pulled inexorably onward. For what felt like hours, Cade's world was a misery of dark, rushing water that choked and battered him in equal measure.

Sand rasped against his side as he tumbled beneath once more, and he kicked out, reaching the air with what felt like the last of his strength. A patch of reeds near the bank slapped against his face, and he grasped at them, choking in terror as they snapped in his hands, but gave him just enough purchase to snatch another handful. Then, his eyes blurry with water, he dragged himself into a thicket, his feet tiptoeing on the riverbed. He hauled his torso forward, his body screaming for air, until he finally crawled onto the bank.

He vomited the water he had swallowed onto the wet-slick grass. Only then could he collapse onto his back, staring at the foliage far above him.

He flopped his head to one side, gazing back up the river. No sign of the boat. No sign of anyone.

Cade was alone.

CHAPTER
18

FOLLOW THE RIVER. THAT WAS WHAT LOGIC TOLD CADE TO do—after all, if the boat hadn't passed him by, then it must have beached itself farther up.

If only it were that simple.

As he limped along the bank, pushing through the snarled weeds and bushes that grew there, he saw it. Hissing in frustration, Cade fell to his knees.

The river branched in two upstream, and he had no idea which branch had brought him there. He would have flipped a coin if he had one, but he had nothing in his pockets—his only weapon, the hand axe, was lost somewhere at the river's bottom.

He looked at the rushing water. The river had narrowed somewhat—he could probably throw a football and hit the other side at the narrow point where the river forked. But at the same time, it had picked up speed.

There was no getting to the other side, even if he thought it was the right direction. So Cade followed the bank he was already on, taking the easiest path he could forge. On he went, pushing through the reeds and bushes, his eyes darting back and forth for signs of danger. But soon enough, he found himself the subject of interest from the local wildlife. Luckily for him, they were not of the reptilian variety.

These were dragonflies, and they buzzed around his head like miniature helicopters. Each specimen was enormous, as large as a seagull and twice as fast. Their carapaces were iridescent, made up of every color of the rainbow, swirling around him as he picked his way along the tangled mire that was the river's edge.

It got so bad that he could barely see a few feet in front of his face, and they were not shy about getting in close, some even settling on his shoulders.

In particular, they seemed to be attracted to the blue of his uniform, chewing at the material ineffectually with their mandibles. It was only when he dropped down into the mud and rolled around in it that the insects began to disperse, his colorful clothing now a dull brown.

That had probably been a good idea anyway—if a predator was nearby, his blue uniform would have stuck out against the green like a sore thumb. A shadow blotted the sky above him, and he sighed.

"Go away, bugs. I'm not edible, okay?"

And then, as if it had been there all along, he saw the Codex hanging above him like a miniature moon.

"What are you doing here?"

"I must retain close proximity to contenders at all times. It's for your own good."

Cade sighed again.

"You said that last time. Why aren't you with the others?"

The Codex zoomed closer.

"You, Cade Carter, were the first contender to be identified. I will keep following you, Cade, until an alternative contender is assigned."

"Seriously?" Cade asked.

"Yes."

"Stupid thing," Cade muttered. "Where's your countdown timer anyway?"

He regretted his words as soon as they left his mouth.

"Here."

Moments later, the timer flashed into existence.

```
05:06:18:09
05:06:18:08
05:06:18:07
```

"Put it away, would you?"

The timer disappeared, and Cade breathed a sigh of relief. It was nice to have company of a sort. And perhaps another chance to answer his questions.

"What's it counting down to anyway?"

"The qualifying round," the drone replied in its bored-sounding, robotic voice.

"What happens in the qualifying round?" Cade asked.

"The scope of your question is too broad. Please narrow parameters."

Cade sighed. This thing didn't want to tell him anything.

"Well, could you at least guide me back to the *Witchcraft*?"

"Action prohibited."

"You're useless," Cade said, settling on a rotting bough beside the river for a rest.

Cade thought for a moment. Maybe if he rephrased the question . . .

"Can you tell me about the *Witchcraft* and where it came from?" Cade asked.

"Yes."

He laughed, despite himself. The thing was as slippery as a greased eel.

"Go on."

"The Witchcraft *is a twenty-three-foot luxury cabin cruiser that disappeared in 1967 with its owner Daniel Burack and his friend Father Padraig Horgan, somewhere within the Bermuda Triangle."*

Cade felt his hackles stand on end. The Bermuda Triangle. Disappeared. This was all too strange. But was it true?

"Why can you tell me that, but not guide me to it?"

"I can identify remnants using recorded data from Earth. I can also identify locations where remnants were last scanned. Had you scanned the Witchcraft *recently and it had subsequently remained in that place, I could have guided you there."*

Cade realized that *remnants* must be the Codex's term for historical artifacts such as the Olmec head, and he assumed scanning was what the Codex had done when it had flashed the statue with blue light.

Speaking of which.

"Interesting," he said. "Can you guide me to the Olmec head?"

"*Yes.*"

Despite his unease, Cade couldn't help but laugh again. That would at least tell him which direction to go, since the boat had passed it not long before the accident.

"Guide me to the Olmec head."

"*Of course.*"

The drone zoomed closer, then suddenly Cade found himself staring into a rectangle of blue light. It reminded him of the strange force field he had encountered in the canyon, for it had the same semitranslucent opacity. But this time, there was a pattern on it.

It took Cade a moment to realize what it was. A map.

But not just any map. It was a map of the caldera, the expansive volcanic crater seen from a bird's-eye view. Or at least, a part of the caldera. He could see the gently curved edge of the mountains, and the vast swath of the desert beyond.

And there, somewhere in the expanse of a green canopy on the other side, was a flashing red dot that he guessed symbolized himself, right beside a thin blue capillary that must delineate the river. There were also smaller, glowing blue dots scattered across the projections.

"Which is the Olmec head?" Cade asked.

"*This one.*"

A blue dot flashed, and Cade breathed a sigh of relief. It seemed it was on the same branch of the river he was walking along. If he continued in the same direction, he'd come across the boat. Or failing that, he could follow the river back to the keep.

The thought of being alone in this world filled Cade with a dread so deep and dark that he had to shake it from his mind. One problem at a time. Less thought, more action.

Cade reached out to touch the map, and to his amazement, he was able to manipulate the image in much the same way he might on a smartphone, zooming closer. And what he found was even more interesting. There was another blue dot, not too far from him. Another "remnant."

"What's that?" Cade asked.

"*Remnant identified as Captain Cole Dylan Benjamin Moore of the Seventh Cavalry Division in the US Army.*"

Cade's pulse quickened. A soldier? Or, at least, the last known location of one. There was no way he was going to ignore it. Yes, his friends might be ahead—the boat might even make it through the rapids while he was away from the river, passing him by.

But to meet someone else, someone armed, who might know more about this place? There was no way he was passing this up.

He took a deep breath; this could be a fatal choice. Then he turned and, for the first time, pushed his way into the jungle.

The waxy leaves slapped against his feet as he waded through the sea of vegetation. And it only took a few steps for his world to completely change.

There was so much life in this place. Insects whined around his head; mosquitoes the size of hornets made him glad the uniform he wore was so tough. A millipede as long and thick as a snake twisted its way up a tree beside him, avoiding the veritable river of giant red ants that seemed to cut a swath through the jungle floor ahead of him.

Cade made an awkward leap over the marching ants, careful not to disturb them. They were as big as beetles and looked twice as deadly, the guard ants that lined the edges of marching workers opening and closing their mandibles.

Above and around him, the calls of various creatures echoed. Chirps, whistles, even low, throaty bellows seemed to shiver the very air. He could not see them, but far larger animals than insects were nearby. It would be best to keep moving quickly. At least when he'd been by the river, he'd had the option of throwing himself in again to escape any predators.

He continued on, slapping at any insects that ventured too close. It was even hotter in the jungle, and soon his muddy clothes were drenched with sweat. Now that he was in among the trees, he found the jungle had a strange, double-layered quality to it—the tall sequoia-type trees created an epic ceiling, with smaller trees soaking up the meager rays in a second, scattered layer below.

Meanwhile, lush vegetation of waxy-leafed bushes, snarling vines, and fallen branches made up the very bottom layer. But to Cade's surprise, he made good time through the forest floor, not least because of the strange natural pathways that crisscrossed the area.

He might have called them bush trails, made by the countless treading feet of large animals like boars and deer. But some of these were as wide as roadways, and Cade did not want to imagine the size of the creatures that had created them.

Still, the Codex followed him, and he could see his red dot was almost on top of the blue dot. And yet . . . there was nothing in front of him. Nothing but tall trees. Whenever this Cole Moore had been scanned, he was long gone now.

"Codex, when was Cole Moore last scanned?" Cade asked.

"Three years, two months, fourteen days, twenty-two hours, and seventeen seconds ago."

"You're all about the detail, aren't you," Cade said, inwardly cursing. "I wish you'd told me that before."

"Would you like me to give more detail when answering your questions?"

"Sure," Cade said sarcastically. "As much as you can."

He sighed. He should definitely have asked more questions before he hurried over here. In fact, they all should have been asking it questions—it was the only thing that had any answers. There had been no time . . . or at least, not since they had known it would speak to them.

Still, he might have gone in regardless, if only to look for clues. Even if the soldier was nowhere to be seen.

Defying logic, Cade searched the area, hoping for footprints, tree markings, anything at all. It was then that his eye caught something glinting among the roots of a nearby tree. He bent and picked it up. It was a Zippo lighter, empty and rusted. A name was engraved on its side: C. Moore.

Had the soldier dropped it? He looked up, more out of instinct than anything else. And there, hidden among the branches at the top of the tree, was a body. Or what remained of one.

Despite being so far below, Cade recognized the army uniform, though it was obscured by the foliage. It looked like

Moore hadn't wandered off after all. He had died, up in that tree.

Cade's belly twisted with disappointment. He had never felt such loneliness, such a desire for companionship. He'd thought he might find someone here. Instead, he'd wasted precious time, time that could have been spent getting back to the others.

Although . . . this body *had* already yielded results. He had a lighter now, even if the fuel inside had long since dried up. What further treasures could be up there, hidden in the soldier's pockets, or hanging off a branch? A gun perhaps?

But how to get up there? He could climb the branches, but the top was fifty feet in the air. It was a daunting task. One slip, and it would be over for him. For a moment he pictured himself dragging his body along the jungle bottom with broken legs, a tide of ants picking him apart, piece by living piece. He shuddered and pushed the thought aside.

In the past, he might have played it safe, but now he wasn't so sure. Pleading guilty had been playing it safe . . . and he'd give anything to change that.

But here, now? This was his best hope of giving himself a fighting chance. He'd roll the dice.

Cade wondered what Cole had been doing up there. The treetops certainly seemed like the safest place to sleep, or hide. But how had he had died up there? Perhaps he had been injured and managed to escape to the tree's relative safety before succumbing to his wounds. Or perhaps it was where the . . . whoevers . . . had left him. Maybe he had already been dead.

There were a lot of questions, but he wasn't going to find

the answers loitering around there. Cade spat on his hands, then gritted his teeth.

"Here goes everything," he muttered.

He jumped onto the trunk and heaved himself upward, glad of the rough bark of the lowest branch. As he pulled up, he pressed his feet on either side of the tree, using the friction there to grip and push with his legs, then grasp the next branch higher with his arms. Now he was able to use the previous branch as a foothold, and he hung there, already tiring.

It wasn't so bad—there was a clear path to the top, a ladder of intermittent branches and footholds. He just couldn't look down.

He reached up and repeated the motion, sweat sticking his shirt to his back. Then again, and again. He tried to ignore the mosquitoes whining around his head. Pull, grip, pull and grip again.

Suddenly, the tree shifted, tilting Cade forward and then bending back, as if a gust of wind he could not feel had blown through the branches above. At the same time, he heard a sound just beneath him, like a champagne cork popping but many times louder.

His legs came free, and for a desperate moment he hung there by his fingertips, his nails digging into the bark. Choking with fear, Cade caught his toe on the trunk, giving him the leverage to pull up to the next branch.

Cade didn't stop to look down. All he could do was continue his ascent, dragging himself onward with all the speed he could muster. The tree lurched a second time, and Cade felt his gorge rise as he swung back and forth. Still he climbed.

On and on he went, the sweat streaming down his face and stinging his eyes, arms burning with effort, legs cramping.

And then he was there, in among the leaves of the tree's top. He perched on the nearest branch and hugged it for dear life, gulping down air as the world spun beneath him. Vertigo almost brought up the figs he had eaten for breakfast, but he forced it down, knowing it could be his last meal for a while.

He took deep breaths, closing his eyes until the nausea receded. Then he opened them, blinking the sweat away.

But as his view of the ground came into focus, a silent scream of horror hissed from his parched throat.

A dinosaur had arrived.

CHAPTER
19

05:05:43:21
05:05:43:20
05:05:43:19

THE CODEX FLOATED ABOVE THE DINOSAUR'S HEAD, AND THE creature leaped for it, its jaws snapping. The sound of teeth clashing was the same one he had heard as he climbed the tree, and Cade felt another wave of nausea as he realized how close he had come to being devoured.

It was a theropod, based on its physique—two legs, a small pair of feathered front claws, a long tail, and a gargantuan head that seemed too big for its body. A carnosaur, if Cade had to describe it, which was an antiquated, catch-all term for the larger theropods that matched a T. rex in shape and size. Smaller theropods were usually known as raptors, of course. Everyone knew that.

For a few heart-pounding minutes, Cade could do nothing but stare at the monstrosity below him, both amazed and horrified to see such a creature up close. Spiny black quills covered its body, and an orange growth upon its head looked for all the world like a rooster's comb. Its movements were slow but controlled, its feathered tail switching back and forth as it stared up at him through two surprisingly small eyes, but with a no less terrifying gaze.

"Think . . . think . . . ," Cade muttered.

As a child, Cade had been obsessed with dinosaurs. His father had entertained his hobby, glad Cade was interested in any sort of history. Cade's memories of their conversations were hazy at best, but he remembered when his father had laughed at Cade's favorite dinosaur poster.

His father had said that prehistoric creatures were unlikely to match what Cade had seen in the movies, or in his picture books. He'd said that the animators and artists had done little more than drape a thin layer of muscle and skin over reconstructions of the fossilized bones, ignoring the fat, skin folds, bumps, lumps, spines, flaps, fur, and feathers that must have coated them. Of course, Cade didn't believe him.

His father had won the debate when he'd shown Cade pictures of three animal skeletons and asked him to tell him what they were. To Cade, they had looked like monsters.

What appeared to be a fanged cyclops skull had turned out to be an elephant's instead. Another had looked like a giant snake with a curved trident for a head—that one ended up being a blue whale. The final one looked more normal, and Cade had been given as many guesses as he wished. He had guessed cat, dog, monkey, dog, possum, weasel. It was only after he had given up that Cade's father had told him it was a raccoon.

Turned out his dad has been right, if this was indeed a dinosaur. Of course, none of this helped him with his current predicament.

"What exactly are you?" Cade whispered. Too loudly.

Beneath, the carnosaur reacted to his voice and rammed its head against the tree. Cade's stomach twisted as the bough he was perched upon swayed back and forth, and the soldier's body almost dislodged from the hollow it was wedged in.

There was a brief flash of blue light, then the voice of the Codex drifted from below.

"The closest known relative of this animal is Gorgosaurus libratus, a tyrannosaur that lived approximately seventy-five million years ago. It was a large bipedal, carnivorous theropod. Adults had an estimated length of nine feet and weight of 2.5 tons. The first fossils were discovered in—"

"Quiet!" Cade hissed as the creature's tail swished with excitement at the noise. Perhaps it hadn't been such a good idea to ask for more detail from the damned machine.

So it *was* a dinosaur, though one the Codex couldn't identify exactly. Impossible. Unless . . . it had descended from this "Gorgosaurus" creature?

But that would be unlikely. Seventy-five million years of evolution would have turned it into a chicken, or some other vastly different-looking creature.

Few creatures looked anything like their ancient ancestors. Human ancestors had been no more than shrewlike mammals back when Gorgosaurus had lived.

With no explanation coming to mind, Cade finally managed to tear his eyes away from the carnosaur and turned back to the task at hand. The soldier. Surely he must have a weapon. Something, anything that might help him.

To Cade's surprise, when he found the courage to look at the man's remains, he felt little revulsion. It was all bone, held together by the uniform and the hollow the body was wedged into. The skeleton had been picked clean by whatever creatures and insects had found it. Three years was a long time for nature to take its course, leaving a grinning skull nestled inside an upturned collar.

Cade rifled through the man's pockets, careful not to dislodge the delicate bones beneath. A pencil and a notebook, though the pages had been soaked by the rain so many times that it was little more than a lump of papier-mâché. A pack of cigarettes was in similar condition—though Cade could make out faded Japanese writing on the outside. There were Japanese coins too.

Thinking back on his history, Cade guessed that Moore had probably been a soldier during the US occupation of Japan, just after the Second World War. Not that this helped him much. He stuffed the items into his pockets, somewhat disappointed but eager to get to the real prize. Because wedged beneath the captain's legs was a long, canvas duffel bag.

Forcing himself to take it slowly, he tugged it free and was glad to feel a heavy weight there. Whatever was inside would be more than scraps of paper. Maybe even a rifle.

The zipper was rusted shut, but the stitching along the edges was ragged enough that Cade managed to tear a large rent down its side. But when he reached within, his hand came away slick. There were pole-like objects inside, and each one was wrapped in oilcloth.

He took the one nearest the top and unraveled the cloth, careful to not let its contents fall to the ground below. He was hoping for a service pistol or a rifle. But what he found instead was much more archaic.

It was a sword. A samurai sword by his guess, with a leather-wrapped handle and scabbard. He imagined the rest of the objects were swords too, but he dug through the bag all the same. He was right—all swords, it seemed. No guns, no documents, no clothing. Just swords.

"Great," Cade muttered.

An hour ago he would have killed for a sword. But it wasn't exactly going to solve his dinosaur problem. And now he was beginning to feel thirsty. He tried not to think of the cool river less than a hundred feet away from him.

He looked down, and his eyes met the carnosaur's. The beast was sitting like a dog at a dinner table, glaring up at him with razor focus. Cade didn't think it would be leaving anytime soon.

CHAPTER
20

05:00:39:17
05:00:39:16
05:00:39:15

THE SUN WAS ALREADY BEGINNING TO SINK BELOW THE HORIzon, and Cade's heart sank with it. Every hour that passed, the others could be moving farther away from him. His choice to pursue Cole had been a fateful one, and now he was suffering the consequences.

To be alone, in the midst of all this strangeness. Unthinkable.

"Codex," Cade whispered, more out of loneliness than anything else.

The drone floated up to meet him, its iris seeming to stare passively at him as it hung in the air beside him. Below, the carnosaur seemed unperturbed by the movement, but remained where it was, staring up while resting on its haunches. Cade had not spoken to the Codex in a while, hoping that if he remained still and silent, the predator would get bored and leave.

No such luck.

Cade had been pleasantly surprised to see the swords—fourteen in total—were sharp and free of rust; the oil that coated them had kept them almost as good as new, despite the years they had likely spent within the bag. One of them was now in his hands—it made him feel better.

For some time he had fantasized about sliding down the tree and leaping from above, beheading the beast in one great blow, movie-style. But Cade was sure that even if he could pull off such a feat, he would break both legs when he landed. More likely, the carnosaur would be waiting with its jaws open wide. He simply be serving himself up like a treat thrown to a pet.

Just like in the new school, Cade was back to being both bored and scared at the same time. He looked at his sword instead, inspecting it in the ailing dusk light, before it was too dark to see.

The slightly curved blade was as long as his arm, with dappled streaks that flowed like water along the steel. The handle was made of simple black leather that creaked when he gripped it but felt firm in his palm. Its near perfection was only marred by the slightest of marks here and there along the blade, telling Cade the sword had seen battle before.

He tested the edge against his arm and winced at its sharpness.

As for the scabbard, it was coated in a black lacquer, with a long red ribbon knotted to its side. Cade created a loop with the ribbon and draped it over his head in a makeshift sling. Now he kind of regretted it; the sword dug into his back, but he was too tired to do anything about it. Not to mention that any movement excited the carnosaur below, and he was still hoping it would get bored and walk away.

"Tell me about this sword," he whispered, curious about where it had seen battle. "Quietly."

"*The Honjo Masamune, forged by Japan's greatest swordsmith, Goro Nyudo Masamune, in the fourteenth century. Considered to be the finest sword ever made, it is one of Japan's most important historical artifacts, handed down from shogun to shogun. It went missing in 1946 when the sword was confiscated, along with thirteen other swords, by Sergeant Koridie Beimo during the United States' occupation of Japan, according to Mejiro police. The swo—*"

"That's enough," Cade hissed, cutting the drone off. "Maybe dial back the amount of detail a bit, okay?"

"*Understood,*" the Codex replied.

Interesting. It didn't say "yes" this time. Perhaps it was getting better at talking to him and comprehending what he meant. Now if he could get it to understand sarcasm, they might have a real conversation.

Ignoring the Codex, Cade stared at the sword, turning it over in his hands. Somehow, he had stumbled across a treasure trove. But something didn't add up.

"Koridie Beimo . . . Cole D. B. Moore," he murmured to himself.

Whoever had written down the name had garbled it, the American nomenclature too foreign for them to transcribe it correctly. Then, somehow, Moore's body had ended up here with the swords. And Cade after him. What were the chances?

But then he had followed the blue dot, had he not? It seemed whoever, or whatever, had placed them there had made a habit of taking lost remnants from the past. The Ninth

Legion. The *Witchcraft*. Even the Olmec head. All placed here, and left to rot?

No. They *wanted* the contenders to find them. Pieces in a game that Cade did not understand. A game he was going to lose if he didn't do something soon. So, as the last light from the sun faded away, and the strange double moon appeared on the horizon, he considered his options.

He could wait until the carnosaur left, but he suspected the creature would outlast him—there was a running river for it to drink from nearby, and the carnosaur wouldn't leave until it ate him, that seemed clear by now. So . . . why not let it eat him?

Well, not actually. But make it think it had.

"Codex, I want you to float over to that tree over there," Cade said. "Try not to get the creature's attention."

To Cade's surprise, the drone zoomed off, and beneath, the dinosaur swished its tail with excitement. Time to put his plan in action.

First, Cade coated himself in the oil from the swords as best he could, going beneath his uniform and rubbing the oily cloths they had been wrapped in all over. That would help mask his scent, or at least he hoped it would. The oil was not particularly pungent, though it smelled faintly of garlic for some reason.

As an added bonus, the mosquitoes that had been whining about his head seemed far less interested in him all of a sudden. He was getting used to feeling filthy, but it felt strange to be so greasy on top of all the grime.

Finally, he slowly pulled Cole's remains from the hollow in the tree and cradled them in his arms.

"I'm sorry," Cade whispered.

Then he unleashed a wild scream and hurled the body out into the night. He had just enough time to see the carnosaur's maw gape open in a flash of yellow pink before pressing himself into the hollow that the corpse had once occupied.

There was a snapping, rattling sound as the dinosaur whipped its desiccated meal back and forth. Cade held his breath, his heart thundering so hard that he could hear his own pulse in his ears.

If this didn't work, he was a dead man.

CHAPTER
21

H E HEARD IT LEAVE. ALMOST FELT IT, AS IF HE COULD FEEL its paces through the vibrations in the tree. He wasn't sure if it was the oil covering his smell, the soldier's body, or just that the beast could no longer see him.

Still, he did not move a muscle for hours in case it lay in wait for him, nor did he speak to the Codex in case it heard his voice. Instead, he listened to the sounds of the night—the unfamiliar hoots, squeals and chirps of creatures he could not see or imagine.

Soon, sleep snatched at him. Time blurred as his head nodded against his chest, fits and starts of slumber that did little to relieve his exhaustion.

04:10:57:36
04:10:57:35
04:10:57:34

It was only when the sun breached the horizon that he finally allowed himself to wake, helped along by the whine of insects and a cacophony of sound that greeted the morning. He would have thought all the twittering and screeching was birds—had he not remembered that he had just seen a creature that had lived hundreds of millions of years before birds had been around.

Then again, birds were descended from dinosaurs. Birds *were* dinosaurs, in fact. Survivors of the great meteorite that had taken out most of their species and given other animals a chance to thrive in their place.

Cade shook his head, wincing as pain lanced through his skull. Dehydration had set in, and he had the kind of migraine that would floor most people for the day. Now he had to trek through the sweltering jungle, weak and hungry as a newborn lamb and almost as helpless. Only the sword, still strapped to his back, gave him any sort of hope. He threw the rest of them down, flinching at the clang of metal as the duffel hit the ground.

It took Cade almost an hour to slide down the tree, each movement making his head spin and leaving him clutching at the branch until the world came back into focus. He had never wanted a drink so badly.

When he reached the ground, he collapsed to his knees. It felt like an age before he had caught his breath and felt strong enough to move again.

For a moment, he examined the huge indents on the ground, like a robin's claw prints in the snow but blown up a hundred times their size. Cade had almost convinced himself he had imagined the carnosaur, but here was the evidence, stark as a hand in front of his face.

Cade took the handles of the duffel and put his arms through them to make it a backpack, then tugged each strap over his head, crisscrossing them over his chest to make them tighter. The duffel hung over the scabbard somewhat awkwardly, but at least the tear he had pulled the sword through was small enough that none of them would fall out if he had to run.

It was heavier than he expected, and for a moment he contemplated abandoning it. But if he did manage to find the others, they could all make good use of the weapons. They were certainly better than sharpened rocks.

Reeling slightly under the weight of the swords, Cade made his way back through the trees, this time with sword in hand to defend himself. But if there were dangerous creatures around him, he didn't see them, for it was all he could do to stay standing, his eyes set only on the ground in front of him. The edges of his vision were blurred, and his tongue cleaved to the roof of his mouth like a wad of dry leather, but he forced himself on. He was desperately vulnerable, and the sooner he reached the relative safety of the river, the better.

He felt a flood of relief when he found the rushing tributary once more—for a moment he had been worried he'd gone in the wrong direction. Kneeling in the shallows, he took the time to gulp great mouthfuls of water, slaking his thirst if not the hunger that cramped his belly.

It seemed that it took no time at all for his migraine and the dizziness to subside, reduced to a dull ache that was manageable and improving with every minute. For a while Cade simply stayed there, ducking his head beneath the water and letting the current wash his hair clean of the grime and sweat of the day before.

At the back of his mind, he knew that it might have been a mistake to drink the water. His brief time with the Boy Scouts, many years ago, told him that he should have boiled it first, perhaps even filtered it through a sock filled with charcoal. But boil it in what, and how? No, he'd had no choice, even if his guts might now be swimming with primordial bacteria.

Pushing the worries aside, Cade considered his options. Really, there was only one, the same as before. Continue back the way he had come, up the river until he reached where he hoped the others had succeeded in stopping the boat before the rapids.

So, with a groan, Cade staggered on. Now he remained on lookout, his eyes roving the jungle's edge as he picked his way along the bank. At the first sign of danger, he would throw himself into the water, preferring the chance of the rushing river's embrace to certain death inside a predator's stomach.

The sword was heavy in his hands, its length tangling in the reeds as it drooped. Finally, he sheathed it in the scabbard on his back, knowing that if it came to fight or flight, he would likely take the latter approach. It was not an easy maneuver— the sword was too long for him to slide in at a comfortable angle.

As the minutes ticked by, Cade's heart began to lift at his progress. He was making good time, and so far there wasn't a creature in sight. Surely he would find the others soon. Had the river really taken him that far beyond the rapids?

Cade was about to ask the Codex to open the map again when he heard it. The snapping of a twig, almost indistinguishable above the sound of the river. It was enough to make him stop and look across the water.

There were bushes there, interspersed with hanging lianas and low branches. For a second, Cade thought he had imagined it. But then he saw them, half-obscured by the vegetation. Yellow eyes, watching him.

He stopped, and as if the creature realized it had been seen, it lifted itself from a stooped crouch and stepped into view. Cade's heart sank. Standing across the river . . . was a raptor.

But this was not the scaly, lizard-like raptor from *Jurassic Park*. No, this was a different creature, though no less terrifying. It stood almost as tall as the film's animatronics, with the same basic body shape, but that was where the similarity ended.

For the creature was covered in spiny plumage, tawny as an owl's, with the same patterning that had helped it blend with the foliage. At the end of its raised tail, a plume rose and fanned out as the creature lowered its body and hissed, and now Cade could not take his eyes off the enormous talons on each of its feet—the largest of which matched the length of a butcher's knife and was sharp enough for the same job.

"Oh sh—"

Cade was cut short as fresh horror stole the words from his mouth. A second raptor emerged from the trees. It was a touch smaller and drabber in appearance but with the same hungry gaze that never strayed from Cade's face.

More rustling. Another appeared. And another. Before Cade knew it, five raptors were watching him across the river, their lips drawn back as they hissed, saliva glistening on their sharp yellow teeth. A pack.

He stood still as a statue, knowing that one move could set them off. The river that flowed between them was deep, though he had reached a bend, where the current was slower and the width narrower. Could raptors even swim? Or had he lucked out?

It was at that moment that the alpha raptor opened its mouth and emitted a sound like none other Cade had heard before. It was a strange, cackling honk that reverberated through Cade's chest and into his bones. For the briefest of moments, silence reigned, the ambient calls of the jungle quieted by the noise.

Then, before Cade could react, the creatures advanced into the river as one, splashing through the shallows and into the deeper water. Cade allowed himself a heartbeat to watch as the current drifted the raptors downriver, but it seemed in no time at all they were halfway across, if a little farther away from him.

Without a second glance, Cade sprinted into the jungle, his heart hammering in his chest, branches tearing at his clothes and hair. Soon he was running between the trees, jumping over moss-covered rocks and fallen branches. The duffel and scabbard bounced on his back, hampering him, but they held the only weapons he had, and he dared not slow to uncross the straps across his chest.

His vision was filled with a maze of trees and tangled vines, but all he could do was zigzag through them, snatching glances over his shoulder. Now, he could hear the yawping of the raptors, echoing through the trees and getting louder and louder.

Frantically, he searched for some tree to hide in, but this deep in the rain forest, he was surrounded by the huge cylindrical sequoias that he couldn't hope to climb. So he ran onward, even as his breath burned in his chest and his legs screamed for rest. To top it all, the forest floor was thickening with low bushes, snatching at him as he tore his way through. Soon his world devolved into a mess of shoots and leaves.

Suddenly, he saw a strange tree with a broad network of thick roots around its base. They were latticed and twisted to form a barrier, but one gap was wide enough for him to squeeze through, and squeeze he did, heaving with all his might as his shoulders were trapped between the roots. He could hear the thrashing of branches behind him, and it seemed that any moment teeth would close around his legs.

He wrenched himself forward, pushing until he was deep among the root network, staring out at the trembling vegetation. He wanted to tug the sword free, but the space was too tight to do it quietly. So when the raptors finally emerged, he found himself pulling his knees up to his chest, praying that they would not see—or smell—him.

But that hope seemed to be in vain. If the pungent oil that had coated the swords had helped mask his scent from the carnosaur before, now it was a beacon to the creatures tracking him. It took but a moment for the alpha to approach, lowering its head and pushing it through the tangled roots and vines, its eyes fixed hungrily on Cade's own.

With a hoarse caw, it thrust forward, and Cade's vision

was filled with the raptor's pink gullet. Then the teeth crashed down just an inch from his face, and Cade whimpered as he turned his head to the side. The stench of rotting meat wafted across Cade's nostrils as the creature snapped and thrust to get closer to him, its sides caught in the tangled vines and roots.

With every thrust from the raptor's legs, tearing and scrabbling at the earth, the jaws inched ever closer. It wouldn't be long before they closed around the soft flesh of his cheeks.

Cade's hands scrambled in the dirt, hoping to find a rock, a stick, anything to defend himself with. Instead, his hand caught on his belt, the one that came with his uniform. Choking with horror, he unbuckled it and pulled it free.

As the raptor hissed and leaned back for a final lunge, Cade rammed the belt between the beast's chops, pushing with all his might. The raptor hawked at the intrusion—gnashing down on the foreign object in its mouth and yawping in surprise when it didn't snap in two, instead sinking into the leather.

Cade heaved, and the belt slipped over the razor teeth to sit on the gums at the back of its mouth, his fists now pressed on either side of its head. For a moment they stared each other down, eye to eye. Finally, after a brief tug of war, the raptor choked, spluttered, and withdrew. The belt dripped with saliva but remained intact, though its edges were ragged.

Cade took the brief respite to get a better grip, looping the loose ends around his wrists and knuckles. Moments later, the raptor charged again, its mouth closing around the belt once more.

Its strength was immense, the clawed feet scrabbling in

the earth as it shoved. Saliva flecked Cade's face, but he locked his elbows and held on for dear life. Again, the raptor withdrew, and Cade didn't wait for a third attempt. Instead, he ducked his head and tugged at the sword handle with all his might, half drawing it, then using the flats of his palms to pull the blade free the rest of the way. It fell to the ground, even as the predator went for a third assault.

He seized it from the earth just in time, lifting the blade. Too high. Rather than impaling the beast, it slid across its sinuous neck before catching in a root, nearly jarring the weapon from Cade's hands.

But it was enough to halt the beast, blood trickling down its spiny plumage as it snapped at him over the sword. Cade gritted his teeth and shoved the handle forward, levering the blade deeper across its chest. It screeched in pain and withdrew once more.

Elated with his small victory, Cade let himself hope that the raptors would leave. Instead they remained there, pacing back and forth. As the minutes ticked by, they seemed more wary, only approaching the roots and snorting at the soil. Cade could do nothing but sit in the shadows, hoping against hope that they would give up.

CHAPTER
22

THEY PROWLED OUTSIDE HIS MAKESHIFT SHELTER, THEIR yellow eyes staring hungrily at him. Another waiting game, it seemed, but this one was far more deadly. This time, Cade didn't have another body to present them with, nor a new smell to mask his scent. Nor could he sleep, or relax. One lapse of concentration, and he was raptor food.

Hours passed, the shafts of light filtering through the roots moving in tandem with the sun above.

The sword oil mingled with his sweat as he crouched inside the roots, watching his hunters settle down, as patient and still as alligators. By the time evening arrived, Cade realized they wouldn't be leaving anytime soon.

```
04:01:36:23
04:01:36:22
04:01:36:21
```

"Can you help me?" Cade asked, turning to the Codex.

"I would be happy to assist you, Cade," the Codex replied. Its voice, though monotone, seeming to his ears more cheery than usual.

"Do you have any advice for this situation?" Cade said, trying to frame his question as specifically as possible. If he heard that damned machine repeat that "parameters too vague" line one more time, he would smash it in with a rock.

"I'm afraid I can't help you, Cade," the Codex said, following what seemed like a mono-second longer than its usual response time.

"Are you?" Cade asked, bitter. "Afraid, I mean?"

The Codex's lens seemed to stare at him.

"No," it said, descending closer to him. *"Earlier, I detected frustration indicators in your responses to our conversations, and have adapted my articulation to accommodate. Would you prefer I revert to my prior, more literal speech patterns?"*

Cade shook his head.

"Do you feel anything in that mechanical shell of yours?" he spat. "Because I do. I'm goddamned terrified."

Great. He was treating the thing like a therapist now.

"No," was the Codex's simple response. *"I do not."*

Cade turned away. There would be no help forthcoming from the Codex.

Instead, he searched among the root network, hoping to find some lost remnant to use to his advantage, in case the mysterious game masters had placed something there for him. But all he found was dead leaves, sticks, and soil.

The sticks were brittle and bone dry. He had tried latticing the largest of them through the roots in front of him into a barrier, but even these snapped easily enough and would make a poor deterrent if the raptors decided to attack again.

At this point, he almost wished they would. Perhaps if he killed one of them, the others would leave him alone.

The alpha was licking the blood from the base of its neck, somehow able to contort itself like a snake to reach the wound. The four others seemed to be blocking Cade's escape, pacing around his tree slowly or crouching in wait on the peripheries of his vision.

They were like wolves on a hunt, and Cade took satisfaction in confirming one of paleontology's greatest questions: Did some dinosaurs hunt in packs? Apparently they did.

"Come at me," Cade yelled.

The noise startled the predators, and they cocked their heads, curious. But it did little to arouse another attack. Cade knew that if he emerged from his hiding place, they would likely surround him and tear him to pieces. He only stood a chance if they attacked him one by one through the gap.

More minutes ticked by, and Cade passed the time by itemizing what he had at hand. A dozen or so sheathed swords, stashed inside an improvised backpack. A dozen or so oil rags. One school uniform (ragged). One rusty lighter (empty). Miscellaneous sticks and leaves.

Then there was the Codex, still hovering in the air somewhere outside his hideout. Somehow, he didn't see it being much use to him now. It had told him earlier that he was facing a relative of a genus of raptor called *Deinonychus*, but that was about as useful as being able to name the gun that was aimed at your head.

It wasn't much to work with. He tested the lighter for the first time, struggling to move the spark wheel. Once he had loosened it from the rust, he was pleased to see it sparked easily enough, even if there was no fluid inside to keep a flame. If he ever needed a campfire, it might come in useful.

A stupid question crossed his mind, but he indulged it. Even assuming he escaped the raptors, would he want to make a fire? He had gone camping with his Boy Scout troop when he was a kid, and he had learned that fires were a double-edged sword.

Mostly, they acted as a deterrent to wild animals, who were scared of the heat and light, not to mention the dangerous humans who often came with it. But at the same time, they attracted bears, who had come to associate humans and their fires with leftover food.

Somehow he doubted that the predators in this world had formed the same connection. It was unlikely that there were many happy campers out there, leaving bags of marshmallows unattended. So. Fire. Was that the answer?

He didn't have any better ideas. It seemed sensible to pull some of the rags from his bag. Each still smelled faintly of garlic, which made him think they were soaked in vegetable oil. Not the most flammable of oils, but it meant the cloth might hold a flame longer, and light more easily too. He tied three of the rags around the top of the longest of the fallen sticks, then knotted them tighter with a strip of cloth cut from the sleeve of his uniform, which was made from fire-resistant material—according to the label. Now he had a torch.

He did this again, but with smaller sticks and two cloths, until he had five smaller torches. These he would use as fire throwers . . . in theory anyway.

Next, he took the driest of the dead leaves and placed them in a pile. With that done, he took a desiccated stick and sliced the bark away with the edge of his sword, getting to the crumbling core within. Once there, he scraped thin strips of it into wood shavings, just as his Scout leader had taught him to. Within a couple of hours, he had a veritable bird's nest of the stuff, piled on top of his hillock of leaves.

Finally he was ready. With bated breath, he flicked the lighter, aiming the meager sparks at the pile of shavings. Nothing. They landed and disappeared without so much as a fizzle.

Again and again he ran his thumb along the spark wheel, grunting with frustration each time. He continued until the skin of his thumb was pink and ragged from the motions, then switched hands and kept going, hoping that the fire would catch before the ancient flint inside the lighter ran out.

Sweat ran down his face and stung his eyes. The humidity was stifling, a strange juxtaposition to the thirst that had now returned with a vengeance. The air was too damp to start a fire like this.

He put the lighter aside and considered his tinder pile. The wood shavings at the top were as thin as he could make them. But it seemed he would need something even more delicate and fibrous. And somehow more flammable.

Cade turned his eyes back to his inventory of items. It hit him then like a bolt of lightning. The oil cloths! Of course, he couldn't simply spark his lighter on one and set it aflame; vegetable oil wasn't nearly flammable enough for that to work— it was why he wasn't concerned that his skin was coated in it.

But what he could do was take that cloth and turn it into a far better form of tinder.

He took the edge of the least greasy cloth strip from one of his torches and stretched it over the edge of his sword. Then he rubbed it back and forth, scraping the cloth until its edge had frayed into ragged fibers. These he ripped off and placed atop his wood shavings until he had what resembled a small cotton ball. That was more like it.

By now, dusk had begun to fall, the sunlight turning to a dull orange glow as its source descended below the horizon. Soon it would be too dark for him to see . . . perhaps that was what the raptors were waiting for. His time had almost run out.

Still, he had to try. At the very least, the fire would give him light—enough to defend himself if they attacked again. So he raised the lighter once more and forced the wheel down, cascading sparks onto the heap in front of him.

Smoke. The smallest trace of it, and the flare of a single thread, slowly burning down. Cade lowered his head and blew gently. For a second his heart sank, the glowing strand disappearing. Then, as if by some strange magic, the cotton ball sputtered and burst into flame.

Resisting the urge to shout with relief, Cade blew again and again, clenching his fist in victory as each successive layer took the fire. First the shavings, then the leaves, and finally, the small sticks beneath. The fire was soon crackling cheerily, its smoke filtering through the roots and toward the dimming sky above.

Cade heaved his backpack onto his shoulders and gripped the sword in his right hand.

It was time.

He hurled the first burning torch out into the dusk light, aiming it at the nearest raptor. His throw fell pitifully short, but it had the desired effect. The raptor yawped in surprise, leaping back with its hackles raised. The others, who had been squatting patiently, now stirred and raked the ground with their talons.

"Piss off," Cade yelled, shuffling closer to the root hollow's entrance and hurling another torch. This one bounced off the alpha's chest, and it squawked in annoyance, stomping at the flaming torch as if it were a rodent. It shrieked in pain as the sputtering fire set alight its feathered talons, and Cade's nostrils filled with the acrid scent of burning plumage.

He hurled another, this one hitting a third raptor square in the face, dashing sparks across the soil and eliciting a screech of rage. To Cade's surprise, smoke began to curl from the leaf-strewn ground, and the flicker of flames could be seen, spreading from the fallen torches. More. He needed more.

"Come on," he growled, emerging from the entrance. "Try me."

A fourth torch now, then the fifth, the former missing its intended raptor completely, the latter grazing its plumed tail. Now Cade only had his final, longer torch left. He crouched low and swept it close to the ground, the sword held above his head.

Already the leaves that he touched with it were taking flame, helped along by a soft breeze that fanned the area.

"I said come on!" Cade cried, feinting toward the alpha. It leaped back, limping on its burned foot.

"Yah," he snarled. "Yah, yah!"

With each shout, he swept the ground with his torch, sending burning leaves tumbling in the air. The air was now filled with smoke, a half-dozen smaller fires starting among the detritus layered over the clearing. The alpha made a tentative step toward him, favoring its uninjured foot.

Cade threw caution to the wind, leaping over the fire in front of him and swinging the torch like a baseball bat. The alpha almost fell over itself in its haste to escape. Cade kicked a pile of flaming leaves and sparks at the creature. This time, it turned and ran.

He watched in disbelief as its lashing tail disappeared into the undergrowth. The others followed, but not without a series of angry croaks and honks echoing in their wake. One moment Cade was surrounded, the next he was alone in the clearing, lungs burning from the smoke.

Now the bushes were beginning to take flame, the green leaves sending up a black smog that was swiftly turning the area into a death trap. Cade crouched low and took a few deep breaths of smokeless air, calming the hammering in his chest and the thousand thoughts rushing through his mind. He counted slowly to ten, giving the raptors time to move away. Then, as the adrenaline began to pass and exhaustion set in, he turned and ran into the undergrowth.

CHAPTER
23

HE RAN UNTIL HE THOUGHT HIS LUNGS WOULD BURST, THEN ran some more. Half an hour might have passed, and there had been no sign of the raptors.

Even so, it was not exhaustion that made him finally stop, but rather the looming shape in front of him.

At first he thought it was a mountain, its great shadow blocking the setting sun and casting the forest in shadow. When he stumbled through the thinning trees and into the clearing that surrounded it, Cade could not help but fall to his knees and stare. Stare . . . at the pyramid.

It was made from cobbled stone, built in square layers like a wedding cake with a steep stairway cut into its side. The size was vast, taller than the giant trees themselves, and its age was apparent by the thick vegetation and vines flowing down its walls.

Cade's best guess was that it was of South American origin, though he couldn't be sure. Then he realized he didn't need to be in doubt. He turned to the Codex, dutifully following behind him, the mechanical orb some feet in the air.

03:23:33:49
03:23:33:48
03:23:33:47

"Codex, what is this place?" Cade asked.

"Remnant identified as the Mayan city of Hueitapalan, first mentioned by the conquistador Hernán Cortés in 1526. It was last seen by aviator Charles Lindbergh in 1927. There have been no further sightings."

A city? Did that mean there were more buildings beyond the pyramid?

Cade groaned and struggled to his feet. His entire body ached, and all he wanted to do was find somewhere to sleep for the night. It seemed to him there was no safer place than the top of the structure—unless he was planning on climbing another tree of course. The latter seemed entirely beyond him at that moment. At the very least, scaling the pyramid would give him the lay of the land, maybe help him spot the others or some sign of human civilization. And he doubted any predators would be able to notice him there.

Investigating the "city" could wait until tomorrow. He approached the pyramid's base and let the bag of swords fall from his shoulders, groaning with relief as the straps came away. It would be waiting for him in the morning. He only wished his torch was still burning, for the structure's top would have made for a perfect signal fire. But it had sputtered out just minutes before, and he had thrown it aside. The forest fire he had left behind him would have to do.

Gritting his teeth, Cade climbed. He took it as fast as he dared—the sunlight was fading fast and he wanted to reach the top before nightfall. He wanted to see the rest of this so-called city, maybe determine which way the river was. In his frantic, desperate sprint through the jungle, he had lost all sense of direction.

The world seemed to fall under a sepia haze as he mounted the stairway, wincing as the pulled muscles in his legs stretched with each step. If it hurt now, he was not looking forward to the aches and pains the morning would bring. But one problem at a time.

Cade lost himself in the climb. It was cathartic in a way to focus on this one task. Some way up, he turned to look behind him, and in the dimming light he could see the glow of the fire, still raging deep in the jungle. In another world, another time, he would have worried about the consequences of the conflagration. Here, he could only grin at his handiwork.

Maybe the others would see it and come looking for him. He snorted at the thought.

Well, probably not.

As he ascended, he began to notice the patterns carved in the rock. The twisting snakes etched into the stairs' edges. Statues that bordered each level, worn away by the wind and rain. Detailed likenesses now reduced to little better than a child's clay figurines—a deformed leopard here, a noseless monkey there.

At this time of the evening, the noises of the jungle were changing from the chirps and hoots of the morning to the nighttime buzz of the insects. And something else. A sound that he had heard before and that sent chills down his spine despite his exertions. A stuttering honk, reverberating through the open air. Slowly, Cade turned.

The raptors. Emerging from the trees, their long tails thrashing excitedly behind them. They were the same ones as before, he could tell by the alpha. Despite a noticeable limp, it still led the pack, with the others following at a respectful distance.

Even with his heart somersaulting in his chest, Cade could not help but be fascinated by the dynamics of the group. A paleontologist would give their right hand to see what he was seeing. Only it seemed Cade would have to give a lot more than a single hand.

As if it sensed his eyes upon it, the alpha leaped up the first steps, croaking in pain as it tottered on its burned foot. Cade didn't waste another moment. He didn't think, didn't plan. Instead, he threw himself up the pyramid with everything he had, ignoring the throbbing of his thighs and the twinging of his tendons. All that mattered was to reach the top.

They were faster than him, hopping up the stairway with surprising agility. But Cade had a head start, and, after a minute of mindless panic, he scrambled up the last step. The yawping ululations of his pursuers grew louder as he spun, tugging the blade from its scabbard.

The alpha was almost on him, but now it slowed, waiting for its companions to catch up. The stairs were steep, too steep for them to attack upward with their taloned feet—they could only use their mouths. It narrowed the odds, though Cade wouldn't bet on himself.

Still, he had another advantage here; the stairway, broad though it was, remained the only way up. There was a drop on either side to the next level below of the pyramid. Not enough to kill one if it fell, but too high for a raptor to climb up and flank him. So Cade lowered the blade and prepared to defend the six-foot-wide stairway, hoping that the high ground would give him the advantage.

The first attack came from the alpha itself, a quick back-and-forth with its head, testing Cade. He slashed wildly, missing, even as the next one tried to pincer in from his right. Cade backswung at it, almost unbalancing himself, but he was rewarded for his effort. The offending creature scrambled back and slid over the edge, screeching in panic as it fell to the level below.

A flash of pain brought him back to his senses, the alpha's teeth closing on his ankle, then withdrawing before Cade could return the favor. The tough leather of his boot had taken much of the damage, but he had felt the teeth sink in, and the sensation of blood soaking into his socks. An eye for an eye. A foot for a foot.

The alpha jabbed its head again, feinting like a cobra and darting out of reach before Cade could swing. Behind it, two of the waiting raptors skirted the stair's edge, and Cade was forced to step left and right, warding them off.

Again and again they skipped back and forth, forcing Cade to overextend, risking more with every thrust. One thing he knew—he was no swordsman, wielding the weapon like a baseball bat.

He couldn't last much longer. The sword was heavy, and his reserves were spent. He was flagging, and the raptors knew it. Their cries were growing excited, and their charges more aggressive with every desperate swing he took.

Cade couldn't outfight them, or outlast them. He had to outthink them, just like last time.

By now, he had noticed a pattern. It was all about the alpha. They followed its lead. Advancing when it attacked, pulling back when it withdrew.

So he had to kill it. But how? His sword had not come even close to connecting—the predator was too fast, too clever.

He needed to bait it. And he knew exactly how.

"Try me!" he yelled out, startling the raptors for a brief second. In that moment, Cade swept the blade at the two raptors on either side of him, sending them skating back, one scrabbling at the edge before toppling over. At the same time, he stamped his uninjured foot at the stair's edge.

The alpha took its chance, and Cade yelled out in both agony and triumph as the teeth chomped around his boot, catching in both the leather and the meat of his calf.

He chopped down, but the pain of it all had thrown him. The swing lacked power, lacked speed. His heart fell in tandem with the sword.

But the blade bit . . . and passed like a hot knife through butter, severing the head and tumbling the alpha's corpse down the steps. Blood sprayed, hot and caustic. Behind, the three smaller raptors paused, their malevolent eyes still fixed on him while a fourth scrambled back onto the stairs from the level below.

The corpse settled at the nearest raptor's feet, and Cade kicked out, sending the alpha's head after it. It bounced like a macabre basketball, disappearing over the stairs' edge.

"How's that?" Cade shouted in hoarse triumph.

He marveled at the sharpness of the sword, and at the fact that his plan had worked at all.

After all these years. Still sharp as a razor.

Yet the raptors did not move. Not until the next largest of them lowered its head and lapped at the blood. Cade's heart fell, and he could hardly believe the grim sight. The new alpha stepped over the corpse, raising its bloodied muzzle at him.

It was as if some sick succession had passed between the predators. *The king is dead—long live the king.*

The wounds in his legs compounded with his exhaustion, and Cade fell to his knees. He held the sword outstretched, its tip wavering as the creature advanced.

"Dammit," Cade said.

CHAPTER
24

THE RAPTOR'S HEAD SNAPPED TO THE SIDE, AND THE BEAST screeched, retreating down the steps. Cade's eyes widened. For a moment he thought it had been shot, but there had been no sound. His mind racing, Cade used the last of his strength to yell out and lurch down the stairs, swinging his sword with wild abandon.

The raptors skittered back, unsure of themselves once more. Then a second projectile hit home, knocking the new alpha's leg from under it. It tumbled down the stairs, taking a second one with it in a tangle of feathers and limbs.

Again Cade charged, his voice hoarse as he roared a challenge, legs trembling beneath him. This time the raptors retreated, helped along by a third stone, cracking against the side of the pyramid. For that was what it was—a stone. Hurled from somewhere below with unnatural speed.

The raptors stopped halfway down before hesitating in

their descent. In that brief moment, the four remaining raptors stared at him. Another stone hummed by, missing the closest raptor by a hair's breadth and making it hiss in surprise. Then, as if by some unspoken signal, they turned tail and descended in leaps and bounds, voicing their displeasure in a series of caws and hoots.

"That's right," Cade called after them, though his voice was little more than a croak now. "You better run."

He dared not take his eyes off them, waving the sword threateningly until they disappeared into the undergrowth. Within moments, all that was left was the alpha's body, blood pooling around it on the ancient steps.

Relief flooded through him, and he sat down on the stair, his blade clattering beside him.

Only then did he allow himself to look for his savior. It was dark now, but the red moon was full and cast a wan, red-orange light over the world, coupled with the silver glow of its white satellite.

Enough to see the bottom level . . . and a shrouded figure there, crouched upon the pyramid's edge. He could see only that the figure was a person, their face turned up at him, pale in the moonlight. Even as he watched, his new ally scrambled down to the ground before haring away on a white, spindly legs.

"Wait," Cade rasped. "Come back!"

But it was no use. And there was no way Cade would catch up, not with his injuries. Instead, he scrambled back up the stairs and hurried to the far edge of the crumbling top. Beyond, he could finally see the city of Hueitapalan, revealed in all its glory in the moonlight.

Ziggurats and other structures were scattered like game pieces along a wide, paved plaza, with stone pillars and arches lining the cobbled streets. Already, nature had made inroads into the city, with saplings growing throughout, and vines and ivy coating the buildings like drizzled green icing.

Cade peered out over the scene, keeping his body pressed against the pyramid's stone top, poking only his head over the parapet. He was just in time to see his savior disappear into the nearest structure, a stone palace complex with a large, cave-like entrance at its base.

"So that's where you're hiding," Cade whispered.

He crawled to the edge of the stairs again and saved his injured legs some pain by making his way down like a toddler, bumping his buttocks along each one until his backside was bruised and he had made it to the bottom. Every second he expected to see the raptors burst out of the jungle for him, but it seemed luck was on his side and the predators had gone in search of easier prey.

Still, Cade didn't feel like hanging around. He could smell the alpha's blood, a sharp, metallic tang that almost left a taste in the air. Raptors were by no means the worst predators that inhabited the jungle, and he was sure that, before long, new creatures would arrive to feast on the dead alpha's remains.

No, he needed to get away from here.

For a moment he considered the bag of swords, but decided against trying to take them, instead sheathing his own blade and continuing on. He was feeling lightheaded now. The blood in his boots squelched as he struggled to his feet and limped for the next pyramid. Each step left him dizzied, and twice he fell.

He gripped at the grass poking between the cobbles, hauling himself forward. Strength leaving him, he was reduced to a half crawl, half stagger, until the murky entrance to the complex loomed above him.

"Hey," Cade bellowed into the darkness.

The sound of footsteps echoed ahead, then stopped. He was being watched.

Cade dragged himself to the wall and dragged himself to his feet, digging his fingernails into the crumbling mortar. The world spun as he steadied himself, then headed deeper inside.

He managed no more than a half-dozen steps before he fell again. Surrounded by gloom, he could only prop his back against the wall. The Codex hung above him, its lens watching him impassively.

```
03:23:11:08
03:23:11:07
03:23:11:06
```

"You're gonna save me, then leave me to die?" Cade moaned, his head lolling to the side. He was fading fast, though whether from shock, dehydration, or blood loss he couldn't tell.

There was a tug on his boots. Then Cade was yanked forward, dragged deeper into the blackness. Time seemed to slip by as stone scraped against his back, his arms trailing behind him. He felt himself turn one corner, then another, too weak to fight back.

As they turned again, flickering light cast the walls in a

wan glow. Ancient carvings flashed there, the scenes playing out like a tapestry. Warriors in feathered headdresses clashing, clubs and spears raised high. Monstrous animal-headed gods watching from above. And the telltale square hieroglyphs beneath, telling the story of it all in an unknown language.

In another lifetime, Cade would have given anything to see such historical wonders. Instead, he gagged as nausea overcame him, the edges of his vision darkening as he held on to consciousness by his fingertips.

Were these to be his last moments?

He felt himself lifted from the ground, heard the grunt of his rescuer struggling with his weight. He was laid down on something soft.

"Beebay," a voice whispered.

Beebay?

Something was pressed to his lips, and cool water dribbled into his mouth. Cade sucked thirstily, gulping it down until the drink was taken away. It seemed almost instantly that strength returned to him, or at least enough to sit up.

He was lying on a stone plinth, padded by a fur covering. At his feet, a hooded figure was picking at his boots, struggling with the knots.

Cade leaned forward and unlaced them, then winced as each boot was tugged off, one by one, followed by his socks. A shrouded face flashed up at him, nodding in thanks.

Only now did Cade look at his wounds. There were jagged bite marks, worse in the right leg he had proffered the raptor than the left one it had bitten before. They were caked in blood, but to Cade's relief, the bleeding seemed to have mostly stopped. The wounds were more superficial than he had first thought, though his socks were soaked red.

"Thanks," Cade said. The figure didn't look up.

Water was poured over the injuries from a flask, running red as the crusted blood dissolved and set the wounds oozing once more. Next, his rescuer reached into a fur bag, hanging by a strap in the corner of the room, and returned clutching a fistful of what looked like honeycomb, complete with pearly white larvae inside. Holding it above the wounds, the figure carefully trickled the warm, golden liquid into Cade's cuts. It burned like hell, but Cade knew that honey had been used as an antiseptic for centuries.

Indeed, Cade remembered it was so effective that honey was the only food in the world that didn't have an expiration date. Even jars found in millennia-old Egyptian tombs had contained perfectly edible honey.

His mind was reeling, darting from one inane thought to another. It made him feel a little sick to smell the sweet, cloying liquid rubbed into his cuts by the figure's hands.

Even as Cade opened his mouth to speak again, his savior ducked away, this time returning with an amphora, its top corked. Cade's interest was piqued. He was desperately thirsty, and he dreamed of cool ice water.

But when the figure opened it and gently shook its contents into their hands, it was not water that came out . . . but ants.

Or rather, one ant. The hooded figure quickly stoppered the jar and gripped the insect beneath its head. Then they moved to place it on Cade's leg.

"Hey!" Cade yelled, jerking away. "What are you doing?"

Eyes glanced up, filled with annoyance, and Cade was startled to see a young man's face. One eye was a pale blue, contrasting sharply with his olive skin, while the other was a dark brown. A calming hand was laid on his leg. The message was clear. Stay still.

Cade relaxed, and watched as the fingers squeezed and manipulated the ant until its mandibles opened. Then he pressed the sides of Cade's largest wound together and lowered the ant. Cade winced as the mandibles dug in, suturing the skin together like a staple. Then the boy squeezed and twisted the thorax away, leaving the ant's head in his leg.

It wasn't pretty, comfortable . . . or sanitary for that matter, but the wound's oozing had stopped. The boy picked up the jar again, and Cade lay back, letting him get to work. After ten minutes of repeating the procedure, his rescuer finally stopped. Cade's legs were clean of blood, with the half circle of bite marks held closed with the black beads that were the ants' heads.

Now, as the boy stood back and admired his handiwork, Cade could finally get a good look at him.

He appeared a year or two older than Cade. Skinny as a rake and as short too, he cut a diminutive figure. His hooded cloak was made from a patchwork quilt of furs and leathers, and beneath he wore a tunic that might once have been red but was now faded brown and covered in mud and filth.

Perhaps most unusual was his hair. A white stripe ran across his matted fringe in a single streak. Cade might have thought it dyed were it not for their circumstances. That and the boy's eyes. They were wide set, unusually so. There was a genetic condition of some kind at work here, but Cade couldn't name it. Not that it mattered. He was immensely grateful to this person, who was now wrapping his legs in a damp, yellowed cloth.

Once that was done, the boy sat on the edge of Cade's plinth. Only now did Cade guess that it was a sacrificial altar. There was some irony here, but he was too tired to work out what it was.

"Thank you," Cade said, clasping the boy's hands with his own. "I'm Cade. What's your name?"

The boy stared at him blankly and shook his head. Cade realized he probably didn't speak English. He tried again, pressing his hands to his chest.

"Cade," he said.

The boy smiled, his eyes lighting up in recognition. He repeated the gesture.

"Quintus."

Cade's heart began to beat faster. Because he recognized the name. Recognized it from his old Latin textbooks and the historical fiction he had grown up reading. Quintus. The name was Roman.

CHAPTER
25

QUINTUS WAS NOT A TALKATIVE SORT. NOW THAT CADE KNEW the boy was Roman, he realized "beebay" was actually *bibe*, or "drink" in Latin. But when Cade tried to engage him in conversation with his own rudimentary attempts at the language, the boy simply shook his head and wandered over to a pile of stone slabs, which he was using as a makeshift table.

Upon it, Cade could see dried strips of some form of jerky. His back facing Cade, Quintus set about eating them, the sound of chewing permeating the small space.

In his famished state, Cade could smell the gamy meat from across the chamber. His mouth flooded with saliva, and his stomach cramped with fresh hunger pangs.

"Hey, can I get some of that?" Cade asked.

Nothing.

Sighing, Cade looked around the chamber and was glad to see the Codex hovering above him. For some reason,

Quintus had not seemed surprised by its presence. Cade was beginning to suspect the boy came from the keep. Luckily, he knew how to confirm his theory. He turned to the Codex.

03:22:52:13
03:22:52:12
03:22:52:11

"Who is this?" Cade asked.

"All records of this individual's name have been lost or destroyed," the Codex said in its dull voice. *"But he was a member of Legio IX Hispana, which disappeared from record in AD 108 or AD 120, depending on scholarly interpretation."*

Now they were getting somewhere. Cade felt his heart quicken, remembering the vigorous debates he'd had with his father over the fate of the missing legion. Here, the answer sat right in front of him.

But what was Quintus doing in this place? It was hard to say what the chamber's purpose had once been, but there were holes in the ceiling where light might have filtered in had it been daytime.

The entrance was a low passageway, while the contents of the room itself showed signs of an attempt to make it homey. A few furs along the floor, bright feathers dangling like fairy lights from the ceiling. A small bowl made from an animal skull contained a burning wick and a pool of animal fat within, which cast a glow to the space.

The room was almost as small as a college dorm room, and clearly the sacrificial altar did not belong here. He suspected this was a storage space, nothing more. Quintus had likely chosen it due to its low and easily defended entrance, and its distance from the outside. Cade noticed a smaller stone slab that Quintus must have been using to block the passage when he slept.

There were also weapons there. A short-sword, one that Cade recognized as a Roman gladius, and a slingshot. Not the Y-shaped-slingshot kind used by kids in comic books, but the slings that had been used in ancient warfare—a rope with a loop for the finger on one end, a leather pouch to hold the pebble in the center, and a loose end on the other side. The weapon would be held at both ends, whipped over the head and the rope released, sending the projectile flying. A simple enough weapon, but an effective one.

Clearly the young man was good with it. Good enough to hunt down meat, if the gutted, bipedal, lizard-like dinosaurs hanging from a nearby drying rack were any indication. Curious, Cade asked the Codex what the creatures were. The room flashed blue as it scanned them.

"Compsognathus is a genus of small, bipedal, carnivorous theropods, which lived approximately 157 million years ago," the Codex said. *"It was first discovered in 1849 by—"*

"That's enough," Cade said. "Less information from now on, okay?"

He recognized the name from the dinosaur picture books he had read as a child. Compies, the book had called them.

Strange. The carnosaur beneath his tree earlier was a relative of a dinosaur that existed 75 million years ago. Yet here they both were. Not to mention a Roman, and a modern-day teenager. If there was some explanation for this, Cade didn't know it.

His stomach twinged again.

"Hey," Cade said, suddenly desperate. "I'll trade you for it, okay? Got a bag of swords not too far from here."

Still no reaction, only the sound of the boy chewing.

"Hello?" Cade said, louder this time. "Can you hear me?"

More chewing.

"Hey!" Cade yelled. He winced, rubbing his dry throat.

Quintus stopped and cocked his head. He turned around, his eyes curious.

"It's rude to ignore people, you know," Cade muttered.

Quintus shrugged apologetically and pointed to his ears, one after the other. Then he shook his head.

"Oh," Cade said, feeling embarrassed. "You're deaf."

So. Communication would probably be challenging, if the language barrier wasn't already a problem. He motioned to the food and mimed eating it.

Quintus smacked his head, embarrassed, and handed some of the strips over. Cade unceremoniously stuffed them into his mouth. It was a chewy, gamy mass, but in his starved state it tasted like ambrosia. He gulped it down and rubbed his belly, showing his appreciation.

Quintus grinned, then took a seat on the table and examined Cade's clothes with an inquisitive eye. Cade did the same, and somehow it did not seem strange as the pair looked each other over, trying to determine where the other came from. Or was that *when*?

The Roman's eyes lit up all of a sudden, and he turned and

went to the corner of the room. There was an animal skin there, much like the others that decorated the room. But this one had been fashioned into a crude poncho, with a deep hood and enough of a cloak to reach his lower back, the front clasped by wooden toggles.

Quintus held it out, and Cade took it with a grateful node and a smile. He only wished he had something to give the boy in return, but the young legionary seemed happy enough as Cade threw it around his shoulders and pulled the hood over his head. It was warm, with the fur turned inside to tickle his ears.

"Thank you," Cade said.

Clearly, Quintus did not think his clothing suitable attire for the relative chill of the planet's night.

Again, the two stared at one another.

"Why did you leave the keep?" Cade murmured, scratching his chin. "There was food there, and it was a hell of a lot safer than here. Unless the game was worse, of course."

Quintus watched Cade's lips as they moved, then shrugged. Could he lip read? Not in English, but perhaps . . . Latin.

Cade tried again, this time in his half-remembered pidgin Latin.

"Where do you come from?"

Quintus replied, but Cade struggled to understand the words. There were flashes of understandable Latin, but whether it was an accent, slang, dialect, a speech impediment from his disability, or some combination of all four, a lot of it was indecipherable to him. The Codex hovered above, and Cade had a flash of inspiration.

"Codex, can you translate what he is saying into English?"

"*Yes.*"

Jackpot.

"Please do so."

"*Sure.*"

Cade grinned. It was getting better at speaking to him.

The Codex floated closer to him until it hung by his ear. It was likely not the first time it had done this—who knew how long the Romans had used it before Cade had come along.

Elated, he motioned at Quintus to speak again. The boy rolled his eyes and repeated what he had said before. This time, the Codex spoke quietly as the boy was talking.

"*You wouldn't be the first to not understand me.*"

Cade nodded, but of course Quintus had not heard the Codex speak. Cade gave him a thumbs-up and pointed at his ear and the Codex, as if to say he understood. Quintus perked up at that and spoke again.

"*You understand?*"

Cade nodded.

"*My prayers have been answered. Perhaps Jupiter is not as deaf as I am.*"

Cade tried his question again.

"Where do you come from?"

The answer came quickly this time.

"*That is a question with many answers. I was born in Rome, but spent much of my life in Caledonia as a legionary in the Ninth Legion. We were under attack by the Caledonians when I appeared here. That was almost a year ago.*"

Caledonia. That's what the Romans had called Scotland.

Cade furrowed his brows, racking his brain for a question in Latin—why hadn't he paid more attention in class? Quintus shrugged and kept talking, seemingly glad to have the opportunity to talk to someone.

"Suddenly, I found myself in a desert. Strange though it seems, my legion and I were transported along with the battlefield we were fighting upon, which was scattered with the bodies of the dead."

Cade's eyes widened. So, that was where the bodies had come from, and the strange square of land in the middle of the salt flats.

"Stranger still, there were others waiting for us there. Other Romans, who had been there for many years. Soldiers from my future, and soldiers from our past."

More revelations, though somehow they didn't surprise Cade. That answered why there were coins from so many time periods. Or how, anyway.

"I was taken to a fort into the mountainside," Quintus went on. *"Built by the first Romans to be brought here, from the earliest days of our republic, when the legions rescued from the shores of Africa were lost in the great storm."*

Cade knew who he must have been speaking of—the famed lost army of the First Punic War. Retreating from a failed invasion of Africa, the Romans had loaded their army onto their fleet, and a storm had destroyed it utterly on the voyage back to Italy. To think . . . that perhaps tens of thousands of drowning men had been plucked from a seething sea and left here, on another world.

"But those first men were long dead of old age and had been replaced by other Romans to continue their vigil. It was these latest

Romans who greeted us out in the desert. They were our ancestors,
who survived the battles of Carrhae and Teutoburg Forest, and our
progeny—those who fought in the revolt of Bar Kokhba and others
who were abandoned on the island of Britannia, when our great
empire fell."

Cade could hardly believe it. It was as if someone had been
watching over the world, snatching people up like game pieces
on a board—with a particular penchant for Romans. And all
transported here, replenishing the fort's garrison with fresh
troops each generation. Quintus's legion must have been the
most recent batch.

He recognized the battles and events that Quintus had
mentioned. Of all the people in the world, he, a history scholar,
was sitting here with this relic from the past. If anything, this
confirmed his theory. He had been chosen for a reason—it was
too much of a coincidence.

"What next?" was all Cade could think to say, watching
as Quintus's eyes followed the movement of his lips.

"In truth, I do not know much—few have the patience to talk
to one such as I. I do know that my legion and I had been sum-
moned to do battle with a great foe, as had other Romans before
me. The weakest of us were left to defend the battlements, while
the rest of the men left for battle. We were told they would return
in a few weeks, then they marched into the desert and out of
sight."

Quintus looked somber now, a faraway look in his eyes.

"They never came back. We waited for almost a month, and then
the game began again. The gods informed us we were contenders,
as the Romans before us had been. But how could we survive it when

all those thousands of men had left and not returned? I was one of the first to leave. The others must have left soon after."

Cade swallowed. Thousands of men, gone. What fresh horrors awaited that could do such a thing? But a word stood out among the rest.

"Gods?" he asked.

"The new gods. The ones who make us play this game."

His pulse quickened. Now the answers as to who had brought them here were coming to the light. But gods? Every theory he'd had involved science. The supernatural had never crossed his mind. Could it be that this was the result of the occult, or some dark magic?

And yet—the Codex, the force fields. Those didn't feel magical. They were technology.

But one thing at a time. He needed to know more about what they might be up against if they went back to the keep. He certainly didn't want to live here, scratching out an existence, eating lizards, and getting chased by raptors. And it seemed Quintus knew of no better alternative, or he would have left Hueitapalan by now.

"Game?" Cade asked. He wished his Latin were better; he could have asked more complex questions. It seemed that Quintus would be doing most of the talking.

"The game we must play if we wish to return home and for Earth to stay safe. In truth, I regret my leaving."

Now Cade was even more confused.

"Safe?"

"Action prohibited. Parameters readjusted."

Cade turned to the Codex.

"I think you mistranslated that one."

"I'm sorry, Cade. Your Strategos has removed my ability to translate until the qualifying round is completed."

Strategos? What on earth . . . or wherever they were . . . was a Strategos?

Quintus was talking again, but Cade shook his head. Quintus tried one more time, but Cade pointed at his ear and the Codex and then shook his head again. Quintus hung his head in disappointment, then busied himself with tidying away the amphora and poultice bowl, leaving Cade to fume.

"What is a Strategos?" Cade demanded.

"Answer prohibited."

"Dammit," Cade cursed, burying his head in his hands. "Just when we were getting somewhere."

After a few moments, he tried again. Something about one of Quintus's answers gnawed at him.

"Why should we play this game at all?" Cade asked. "What happens if we win?"

The Codex was silent for a moment, seemingly considering its answer. As if now, there was somebody deciding on what it could, and couldn't, say. The Strategos. Or perhaps . . . one of Quintus's gods. Perhaps they were one and the same.

"Winning the qualifying round will result in prohibitions being lifted and access to higher Codex functions," the Codex said. *"Contenders will also gain access to the leaderboard and the right to represent Earth."*

None of that made any sense to Cade.

"How do we win?" Cade asked. He should have asked more about the qualifying round a long time ago, with more specific questions. But with everything that had happened, it had seemed like the least of his worries.

"Contenders must defend their home base from attack. Complete loss of life or uncontested occupation of the home base will constitute failure, and disqualification."

"Where is the home base?"

"It is in this location."

The Codex projected the map into the air, making Quintus jump. The boy shrank away from it, hiding behind the altar and gazing at it with wide eyes. It seemed the young legionary hadn't seen the Codex project something before, even if the floating object itself did not surprise him.

Cade looked at the map and saw a dot where the keep was, flashing bright red. So they had needed to defend that place all along. He wondered if the keep had been built for that very purpose.

"And what are we qualifying for?" he asked.

"Answer prohibited."

"What will we be defending against?"

"Answer prohibited."

Cade groaned.

"Can you at least tell me what happens if we lose?" he asked. "Or if we don't play at all?"

The Codex answered in its bored voice. And yet each word sounded like a death knell in Cade's ears.

"Planet Earth will be destroyed."

CHAPTER
26

CADE AWOKE TO SUNLIGHT STREAMING THROUGH THE HOLES in the roof. For a moment he lay there, comfortable for what felt like the first time in an eternity, his only disturbance the dull throb of pain from the bites in his legs and the screech of birds and other creatures greeting the dawn. No longer thirsty or hungry, he took a moment to enjoy the feeling. But before he could, the Codex's words from the night before came rushing back to haunt him.

He had spent the better part of an hour questioning the Codex on this, but it had shut down communication. The Strategos, whatever it was, seemed to have decided that Cade had learned enough for that day.

What will happen if we don't complete the qualifying round?

The end of the world, apparently. Was that even possible? Considering everything he had seen so far, anything was possible. Dinosaurs no longer extinct, yet somehow in the same, unevolved form, millions of years later. Romans from centuries ago, all from different time periods, together at once. But what time period *was* it? Were they still in the modern day, or had Cade been taken to the past?

Or maybe transported to the future?

And yet, there was little evidence of things being brought backward in time from his future—unless the Codex and the force fields were some form of advanced, man-made technology from the year 3000.

It was a mystery that would need to wait for another day. One thing he knew for sure—whoever had created this place, they had the power to destroy the Earth. For all he knew, they could teleport it, bit by bit, into the sun.

He pictured his parents, burned away in an instant. The thought of them gone, just like that, filled him with such despair. And the children. Everyone. Every species on the planet, from the smallest bacteria to the whales beneath the oceans.

But worst of all, the *future* of humanity was at stake. Two hundred thousand years of human achievement, and all its unrealized potential thereafter, gone in a flash. Unthinkable. Yet here he was, lazing in the dappled sunlight.

Resolved, Cade rolled from his place on the altar, only to find himself alone, unless he counted the Codex.

03:09:12:51
03:09:12:50
03:09:12:49

No sign of Quintus.

"Quintus?" Cade called.

He kicked himself. The boy was quite deaf—shouting was futile.

Groaning, Cade approached one of the amphorae in the corner and, after making sure it wasn't the one full of ants, took a deep swig. That done, he stuffed his mouth with the last of the jerky, grimacing as the gamy taste coated his tongue. It had tasted so good when he'd been starving the night before.

For a moment, he considered taking the sword, propped in its scabbard against the wall. He decided against it. If he couldn't find Quintus he'd come back and wait for him.

Quintus had pushed a paving stone in the way of the entrance, most likely to keep out scavenging dinosaurs, but Cade managed to scrape it aside and squeeze through. In the light of day, the passageway was far less foreboding, with sunshine pushing its way through chinks in the stone.

There was little sign of Quintus, but from the footprints in the dirt and dust that coated the floor, he could tell the path the young legionary usually took. With nowhere else to go, Cade followed it. To his surprise, his legs did not hurt as much as he thought they would have, though they itched something terrible now they'd began to scab over, and he could feel the ant heads scratching on the inside of his pants legs.

Eventually, Cade found himself standing in the entrance to the temple, an array of buildings laid out before him. It seemed that the small, green bipedal dinosaurs known as compies were everywhere—he could see them hopping and skipping around, chasing the bugs and mice that must live in the many nooks and crannies of the structures.

The compies were not the only inhabitants. Pterosaurs gathered on the tops of the ziggurats that surrounded him, looking much like a flock of seagulls on a rocky beach. The colors that adorned each body were extraordinary and would not have been out of place at a tropical bird's tree house. Only these "birds" were featherless, with bat-like wings and strange, bony protuberances on their heads. Many had toothed mouths instead of beaks, and all seemed to sport dangerous talons.

Interestingly, he could see scores of nests high up, many of them spilling from the mouths of the Mayan gargoyles that adorned the temple tops. They sounded like a pack of seagulls too, squawking and screeching at one another, making the entire city of Hueitapalan echo with a cacophony of noise. It grated on Cade's already frazzled nerves, and he wondered if Quintus could hear it at all.

They varied in size, many no larger than sparrows, others so large that he had to look twice to be sure he was seeing straight. All seemed to roost together, refusing to differentiate by species. Even the few that appeared as gigantic as giraffes had the company of their smaller cousins, and Cade stared as they splayed their wings like monstrous statues, warming up in the morning sun. He quickened his pace then, fearing they might swoop down and snatch him up like Sinbad and the roc.

It was then that he spotted Quintus, crouched behind a large pillar in the very center of the plaza. For a moment, Cade thought he was hunting, for he was very still, his head barely poking out from the great pillar's edge, the sling dangling at the ready from his hand.

But these were no compies Quintus was watching. Cade's heart leaped to his throat, stifling a shout of joy.

At the very edge of the jungle, skirting the border of the city . . . were people.

People!

They wore plate armor and chain mail, and each carried some form of axe or sword. The figures were too far away to identify, but already Cade's mind was drifting to chivalrous knights of medieval England. Men who could understand him. Who could help him win the qualifying round.

Already, Cade's legs were moving, unbidden, and now he turned his shambling into a run, stitches be damned.

"Hey," he yelled out, wincing at his raw throat.

But the noise from the pterosaurs drowned him out. The men had disappeared behind a smaller pyramid, and Cade felt the irrational fear that he'd lost them. Breaking into a sprint, he tore past Quintus, and heard him call out.

He was likely warning him of the pterosaurs, but it was time to throw caution to the wind. He could not believe his luck.

Hell, they might even be contenders too!

Gasping for breath, Cade rounded the pyramid, only to see the men disappearing into the trees. He followed, tearing through the branches like a wild animal, careless of the thorns and twigs that caught on his clothing.

He stumbled into a clearing where the vegetation was knee high. To his surprise, the men were waiting for him, their weapons held ready, bodies crouched for action. There were four of them, but all wore helmets that obscured their faces.

The closest bellowed foreign words from behind his face-plate, brandishing his sword

Cade staggered to a stop, holding his hands up.

He smiled at them, trying to show he wasn't a threat. After a few moments, the nearest of them pulled off his helmet.

His dark hair was cut short, and what little remained was slicked back with sweat. It was no wonder—the day was sweleringly hot, even this early in the morning.

The man returned his smile and muttered some calming words in a foreign language.

Cade took a step closer, and the man beckoned him with a mailed hand.

"Thank god I found you gu—" Cade began.

He never saw the fist coming.

CHAPTER
27

Pain. It felt like it would split Cade's head in two, yet still he forced his eyes open. To his surprise, the world had turned dark. For a single, panicked moment he thought he had gone blind, but then he saw the stars in the sky, just visible beyond the dense foliage of the canopy.

"He's awake," came a soft voice.

A girl's face swam into view, lit by a flickering flame somewhere to his left. A heart-shaped, freckled face, with eyebrows furrowed. Her lips parted, pink tongue poked out in concentration, and Cade felt a cool cloth bathing his brow.

"Easy does it," the girl said, and Cade felt a hand beneath his neck, helping him to sit up.

The world spun, but he managed to stay upright, taking in his surroundings.

He was in a cage. A wooden one, it seemed, made of stakes lashed with rope. Beyond it, Cade could see the armored men hunkered around a fire, with a rudimentary palisade encircling the entire campsite.

And surrounding him . . . were four schoolgirls.

There was no other way to describe them. Each wore a checkered skirt, knee-high socks, and a buttoned blouse, though their clothes were almost as dirty and ragged as his own.

The one who had helped him gave him an appraising look. Her dark hair was pulled into a ponytail, making her furrowed brow all the more evident. Her brown eyes spoke of part-Asian descent, and they narrowed with suspicion as she looked at him.

"Who are you?" she asked.

A British accent. It was refined too, the sort of accent he imagined the Queen speaking with.

"How long have I been out?" Cade groaned.

"They brought you in this morning," the girl said, her voice impatient. Cade peered at the men again, and she snapped her fingers to get his attention.

"Who are you?" she repeated.

Cade shook his head, then regretted it as his skull lanced with pain. He reached up tentatively to touch his forehead and found an egg-sized lump there.

"Cade," he said. "My name is Cade."

She looked at him expectantly.

"Is that it?" she said.

"I could ask you the same question," Cade said. "Who are *you*?"

The girl rolled her eyes.

"I'm Amber," she said, "and that's—"

"Grace," the girl behind her said quickly.

Grace had dark skin, with high cheekbones and braided cornrows. He could tell she was tall, even when she was sitting down. Now that Cade looked, her blouse was spattered red. None of them appeared injured though. He wondered absently whose blood it was.

"I'm Bea," said another girl.

"And Trix," the other chimed in.

The pair were identical twins, and Cade found it hard to imagine parents intentionally saddling them with those names. Both were short girls with elfin faces and blond tresses, though their hair was streaked with dirt.

"Now we're all *acquainted*," Amber said, exasperated, "maybe you can tell us what you *know*."

But Cade wasn't listening. He'd suddenly realized the Codex wasn't there.

"Codex?" Cade called out.

"What are you blathering on about?" Amber said, throwing her hands up in the air.

Beyond him, Cade saw the Codex flicker into existence. Then, as Amber spun to see what he was staring at, it disappeared.

Camouflage. That's new. Maybe it doesn't want them to see it. But . . . these have to be other contenders . . . surely?

"Are you contenders?" Cade blurted out.

"Are we *what*?" Amber demanded.

Cade sighed.

"Never mind," he said. "Look, why don't you tell me how you got here, and I'll fill in the rest."

Silence.

"He knows something," Grace growled. "He knows *exactly* what's going on."

"You think I'd be in this cage with you if I did?" Cade snapped back.

"Maybe you're a spy," Grace said. "Maybe they sent you in here to find out what we know."

"What would be the point of that?" Cade replied. "Sounds like you don't *know* anything."

Trix raised her hands, trying to calm them.

"This isn't helping. How about we go first. Bea?"

The other twin, Bea, gave Cade a shy smile, then cleared her throat as if at a poetry recital.

"We were on our way in the school minivan to a hockey game, driving through the woods," she said, and Cade had to lean closer, her voice was so low, "then suddenly the minivan was tearing through some bushes in the middle of a jungle."

"Where?" Cade asked.

"You tell us!" Amber snapped.

"I mean, where were you *before*," Cade said. Now it was his turn to roll his eyes.

"Duh. England. Shropshire?" Bea said, looking at Cade as if he were an idiot.

"Then what?" Cade said.

"Well, there were eleven of us, plus our coach. And the van gets stuck in the middle of the trees, right?"

She looked at Cade expectantly.

"Right . . . ," said Cade.

"So we get out, try to find the road. Only we can't. And then . . . we were attacked."

She faltered, her voice cracking. Trix put her arms around her sister, comforting the girl.

Could it have been vipers?

"Did they look kind of like . . . hairless chimps with a piranha's head?" Cade asked, realizing just how foolish he must sound.

They stared at him.

"No. We didn't get a good look at them, but it wasn't that." Amber spoke slowly, as if talking to a madman. "Have you seen . . . piranha-chimps?"

Cade ignored her.

"Then what?"

This time, it was Trix who answered, having gathered her courage.

"We ran. But we were the only ones who made it back to the minivan. We hid in there till they got bored and left. Big feathery things, like giant chickens or something."

She paused, her lip trembling.

"After a few days we ran out of water and food, so we decided to go look for help," Grace said, her voice laced with impatience. "That's when these guys found us. They threatened us with their weapons, tied us together, and forced us to walk here, where they had this cage and camp."

"Did they speak to you?" Cade asked.

"We only heard them speak in another language," Amber said, shaking her head. "We have no idea what it is."

"But I think they understand English," Grace said quickly. "The young one was listening to us when we were talking earlier, I swear."

Cade glanced over at the men and noticed there were five of them now. The camp was far too large for just five men and a cage, perhaps as wide and long as the keep's atrium had been. Now that he looked, he saw a long wooden table with benches beyond the fire that could have fit more than forty people.

"They must be part of a larger group," Cade said, crawling closer to the wooden bars.

Amber nodded.

"There were more of them here before, but they were gone almost as soon as they arrived."

She bit her lower lip.

"We think these guys stayed to keep . . . hunting for more people," she said, pointing at the campfire. "They left the youngest one on watch. Do you see him?"

He followed the line of her finger to see a fellow who looked a little older than Cade. As if he could sense their eyes on him, the boy turned to stare at them, until a barked order from one of the men made him turn away.

"And that's it?" Cade asked. "You don't know what they want us for?"

"Well, when we first got here we thought they wanted us girls for, wives or something," Grace said, grimacing. "So it was kind of a relief when they threw you in here."

"Not for me," Trix said glumly. "My money's on cannibalism. I almost didn't touch the stew they gave us earlier."

Cade's stomach twisted at the thought.

They needed to escape. And soon—he suspected that they'd be moved somewhere more secure by daybreak. After all, they had five prisoners now. One for each of them.

"Look, I have a . . . friend . . . sort of," Cade said. "He may have followed us here, might even be watching us from behind the palisade. Maybe we can send him a signal when the guards have gone to sleep, get him to break us out."

"How?" Grace asked.

"Maybe if we flash a light at him," Cade said, peering at the palisade, hoping he might see Quintus's face peering between the wooden poles. "Do any of you have your phones?"

For what felt like the tenth time that day, the girls looked at him like he was insane.

"We all have phones . . . ," Amber said.

"Great, well, do they have any battery left?" Cade asked.

"Mine doesn't have a battery," Grace said, confusion stamped across her face.

"I don't see how my phone is going to help us," Trix said. "It's not like I can use it from here; it's at home. And who would we call?"

"I thought you wanted to make light . . . why are you asking if we own phones?" Bea asked.

Cade went very still, realization slowly dawning on him. He phrased his next question as casually as he dared.

"This may seem like a weird question but . . . what year do you think it is?"

Again, they stared at him.

"1985," Amber said. "Why?"

CHAPTER
28

CADE TOOK SOME TIME TO GATHER HIS THOUGHTS, IGNORING their groans of impatience. 1985. Before mobile phones were a *thing*. Before even the internet! When music was on cassettes or vinyl, and video games weren't even in 3-D. And here they were. Completely oblivious.

"I don't know how to tell you this," Cade said. "But I come from the future."

Amber burst out laughing.

"Like *The Terminator*?" she said.

The others chuckled.

"Well . . . ," Cade muttered.

"I just watched it." Amber laughed. "Wasn't it great!"

She wiped her eyes.

"Oh, it feels good to laugh in all this mess."

Grace wasn't amused though.

"Now's not the time for jokes," she said. "Tell us what's really going on."

Cade scratched his head.

"Did you notice we're on another *planet*?" he asked. "And that you were attacked by a *dinosaur*?"

He looked up at the stars, and though the sky was tinged with the thin light of what must have been a crescent moon, the red satellite and its small white companion were out of sight. The girls must not have seen it yet, what with their minivan being stuck beneath the canopy.

"Dinosaurs don't have feathers," Trix muttered.

Cade groaned and rubbed his eyes.

"Listen, you've been taken out of time and placed on another planet. I come from several decades ahead of you, and I'm in the same spot. I don't know what year it is or where we are."

"Seriously, you're not funny," Grace said.

Only Bea seemed to be taking him at his word, the blood draining from her already pale face.

"That's impossible," she whispered.

"You think we're in the English countryside right now?" Cade snapped. "You think those men there are a bunch of tourists playing a prank?"

There was no laughter now. Only fallen faces and narrowed eyes.

He opened his mouth to speak again and heard an angry bark from the armored men. The words made no sense, but the meaning was clear. Silence.

Cade leaned in and whispered.

"Tell me, after seeing the creature that attacked you, seeing this jungle, that you don't think something *impossible* is going on."

More silence. It was Amber who spoke first.

"Let's say you're telling the truth. Do you have a plan to get us out of here?"

Cade shook his head.

"Well, then, it's back to plan A," she muttered.

Cade furrowed his brow, then winced as he felt the skin tighten on his head wound. That was going to be sore for a long time.

"Plan A?" Cade asked.

"Not so loud," Grace hushed him.

She leaned closer to speak, but Amber gripped her shoulder.

"We can't trust him yet," she said. "He could still have been sent in here to see if we're planning an escape."

"Seriously?" Cade asked.

Amber ignored him.

"Just wait," she said. "And keep quiet."

Cade shrugged. In their shoes, he'd likely think no differently. Pressing his face up to the cage bars, he turned his attention to the next mystery.

Who were these men? They might have been medieval knights, but that time period wasn't Cade's area of expertise.

But even if it was . . . the armor could have been scavenged from corpses. There were a lot of maybes. And none of it helped him work out what intentions the men had with him and the girls.

He might have asked the Codex about the men, but he knew it would scan them in a flash of light—and who knew how they would react then?

Even if he asked it more subtle questions, given its silence the day before and its camouflaged state, he doubted it would respond. If he started asking questions into empty space with no reply, the girls would question his sanity.

He did know one thing though. Cannibalism was unlikely; after all, these men had given the girls food—a pointless exercise if they were about to eat them. He was leaning more toward slavery. After all, it had been almost universally present in human societies right up until the past few centuries, with pockets of it still in existence. It wouldn't be a stretch to imagine the practice rearing its ugly head in this strange world.

Clearly this was only a staging camp, a safe place to sleep before moving them to a new location.

"Who are these guys?" Cade whispered to himself.

And who were the girls? If they were not contenders, and neither were these men, then what purpose did they serve in this world? People abandoned in the jungle as fodder for the dinosaurs? Perhaps these so-called gods enjoyed watching them fend for themselves.

Or perhaps both the girls and the men were all part of a larger game. People for contenders to recruit . . . or to compete with for the scarce weapons and resources left scattered throughout the caldera.

Maybe both. It was impossible to say.

If contenders were the players then these girls were . . . game pieces? The thought of it made him feel ill.

His mind was too fuzzy to think further. All he knew was that he was running out of time, and he had lost an entire day. Already his eyelids were drooping, and he was glad of the hood

Quintus had given him as he nestled deeper beneath it for warmth.

Does unconsciousness count as sleep?

He stared into the camp a while longer, but no new clues presented themselves. A search of their cage also bore little fruit—only a rusted length of chain, one that must have been used on more unruly captives.

The men were settling down beside the fire, having thrown up a makeshift canopy above them in case it rained. No such protection for Cade and the girls.

All remained in full armor, though one of them hadn't curled up beneath the canopy. It was the young boy, sitting moodily on a stool beside the fire. Guard duty. Cade suspected he was new, and low in the pecking order. The group's underling.

The boy was pale, paler than one might expect in this climate. And his eyes were a watery blue, with blond hair that was long and braided. Cade might have thought him a girl were it not for the small, fluffy mustache growing on his upper lip.

The boy looked scared, his eyes constantly roving along the tops of the walls. Perhaps this was his first people-hunting mission. His first time out in the jungle. There was a safe place somewhere here. It was just a shame that in order to get there, Cade would be in chains.

Soon, the sound of snores permeated the camp and the coals of the campfire had burned low. The girls were huddled across the cage from him, on the side facing the campfire. Their backs were to him, and he couldn't tell whether they were sleeping, whispering, or praying. Whichever it was, they wanted nothing to do with him.

But it was warm and dry at least, the ground beneath them covered with a thin layer of straw. So he slept, waiting for whatever plan it was that the girls had concocted to come to fruition.

CHAPTER
29

CADE WOKE TO THE SOUND OF VOICES. HE HALF OPENED HIS eyes, only to see Amber pressed up against the bars nearby, her hand outstretched toward the young guard.

"Please," she was whispering. "Water."

Cade didn't move. It was still night, and the girls were laid out beside her, curled together in a heap. The pail of water they had been given was on its side, the straw still damp from the spillage. One of them must have kicked it over in their sleep.

The guard shook his head, glancing over his shoulder at the sleeping men.

"I'm so thirsty. Please!"

She used her other hand to grasp at her throat, the other still outstretched in supplication. This went on for almost ten seconds. It was only then that the guard stood and came closer, a fur-covered flask held in his hand. He stopped a few feet from the cage, eyeing her like she was a wild animal.

"Please," Amber said hoarsely.

Cade could see she had wiped the dirt from her face, and her hair had been let down to fall about her shoulders. Despite it all, he couldn't help but notice that she was beautiful.

A tear ran slowly down her right cheek, and the guard shuffled closer still. Finally, he held the flask outstretched, and she snatched it from him. Tearing the cork from the top, Amber gulped it down, emptying it, then holding it above her head and tapping it for more.

Cade watched through half-closed eyes as the guard held a hand out expectantly. But Amber was oblivious. Spent, she collapsed back to the floor of the cage, letting the flask fall to the ground outside the bars.

"Girl," he said.

Even from that one word, Cade could detect a strange accent.

"Girl," he tried again.

Amber lay still, the hair across her face fluttering with her soft breaths. The guard took a tentative step closer, his hand hovering over the axe hanging from his belt. But still, Amber remained motionless. The flask lay on the ground, fallen from her palm, her arm outstretched through the bars of the cage.

Another step. Now he was but two feet away, grasping for the flask with his fingertips. Cade tensed. Could he reach him?

Amber lunged. Her hand struck like a snake, pulling the guard off balance. He sprawled against the cage, and suddenly more hands were reaching for him, Grace grasping him by his long blond hair, tugging his head through the bars. Her other hand clamped over his mouth, cutting short a scream. Amber's arm went around his neck. She held him in place as he tried to wriggle free.

For a second there was silence, the only sound the scuffling of the guard's feet against the earth, and a muffled humming as he tried to yell through his nose. By now Cade was up, but all eyes, including the guard's, were turned to the sleeping men beside the campfire. There was no sign that they had been disturbed.

Then Trix was moving, threading her hands through the bars and pulling the axe from his belt. She stared at it, unsure what to do, until Amber took it with her spare hand and pressed it against the soft underside of the guard's chin.

"I want you to know that I will slit your throat if it means getting out of here," Amber whispered.

The young guard stared up at her, his pale blue eyes full of fear.

"Nod so I know you understand me," she whispered.

He nodded frantically, even as the axe grazed his skin and sent a rivulet of blood down his neck.

"Told you he understands English," Grace said, smirking.

Amber rolled her eyes, then handed the axe to Bea.

"Get to work," she said.

It was masterfully done. Cade was impressed.

"That was amazing, Amber," Cade whispered.

"I had a year of sixth form drama," she said.

Cade had no idea what that meant. He shrugged and turned to see Bea sawing away with the axe blade, her hand working frantically back and forth. Not at the thick branches that latticed them in, but instead at the twine tied tightly along the edges that kept the cage's side in place. But Bea's hands were shaking, her nerves getting the better of her.

"Let me," Cade said, holding out a hand. Relieved, she went to give it to him.

"Bea, don't gi—" Amber hissed, but it was too late. The axe was his.

There was a moment of panic, neither Grace nor Amber able to relinquish the guard, while Bea and Trix were frozen in place, horrified.

Cade rolled his eyes and shuffled closer to the bars, then began sawing at the twine himself.

"Guess that's sorted, then," Trix muttered.

With his steady hands, Cade was soon through the first few knots, the cordage parting beneath the sharp blade. Soon there was only one more tie to cut—with it gone, the entire backside would fall from the cage.

"Are we taking him with us?" Grace hissed before the final slice. "Maybe we should ask him some questions first."

Amber shook her head.

"Too risky," she replied. "Outside."

Cade nodded and cut the final strand, with Bea and Trix lowering the side of the cage to the ground.

Then they were out. But a new problem faced them. The gates to the compound were across the camp—past the sleeping men and the fire. And they had to figure out what to do with the guard.

A sick thought crossed Cade's mind. It'd be better if they killed the guard first.

Is this what I've become?

"Axe," Amber said, holding out her hand.

Cade hesitated, wondering if she'd had the same thought. He handed it to her—this was her plan after all. Lacking a weapon, he picked up the length of chain—maybe they could use it to tie up the boy later.

It clinked as he stuffed it into his pocket, and Amber glared at him before pressing the axe against the guard's throat.

"Stay quiet, and I might just leave you somewhere outside where the monsters won't get you."

"Dinosaurs," Cade muttered under his breath.

Amber ignored him, instead looking at the boy, waiting for his answer. His eyes widened in panic, clearly terrified of being beyond the palisade. But the sharp blade of the axe was a far worse alternative. The guard let out a breath and nodded.

"Let's go."

With the guard's neck still in Amber's headlock, the group skirted the edge of the palisade, working their way to the gates. There, Cade could see a heavy wooden bar blocking it. They could lift it in a pinch. But all the while, he searched for clues. Anything that might help him understand who these men were. But there was nothing. Just footprints in the grass, the long wooden table, and the men. This was a staging area, nothing more.

Finally, they reached the gates, and both Cade and Grace lifted the bar, struggling beneath the weight. Only then did the doors creak open. Too loudly. Grace grabbed Cade's arm, stopping him from opening it farther, then one by one, the girls pushed through the narrow gap they had created.

Soon it was only Amber and Cade left.

"Go on," she urged.

It was then that the guard made his move. In a sudden motion, he wrenched himself free from Amber, unleashing a wordless yell. He stood there, as if surprised to still be alive, while Amber's axe hung limp in her hand. Cade's fist was moving before he even knew it, slamming into the guard's chin with a crack.

The guard collapsed, and Cade's hand hurt like hell, but there was no time to check if he'd knocked him out. There were stirrings from the sleeping men. One sat up, bleary-eyed.

Amber grabbed Cade's arm and tugged him through, even as the man called out in a language they couldn't understand, still unaware of their escape. Cade stopped just on the other side of the gates.

"What are you doing?" asked Amber.

"Buying us time," Cade said, yanking his arm away.

He still had the chain in his pocket, and now he ducked back through the gap in the gate doors and threaded the chain around the iron holders that the bar had rested upon, keeping the loose ends in his hands.

There was a shout of anger from within as he ducked back through the doors and pulled them near closed behind him, the ends still sticking through the crack. Footsteps thudded across the grass, followed by more yelling. Cade knotted the chain once, then twice for good measure.

A huge weight slammed against the door, but the rusted chain held, the lumpy knot pressing against the door. He turned, only to see the girls were already running. Amber alone had stayed, the axe raised, lips tight with fear and fury.

"I didn't wait for you," she blurted as Cade raised his eyebrows at her. "I was going to buy them time."

"Yeah, whatever," Cade said.

There was a rough path ahead of them, but the girls had run into the trees, hoping to lose them in the jungle.

A second blow cracked behind them, and this time there was the sound of splintering wood. A bloodshot eye peered through the door gap, followed by a roar of rage.

"It won't hold them for long," Cade said. "Let's go."

They broke into a run, even as more blows fell on the gates.

"Do you know which direction?" Amber panted.

"Anywhere but here."

CHAPTER
30

IT WAS ALMOST IMPOSSIBLE TO RUN IN THE DARKNESS. AMBER and Cade caught up with the others almost immediately, the girls fumbling through the black curtain of night, cursing as they tripped on the uneven ground and the branches tore at their faces and hair.

Soon it got marginally better, their eyes adjusting to the dim light, but progress remained slow. And soon enough, men with torches would be coming behind them. Cade didn't think all would be forgiven if they were caught either.

The group stopped in unspoken agreement when they broke through to a clearing, leaning with their hands on their knees and taking great, sobbing breaths. Cade was struggling to keep up, the wounds in his legs beginning to ache. He was the last to struggle through the trees, huffing with relief at the brief respite.

"I've never touched so many cobwebs in all my wretched

life," Trix wailed, slapping at herself with her hands. "I must be crawling with spiders."

Cade couldn't help but agree with her. He went to stand beside Amber, who was itching and pawing at her hair. He wouldn't be surprised if a few insects had taken up residence there.

"Bastard," Amber snapped.

Cade held up his hands.

"I'm doing my best. Just give me a minute."

"Not you," Amber groaned. "That boy with the pigtails. If he'd just . . ."

". . . let you chain him up and leave him helpless in the jungle to get eaten?" Grace finished off Amber's sentence, a mischievous gleam in her eye. "Maybe after a nice interrogation by the mad girl with the axe? I'm surprised we got as far as we did."

"Point taken," Amber sighed.

"Would have liked interrogating him though," Cade said, straightening. "I would love to know where he came from."

"Don't you mean *when* he came from?" Trix asked. "He's from the future, like you, right?"

She only sounded slightly sarcastic. That was an improvement.

Cade shook his head.

"I'm not sure. From what I know of this place, most people come from much farther in the past than you—there are dinosaurs here after all. But that doesn't mean he's from another time."

"Oh? And what year do you think it is now?" Amber asked.

The sarcasm was positively dripping from every word. Cade answered her regardless.

"If I had to guess, I'd say we're in the same time period as where I came from. I'm yet to see anyone from the future, which would suggest I'm the most 'up-to-date.'"

His words were met with silence. And yet, there was so much more to say. More to tell them.

The qualifying round. Being a contender. The Romans, the gods, the end of the goddamned world. The Codex. Even now, it was still following him, for he could hear its pushing through the leaves above him. It had yet to reveal itself, and Cade wasn't entirely sure why it was invisible at all.

But now didn't seem like the right time to tell them he wanted them to join him in a fight to the death.

"We should get moving," Amber said, staring into the darkness.

"I don't know," Grace said. "We've been running for an hour . . . and there's *things* out here. We keep crashing around, and something's bound to come across us. And we could be running in circles for all we know."

"So what do you suggest?" Amber said. "That we just stay here, wait for those men to get us?"

"It's dark for them too, even if they have torches!" Grace replied. "And there's a reason they sleep behind a palisade. I bet they spent ten minutes looking for us and went back to camp. They're probably as scared to be out here as we are. More so, really, because we don't even know what *is* out here."

"Dinosaurs," Cade muttered.

"Shut up," they snapped in unison.

Cade shut up.

"We wait here, then," Amber said. "But as soon as there's daylight, we move on."

"Should we sleep?" Bea asked in a quiet voice.

"You think we'll sleep . . . out here?" Trix asked.

"Never mind," Bea said, sitting cross-legged on the ground and putting her chin in her hands. Cade joined her, glad that the mossy soil was dry at least. The others soon followed, and they huddled together. Despite the climate, it was chilly, and Cade felt a little left out as the girls put their arms around one another. He sat at the edge of the circle, his hands tucked into his armpits.

In the mad rush, all they had heard was the crashing of branches and their ragged breathing as they tore through the jungle. But now, the night noises were loud and clear. The whine and chirr of the insects was a constant, while the discordant throaty coughs, whoops, and shrieks of the larger creatures made them shudder with every sound. Trix was right—there would be no sleep that night.

Trying to distract himself from the combination of the chill and his fear of nocturnal predators, Cade spoke up.

"So . . . you guys were a hockey team? I didn't think they had many ice rinks in England."

Even through the gloom, Cade saw the withering look Amber gave him.

"Not ice hockey, dumbass. Hockey. You *Americans* call it field hockey."

So much for small talk. Amber relented, her furrowed brows unknitting.

"I was the captain. Grace, the goalie. Trix and Bea were our wingers. The others . . ."

"I don't want to talk about them," Bea said quickly.

Amber rubbed her shoulder and forced a smile at Cade.

"So, tell us about the future."

Her voice was only half-joking. Cade shrugged.

"What do you want to know?"

"Do they have flying cars?" Trix asked.

"Nope," Cade said. "But they have electric ones."

"Did we go to Mars?" Bea asked. "I've always wondered what it would be like on Mars."

"Um . . . ," Cade said. "We sent some robots up there."

"And did they find anything?" Trix demanded.

"Uhhh," Cade said, searching his memory.

He shook his head.

"Gosh, the future kind of sucks," Grace said sarcastically, though Cade was pretty sure she still didn't believe him. They would though. Eventually.

For a moment he considered asking the Codex to reveal itself. Maybe that would convince them? Then again, it would likely freak them out even more.

Cade turned his head. Had he heard a branch crack?

He heard it again. Louder this time. He wasn't the only one. Together, the five of them stared into the darkness. More movement, so close that they could hear the footsteps on the ground. It sounded like a single person . . . or creature.

Had they sent the young guard out on his own to find them? Even alone, an armed, armored soldier could take them all on.

Amber was the first to stand, the axe held in front of her. Grace followed suit, hefting a fallen branch, while the other girls crouched behind them, unsure of what to do. Again, Cade wished he had his sword, but it was still in Quintus's chamber.

He scrabbled his hands on the ground. No more branches—only a rock the size of a man's fist. He clutched it like a stress ball.

A dark figure stepped out of the jungle, red-tinged moonlight glinting off a blade. For a moment there was only ragged breathing, the figure staring at them from the shrouded cover of the bushes he had emerged from. In the darkness, Cade saw he wore no helmet. A chance, then.

He hurled the stone over Amber's shoulder, cursing as the misshapen object fell short, striking the figure's shin.

"Heu, filius canis!" cried a voice, the blade thudding to the ground. The figure hopped on one leg, clutching his shin.

Amber yelled and charged.

"No, Amber!" Cade shouted.

He tackled her to the ground.

"Traitor," Amber screamed. "Get him!"

Cade held the axe against the grass, while Grace lashed at them with her branch, hitting both of them as she flailed in the darkness.

"He's my friend," Cade bellowed.

Because he had recognized the voice, and the white streak in the figure's hair.

It was Quintus.

CHAPTER
31

CADE LAY ON TOP OF AMBER IN THE DARKNESS, STARING INTO her face. Grace's branch whipped down, once, twice, but the blows lacked conviction. He ignored the sting of them, focusing on wrestling the weapon from Amber.

Their faces were inches apart, and he could see the determination in her eyes. She gritted her teeth, snarling as she heaved the axe up. Her strength was surprising, but Cade had the upper hand, literally. Finally, she let the axe fall from her fingers, hissing with frustration. He picked it up and stood. Grace raised the branch threateningly.

"Please," Cade said wearily. "Please don't."

Grace stopped, a look of confusion on her face.

"Quintus?" Cade said. "Oh . . . right."

He gave Quintus a friendly wave, and the boy stepped out of the shadows, the Roman sword back in his grasp. He looked at Cade warily.

"How did you know it was him?" Amber snapped from the ground.

Cade ignored her, saddened by the look of distrust on his new friend's face. Cade *had* thrown a rock at him after all.

"Sorry," Cade said, raising his hands. "I thought you were one of the . . . other guys."

Quintus grinned, somehow catching his meaning, and let the gladius fall to his side. He must have tracked them in the darkness after their escape, and been watching the camp. Cade wondered at the courage of the boy, to follow him through all that. To stay, into the night, waiting for an opportunity to rescue him. That was a debt that Cade couldn't even begin to pay back.

He stepped forward and embraced the legionary. Felt the bones of his shoulders, the leanness of his back. Quintus was half-starved. Cade only wished he had some food to give him.

"Hello, are you deaf?" Amber demanded as Cade stepped away. "I asked you guys a question."

"Well, Quintus *is* deaf, actually," Cade said, grasping her outstretched hand and tugging her to her feet. "But I recognized his voice."

"Oh," Amber said, staring at her feet shamefacedly. "Sorry."

"What did he say?" Grace asked. "I missed it."

"My Latin's pretty bad, but even I remember what *filius canis* means," Cade said, giving Quintus a quick grin. "We used to yell it at one another in class, and it drove the teacher up the wall. It means son of a bitch."

Quintus leaned forward, rubbing his shin with a wince. He didn't seem to mind the conversation going on around him.

Cade supposed the legionary was used to it by now, though he still regretted excluding him.

Meanwhile, the girls were speechless.

"You always forget the swear words last," Cade said weakly, scratching his head.

"Ummm . . . why is he speaking *Latin*," Amber asked.

Cade paused. Of course. They didn't know about that.

"Quintus is a Roman legionary," Cade said.

Amber ran a hand down her face.

"Bloody hell. What film is this from? *Spartacus*?"

"There is no film," Cade groaned, exasperated. "I'm telling the truth."

Amber opened her mouth to retort, but to Cade's surprise, it was Bea who spoke up first.

"I don't give a damn what's true or not. All I know is that I don't want to spend another *minute* in these woods. Can this Quintus take us somewhere safe?"

They looked at the young soldier, who had chosen that moment to pick his nose and examine his findings.

"Hey," Cade said, waving to get his attention. Quintus looked up and smiled again.

"You know how to get back to Hueitapalan?"

He sounded out the syllables of the last word, in case Quintus could read his lips and recognize the city's name. No luck though. Not in this darkness.

"Back to *where*?" Trix asked, incredulous.

Cade pointed into the jungle and mimed walking with his fingers. Quintus's eyes lit up, and he nodded.

But instead of heading for the trees, he walked farther into the clearing, nodding politely to Bea and Trix. He stood between them and looked up, then held up a hand with the thumb sticking out.

"What on earth is he doing?" Trix whispered.

Cade shrugged.

"Hell if I know."

"I know," Grace said. "He's looking at the stars."

Of course.

Cade walked over to Quintus, trying to follow the length of the boy's arm with his eyes. They were lucky—the clearing had been made by a fallen tree, the rotting log somewhere behind them. Through the gap it had left, Cade could see the stars. With everything that had happened the past few days, he hadn't had much of an opportunity to examine the sky properly, having only brief glances as he ran from some danger or another, or seeing hints of it filtering through the canopy.

Now that he looked, it was glorious. He had seen pictures of the Milky Way before, high-exposure shots taken over hours with expensive cameras to capture all the light. But this sky looked like that to the naked eye. Every inch was filled with stars swirling across the firmament like glitter spilled on ink.

There was no moon to be seen, and the constellations seemed random, but that didn't seem to matter to Quintus. After a few seconds, he nodded to himself and strode off into the jungle, leaping over the fallen trunk without even a glance over his shoulder.

"Do we just follow him?" Bea asked.

"Unless you want to stay here," Cade said, not unkindly. "Come on. We can trust him."

Still, the girls stood, unsure at the sound of Quintus chopping a way through the vegetation. Cade followed after him, choosing action over words.

Sure enough, the girls were only a few steps behind him.

"Known him long, then?" Amber asked.

"Met him last night," Cade said.

"Oh, great," Amber said. "And I suppose you stayed up all night getting to know each other?"

"Well," Cade said, ducking a low branch, "we did talk for like five minutes."

"Oh, how *delightful*," Amber said. "Are you old chums now?"

"Look, he saved me more than once," Cade said. "I'd trust him with my life."

"And ours, apparently," Amber added.

"The clearing's that way if you don't want to come."

Silence. Finally, she didn't have a retort for him.

"As far as you know, he could have sold you to the . . . armored guys," Amber muttered.

For what felt like the umpteenth time that day, Cade ignored her. She was already getting on his nerves.

"Maybe you were worth more to him alive," Amber went on. "And that's why he saved you. Maybe he's leading us back to them right now."

Cade shook his head and pushed on through the jungle, following the sounds of Quintus hacking a path. He left an easy trail to follow, cutting a wide berth with his gladius.

Quintus may have been skinny, but there was a wiry strength to him, and he seemed tireless. Progress was still slow, but far more comfortable without the endless leaves slapping against their faces.

He tried not to think about the creatures that might be lurking in the darkness. Nocturnal predators, waiting for a snack to stumble past them.

"Happy thoughts, Cade," he muttered under his breath. "Happy thoughts."

CHAPTER
32

CADE WASN'T SURE IF IT WAS QUINTUS'S GUIDANCE OR BLIND luck that had allowed them to survive the night. Other than some nearby rustling and a fraught hour crouched among the bushes as a dark giant stomped by, they had encountered little of the fauna that populated the caldera.

Even so, it was a relief to stumble into the broad, empty streets of Hueitapalan a few hours later, not least because Cade's legs felt like leaden weights with the consistency of wet noodles. He couldn't resist grinning though as the girls marveled at the tall buildings on either side of them. Without the trees surrounding them, the red moon was clearly visible, with its smaller white satellite peeking out from behind it.

"Well, this isn't Shropshire," Trix announced.

"No kidding," Amber said, turning in a slow circle.

Cade kept quiet. Somehow, he didn't think an "I told you so" would be helpful at that moment.

He only wished that there were some sauropods present so he could win the dinosaur argument too. Unfortunately, Quintus barely gave them a moment to take it all in before he was loping across the red-moonlit plaza, heading for his temple again. Clearly the area was not as safe as it appeared, and Cade decided he preferred to delay his victory than to win the debate by getting eaten.

Together, the six of them staggered into the entrance and down the corridors, following Quintus's unerring course. Cade almost held his breath for the last corridor before collapsing with a deep sigh on the makeshift bed of the fur-covered altar.

He caught Quintus eyeing him reproachfully.

"What? My legs are killing me."

Quintus raised his eyebrows.

"Fine," Cade moaned, standing as the girls walked in.

He offered them the seat, and they sat down gratefully, groaning as they kicked off their mud-soaked sneakers.

Quintus busied himself with the fire, using his gladius and a flint to light it. Soon the girls were wiggling their toes by the flames. Cade collapsed to the ground beside it, warming his hands and feet. He took the opportunity to roll up his pants legs, and it was with some surprise that he saw the ant-head stitches had held.

Quintus caught his eye and gave a mock bow before snatching some of the hanging, gutted compies drying above the fireplace and handing one each to the girls. They stared at the desiccated remains in disgust. Quintus dropped another in Cade's lap and kept one for himself, settling down beside the fire and tearing a hunk of leathery flesh free with his teeth.

"What on earth are these?" Grace whispered. "Looks like a lizard had a baby with a chicken."

Cade bit his tongue at the comment and took a bite of his compy. It tasted like a piece of dry old leather, but he chewed it down anyway.

"They're dinosaurs," Amber said, winking at Cade. "And . . . I don't think we're on Earth either."

He almost choked on his compy with surprise, and Amber let out a laugh.

Well, at least she's starting to believe me.

"So, Cade," Grace said through a mouthful of dry flesh, "care to tell us how you found yourself here?"

Cade took his time chewing, something that wasn't difficult given the consistency. He gathered his thoughts, wondering how to explain it without sounding completely unhinged.

"I was at school," Cade said. "Then suddenly I was standing on a rock. There was this monster beneath me—one of those piranha-chimps I was telling you about. I fought it off."

The room was silent except for the crackle of the fire and the sound of Quintus devouring his meal. He was not a quiet eater, and Cade paused as the soldier smacked his lips and began to crack the delicate bones inside to get at the marrow. Quintus caught them staring at him and grinned, a flap of compy skin hanging from his chin. Then he went back to it, unfazed.

"Um . . . anyways. After that, I ran into a force field before it disappeared."

"Seriously?" Grace asked. This time, it was less a comment of doubt than one of shock.

"Yeah. It's all a game. Someone . . . something . . . made this place, and put us here. And not just us. Quintus and some other soldiers were left here too, somehow taken out of time, just like the dinosaurs."

"And us," Trix muttered.

"I met up with some other guys from my school and we came across a fort that the Romans built," Cade continued. "And then there was this . . . thing . . . there."

This was the part Cade had been dreading. But he had to do it. Rip it off like a Band-Aid. He needed these girls on his side. Needed them to believe him.

"What thing?" Amber asked.

Cade cleared his throat.

"Codex?" he said, looking around the room. "Can you show yourself?"

Instantly, the Codex flickered into view. The girls gasped, nearly falling over the back of the altar as it floated down to Cade's level.

02:13:12:51
02:13:12:50
02:13:12:49

Cade gulped at the sight of the timer. He'd lost so much time. He didn't want to look at it.

"What in heaven's name is that?" Bea whispered, trying to hide behind her sister.

"It calls itself a Codex," Cade explained. "Think of it as Google, but it'll pretty much only tell us about things that originated on Earth. And sometimes the game, if it feels like it."

Amber groaned.

"You've lost me."

Cade thought for a minute.

Oh.

"Of course," Cade sighed. "Google isn't around yet in 1985."

"Silly word if I ever heard one," Trix muttered.

"Okay, so think of it as an encyclopedia, then," Cade said. "You point at something, and it tells you what it was, as long as that information is still available on Earth and the thing comes from Earth."

"You mean we could have done it to those men?" Grace asked.

"Yes," Cade said, hearing a hint of regret in his voice. "But I didn't want to reveal it to them, and the thing flashes when you ask it a question."

"Did you tell it to hide from us?" Grace asked, reproachful.

"Was I conscious when they brought me in?" Cade asked dryly. "The damned thing has a mind of its own."

"Language," Trix said, raising her eyebrows at him.

Cade put his head in his hands.

"We have the next best thing though," Amber said, hefting the axe. "Make it point at this!"

Cade lifted his head and flashed her a smile. She was getting the hang of being in this strange place.

"Okay," he said. "Codex, where does this axe come from?"

The Codex flashed, so bright and sudden in the darkened room that even Cade jolted at it.

"Action prohibited. Object is not a remnant. It does not originate on Earth."

Cade cursed under his breath and earned a reproachful glare from Trix.

"What does that mean?" Amber asked.

"It means it was made here. Somewhere in this godforsaken world, there may be a blacksmith churning these out. In fact, now that I think about it, I doubt pointing the Codex at those men would have told us much at all."

"Why's that?" Amber asked.

"Because I suspect they're descended from people left here long ago. Unfortunately for us, they're the kind of people who take captives to use for who knows what purpose."

"And those numbers?" she asked. "What are they?"

"I . . . it's hard to explain," Cade said.

He waited for Amber's next question, but none was forthcoming. In fact, as the warmth from the fire seeped into the room, Bea and Grace had already begun to nod off.

"Let's get some rest," Cade said. "We're safe enough here."

"All right," Amber said, yawning. "Let's pick this up in the morning."

As the girls made themselves comfortable around the room, Cade considered whether now was the time to tell them about the qualifying round. Ask them to join the fight.

But it was hard to keep thoughts still in his head, exhaustion settling over him like a heavy cloak.

Tomorrow, then.

CHAPTER
33

CADE WANTED TO SLEEP. NEEDED TO SLEEP. BUT THAT DIDN'T seem to be on Quintus's agenda. It felt as if he had only just closed his eyes when the soldier was prodding him awake and tugging at him to follow, even though the sky he saw through the holes in the ceiling was stained with the dim light of dawn.

The girls were sprawled in various positions across the room, with Trix and Bea propped against each other in the corner. The fire had long since burned out, and there was a chill in the room. Amber was shivering in her sleep, so Cade picked up the fur that had fallen from the altar where Grace had been tossing and turning in the night and laid it over her.

He looked to the Codex, and realized he had slept for under two hours.

```
02:11:36:11
02:11:36:10
02:11:36:09
```

It was probably around six in the morning. Or whatever the equivalent of that was on this planet. It seemed a day here could last twenty hours, or thirty. He hadn't been keeping count. Whatever time it was, Quintus was in a hurry, practically dragging Cade into the darkness of the corridor.

Soon Cade was in pitch black, feeling the cobwebs catch across his face as the legionary led him unerringly from one place to another. To Cade's surprise, they were not going the usual route, instead turning down a different corridor, where much of the floors above had fallen through.

Sometimes Cade dropped to his knees and crawled, while other times he edged sideways. Here and there, dawn light cut through cracks in the walls, illuminating hallways filled with fallen pillars, rubble, and encroaching vegetation.

Lianas crisscrossed wherever he looked, with hanging mosses adorning them like Christmas ornaments. Tiny bones crunched underfoot, and all the while the sound of dripping water echoed around. Twice they went up narrow flights of stairs, so steep that Cade had to stop and rest midway before continuing on. This complex was larger than Cade had realized.

They reached the top floor, and even then, Quintus led him inexorably onward. There were paintings on this level, murals that had begun to peel but still showed the tanned, elaborately dressed figures of what Cade guessed were Mayan royalty and jaguar-skin-clad warriors, with the blue sky painted vividly above them.

A final staircase was built into the wall, and Quintus scampered up it, quick as a fox. As they emerged at the top, Cade blinked in the sunlight.

Strangely, the cacophony of noise was even louder than the last time, the screeching of the pterosaurs coupled with distant honks, though his position on the rooftop blocked his view of the plaza.

The stone was slippery underfoot here, and the entire surface seemed to have been decorated in some way, with carved tiles of twisting figures, long since worn away by the rain and wind. Large statues lined the edges, reminding Cade of gargoyles on a medieval cathedral.

Here and there, pterosaurs hissed from their nests, though these were no larger than pigeons. Cade was only thankful that the giraffe-sized beasts he had seen before were nowhere to be found, although from the amount of feces piled on the roof, they might as well have been. By now, the sun was truly beginning to rise, casting the world in a golden light.

He wanted to catch his breath, but Quintus tugged at his hand, muttering in Latin under his breath. There was something he wanted Cade to see, and urgently. So Cade staggered on with a groan, though to his relief his legs ached only from exertion—his wounds well on the way to recovery. Then he saw it, and the discomfort was forgotten.

Three figures were sitting around a campfire in the center of the city. Quintus was snatching at Cade's shirt and pointing, and immediately Cade saw they were wearing the same blue clothing as he himself was.

Cade squinted but couldn't be sure who they were. The fact that there were only three of them was worrying, but he found himself grinning regardless. Especially because of what else he saw down there.

Walking around where the three were sitting . . . were dinosaurs. The city's plaza had become a natural thoroughfare for the largest animals, caused by the lack of low branches and vegetation and the natural funnel of the buildings on either side. Some form of migration was in full swing, and Cade marveled at the magnificent creatures walking below him.

The first that caught his eye was a herd of sauropods, the long-necked, quadrupedal beasts that had a giraffe's neck and head on the ponderous body of an elephant. These were not as large as the plane-sized behemoth he had seen stretching its throat across the river, but they still seemed unperturbed by the trio of humans crouched beneath them as they continued their slow march to the jungle on the other side of the city.

The other boys seemed trapped among the animals, fearful of being trodden on by the great beasts that parted around their small campfire like water flowing around a rock. It seemed they had decided to make camp in the lee of the great, central pillar of the plaza, a giant obelisk that stretched higher than the one opposite the White House. The three might have made a run for it, but the sauropods were not the only beasts that blocked their path to the buildings on either side.

Among them were other creatures. Ceratopsians, known for the most famous of them—triceratops—were also among the crowd. These beaked, horned cows with frilled shields growing from their foreheads lumbered to chew on dandelions emerging from the paving.

Smaller, bipedal lizards skittered back and forth between the falling feet; the compies that Quintus had been living off.

And dozens of others that Cade couldn't name if he tried, made up of a plethora of shapes, colors, and sizes.

All the while, the animals vocalized, filling the dawn air with their orchestral sounds. Deep lowing, coupled with hoots, caws, whistles, and screeches. They were greeting the morning it seemed, and it filled Cade with a wistful appreciation. If only his father had been there to see it.

Cade whooped with relief, but Quintus didn't seem as happy. In fact, now that he saw Cade was pleased to see the others, he began waving his hands and shouting at them. Desperately.

"What's happening?" Cade asked, gripping Quintus's arm.

The boy seemed to understand him intuitively and pointed into the jungle on the side of the city, where the vegetation was thicker. Dinosaurs did not seem to be coming from there, instead coming in from one end of the city and exiting the opposite. Cade couldn't see anything, and Quintus yanked his arm away and continued trying to get the attention of the others below.

But as the light of the sun got stronger, Cade finally saw what Quintus must have seen earlier.

Predators. A half dozen of them by the look of it, crouched among the tangled trees, partially obscured by the shadow of a nearby pyramid. These were no carnosaurs, nor were they raptors, but still terrifying in their appearance and size.

They were like crocodiles in many ways, with the same tail, fangs, and armored scales, though with a larger head and shorter snout. But unlike a crocodile, their bodies were made for speed. They were built like wolves with four muscular limbs. And just like wolves stalking their prey, they seemed to be lying in wait.

Now Quintus took Cade's arm, pointing at something else. A new herd had entered the clearing. Sauropods again, but smaller ones, no larger than elephants. A family group it seemed, with only three adults. Ambling among their feet were juveniles, their gait awkward and bumbling.

They might have just been born that week for all Cade knew, but there was something else he *did* know. Predators hunted the young and vulnerable. If the predators were going to pounce, they would be doing so soon. And the others would be caught in the ensuing stampede.

Despite all this, the group below hadn't noticed Quintus; the noise of the dinosaurs passing by was drowning out his shouts. They needed to do something else to catch their attention, and quickly.

Cade strode to the edge of the building and saw a crumbling stairway on one side. It was so steep that it almost looked ceremonial, perhaps more for decoration than everyday use. In a pinch he could scramble down, but making it back up would be a problem. They would need to reenter the building from the ground floor.

He tried shouting, but with his throat hoarse from earlier, it sounded weak even to his own ears. Every second the sauropod family trundled nearer.

Luckily, the predators were yet to see them, their view blocked by the pyramid they were hiding behind. Cade followed the family's trajectory and saw the point where they would cross the crocodogs' field of vision.

Slap bang in the middle of where the others were resting. He needed to warn them, but he was too far away.

There's nothing I can do.

Even at that thought, Cade felt a twinge of guilt, just as he had felt many times over the past year. It was the same guilt he had felt after Finch had attacked Spex. Was this who he was?

A survivor.

No.

A coward.

Cade set his jaw. There was more at stake than ever.

He began to climb down.

CHAPTER
34

CADE IGNORED THE ACHE IN HIS LEGS, HURLING HIMSELF DOWN the last few steps and onto the crumbling floor. Compies scattered out of his way, screeching their displeasure, but Cade ignored them and plowed on, waving his hands in the air.

"Hey," he yelled, sidestepping a ceratopsian that was blundering past, its great horns jutting like elephant tusks.

Still, they didn't hear. The animal noises were louder on the ground, a veritable thunder of grunting and lowing. Yet none of the creatures seemed perturbed by Cade—the running, shouting boy in their midst.

So he ran on. He could see the others now, Finch and Spex, along with Scott. The three of them were pressed up against the pillar, scared to move among the scores of enormous animals passing them by. Most of the dinosaurs seemed to be giving them a wide berth, though more likely because of the fire than anything else. Finally, Scott spotted him.

Scott stood, a wide grin on his face, but it was soon replaced with confusion as Cade turned his waving into a frantic beckoning motion with his arm. Then Scott was speaking to the others, pointing at Cade. Behind them, the family of sauropods neared, the juveniles ambling ahead in their youthful exuberance.

The trio passed out of Cade's sight as a herd of hadrosaurs wandered between them, honking through their duckbills. Cade cursed. His view was blocked by a wall of moving mottled flesh, the creatures alternating between four legs and two like ungainly kangaroos.

He waited a few panicked seconds. Then he saw the boys jogging toward him, puzzled looks upon their faces.

"Run!" Cade shouted, preparing to lead by example.

But before he could turn, a croaking nose echoed from the jungle, setting dozens of pterosaurs flapping from their roosts and into the skies. Again it sounded, deep and menacing.

Silence fell—and the crocodogs burst through the trees, their long tails lashing back and forth as they tore across the ground.

Pandemonium. The ground shook as a hundred giants thundered in all directions, jostling for position as they headed for the side streets or continued on their way through the plaza. It was all Cade could do to avoid the thundering feet, diving one way or another as they hurtled by.

Scott sped past, followed by Spex. Cade went to follow them, but something barged into him, sending him crashing to the ground. His skull hit the cobbles, stars flaring in his vision, but he saw the culprit, Finch, scramble up and keep on going.

A juggernaut of ceratopsian flesh passed within inches of his face. Head spinning, Cade rolled aside and curled up in a ball, trying to reduce his size as clawed pillars of meat and bone slammed down around him. He counted to five, his eyes tight shut. It was surprisingly hard to open them again.

Luckily for Cade, the stampede had passed him by, but he found himself in a far worse predicament. Because he now lay right between the crocodogs and their prey. Out of the frying pan, into a blazing bonfire.

The sauropod family had formed a protective ring around their babies, but strangely, each had their side turned to the approaching crocodogs, like ancient battleships presenting a broadside. In the other direction, the crocodogs had stopped. One stood on its hind limbs, and Cade realized that they alternated between four legs and two.

It seemed to Cade that these ambush predators had intended for the panic to separate the young from their parents, and they were now forced to reevaluate their plan of attack.

He didn't plan on being their consolation prize, but the predators had spread out in their approach, blocking the way back to the temple. The simple answer would be to run for the nearest building, but he couldn't be sure that running wouldn't set them chasing him instead of their intended prey, and they'd definitely catch up to him before he reached it. The nearest place of . . . admittedly dubious safety was with the sauropods themselves.

He thought of the line from *Jurassic Park*, that the T. rex couldn't see you if you stayed still. That wasn't the case here.

Already the crocodogs were peering at him, cocking their heads to the side.

What was this strange blue-brown creature that hadn't run away from them? Hopefully the answer wasn't lunch.

Slowly, he got to his feet, looking the crocodogs in the eyes, trying not to show fear. It wasn't easy. Up close, he realized how large they were too. Each was almost fifteen feet long and taller than a small horse.

As he forced himself to glare at them, the Codex drifted across his view, unharmed by the stampede. He had almost forgotten it was following him. Time for a distraction.

"Codex," he whispered. "Tell me what those are."

Immediately the drone zoomed toward the closest of them, and the predator fell back, mystified by it. When the blue light flashed, Cade turned and sped away, limping and hopping his way toward the sauropods.

"*Remnant identified as* Postosuchus," the Codex intoned, returning beside him as he ran. "*This species is a member of Pseudosuchia, the lineage of archosaurs that became modern crocodilians—*"

"Shut up," Cade snapped. "Scan all of them."

The Codex zoomed off to do his bidding, while Cade took advantage of the distraction. He staggered beneath the belly of the nearest sauropod, its four legs like tree trunks on either side of him. The juveniles squalled, and the giant above rumbled its displeasure at his presence.

Message received. Stay away from the young ones.

Luckily for him, the crocodogs had not given chase, though they were each in turn snapping at the Codex as it flitted between them. Flash after flash of blue followed before it rock-eted back, though this time it stayed silent. Now, Cade could only wait to see what the outcome of the standoff would be. He hoped the crocodogs would slink off in search of easier prey.

The sauropods certainly looked formidable, and now that he was among them, he noticed that they had what appeared to be bony plating studded along their backs. Useful, should the crocodogs succeed in mounting them.

But it seemed the predators did not share his opinion of their chances. They were prowling back and forth, switching positions and making mock charges, edging ever nearer with each lap. Soon they were only a stone's throw away, eliciting groans of anger from the sauropod above him. Then Cade realized why the giants were facing the predators side on.

A long tail swept through the air, whip-cracking as it broke the sound barrier and bowled the nearest crocodog away. The monster tumbled head over heels until it rested against the foot of a pillar. It didn't move.

The sauropod above him stomped a great foot, the thud reverberating as it swept its tail in warning against more approaches. But the crocodogs were undeterred. As one, they charged toward the waiting parents, leaping fluidly across the ground with a pace Cade could hardly believe was possible.

His eyes widened as one made a beeline straight for him, then the monolithic neck above swung down like a mace. Only this time, the crocodog was ready, leaping atop the dinosaur's throat as it slammed the ground, then scrambling up it. The sauropod lifted the crocodog from view, though the giant's bellows of pain reverberated through the chest above Cade's head. Suddenly, Cade found his path ahead clear as the remaining predators engaged with the adults on either side.

He ran, forgetting the pain in his legs, forgetting the throaty vocalizations of the battle behind him. Ahead, he could see Quintus's palace and the cavernous entrance at its base. But even as he ran, movement stirred in the corner of his vision.

The crocodog that had been knocked into the pillar was getting up.

"Hurry," a voice yelled. Scott appeared in the palace entrance, followed by the others. They waved him on. Quintus was nowhere to be seen.

Cade staggered on, glancing back to see that the injured crocodog had given chase. The creature was scrabbling across the ground in a half crawl, barely using one of its back legs. Yet it was still gaining on him, its claws digging between the cobblestones. Its hungry eyes locked with his, and Cade turned and broke into a faltering run.

The palace entrance loomed larger with every step, but he could hear the panting croaks of the beast behind him. Even as he crossed into the shadow of the complex, his leg was yanked back and he fell. His boot was torn from his foot as he scrambled away.

Meanwhile, the crocodog went into a death roll, shaking the boot in its mouth. It released it a few moments later before dropping into a crouch. It was going to leap.

Cade groped for a weapon. But it was too late. The sky was blotted out as the creature launched itself into the air, and Cade could do nothing but cross his arms over his head.

The impact never came. Only a spatter of warm liquid across his face, and a rasping croak. Cade opened his eyes. Quintus was crouched over him, his gladius outstretched, buried up to its hilt in the crocodog's chest.

The creature coughed again, its lifeblood spraying across the pair of them. Then it fell away, jerking the sword from Quintus's grasp as it spasmed in its death throes. Quintus lifted Cade to his feet, and together they stumbled into the threshold of the complex.

Scott spoke first.

"I think I liked it better at the keep."

CHAPTER
35

THE SCENT OF COOKING MEAT FILLED CADE'S NOSTRILS AS HE tore into the hunk of greasy flesh in his hands. It tasted like fish-tinged chicken, but to his starved stomach it was heavenly, if a little on the rare side.

It was but a few minutes after they had absconded back to Quintus's home in the temple, but not before the young legionary had retrieved both Cade's boot and his own gladius from the crocodog's corpse and lopped off the foreleg, that all of them were now eating, sitting in a circle on the floor. It turned out that Quintus wasn't the best of cooks, nor the most patient, cutting slices with his bloodied sword and handing it out to the others while the meat was still roasting.

Cade made sure to keep his own blade by his side. In part because of what had happened, and in part because Finch had been eyeing it with interest.

Introductions had been made, but the girls were reticent as the three new boys entered the room, not least because of the leer Finch gave them. They had hardly spoken a word since.

In contrast, the guys had taken meeting a quartet of English teen girls from 1985 in stride. Cade had yet to tell the boys of their capture and escape, though.

Cade had felt a profound sense of relief at finding the others, though Finch's presence had marred the feeling somewhat. If they worked together as a team of contenders, their chance of winning the qualifying round must be stronger. All he had to do was convince them.

Now, they sat in silence, their hunger outweighing their curiosity as the smell of cooking meat permeated the room. The compy that most of them had eaten the night before had definitely not hit the spot.

"So, elephant in the room. Or should I say ... weird, caveman-looking dude in the room," Scott began, eyeing Quintus as the boy buried half his face into his piece of crocodog. "Who is he?"

"Quintus. He's a legionary from the Ninth Legion," Cade said. "But he can't speak English and his hearing isn't so good."

Scott shrugged.

"Sounds about right," he said.

"Does he know anything?" Finch asked.

"He says gods brought him here, but he ran away from the keep when his legion marched off and didn't come back. Make of that what you will."

"That legion sure has a habit of disappearing." Finch let out a bitter laugh, then went back to his meal.

"What happened to you guys?" Cade asked, resisting the urge to talk with his mouth full. It felt like forever since his belly had been satisfied.

"We managed to get the boat to shore in one piece," Scott said.

Cade sighed with relief. They would need the food inside it if they were to make the trek back to the keep in time. Of course, he still needed to convince them to take part in the qualifying round.

"It stopped next to that red ship," Scott went on, mumbling through a mouthful of primordial reptile. "Weird-looking thing. It was all broken up, and it looked like an old Chinese boat. I mean really old, with a sail and everything. But it had *Sea Dragon* written on its side in English though, and there was a diesel engine on there. With diesel to spare in rusty old cans."

Cade shook his head. An ancient Chinese vessel, with English lettering and a modern engine? That didn't make much sense, but then, nothing here did.

"Yoshi thinks he can clear out the gunk in the *Witchcraft*'s engine," Spex said. "Fill it with fresh diesel from the new ship. Drive us back up and try one of those tributaries, or try to make it through the rapids."

"Delusional," Finch muttered from the corner.

"We saw footprints leaving the Chinese ship," Scott said, glaring at Finch. "Decided to follow them, see if there were any other people here. We drew straws, and the three of us got the short straw."

"And did you find anyone?" Cade asked.

Scott's gaze fell.

"There wasn't much left of them," he muttered. "No clue who or what they were, but it can't have been more than a few days since they were killed. After that, it got dark, and we got lost trying to make our way back. Ended up here."

"What about you guys?" Spex asked, turning to the girls. "Do you know why we're here?"

Bea gave them a soundless shake of her head.

"Talkative bunch, aren't they?" Finch said, pointing at them with a crocodog claw. "Dinosaur's got your tongue?"

"I heard it almost got yours," Amber retorted. "And the rest of you."

Finch grinned.

"Oh, I *like* you," he said, giving her a wink.

Amber's nostrils flared, and Cade noted the axe laid out across her lap.

"And you?" Finch asked, glaring at Cade with suspicion. "Why didn't you come looking for us up the river?"

"I did," Cade snapped. "But it's not easy when everything out here is higher up on the food chain."

Finch snorted.

"I think you know something," he said, narrowing his eyes. "You didn't fall, you jumped. And you took the Codex with you. Now you show up here with your fancy sword and your Roman friend. There's something you're not telling us."

"You think I'm in on all this?" Cade growled, struggling to his feet. "After what I just did for you?"

Finch spat derisively and muttered under his breath.

"Shitskin."

Cade felt the anger boil up inside him, like bile in his throat. This time, he wasn't prepared to let it go.

"What did you say?" he demanded.

Finch stood and squared up to him, bringing his face an inch from Cade's own.

"You want to do something about it?" Finch asked. "I'm right here."

There was the sound of a blade scraping against stone, and a cleared throat. Quintus looked up at them with a blank stare, but his meaning was clear. There was to be no fighting in his house. To Cade's surprise, Amber and Grace had also stood, though whether it was to help him or not, he wasn't sure.

Suddenly, Finch jerked his head forward, trying to make Cade flinch, then backed away with a sneer.

"Can't trust anyone here," he muttered.

"Now who's delusional," Amber snapped. "Leave him alone and eat your dinosaur."

The temperature in the room seemed to cool a few degrees as Cade returned to his place on the floor.

"Thanks, by the way, Cade, for warning us," Spex said, pushing his thick glasses up his nose. "I should have said it earlier."

"Yeah," Scott said. "You basically traded places with us, you fool."

Cade grinned, though he didn't expect any thanks from Finch. He returned to eating his meal, but the knowledge that time was ticking away was nagging at him. He had the girls here, and several of the boys. This was it.

He sighed and handed his meat to Scott, who stuffed the whole piece immediately into his mouth.

"There's something I have to tell you," Cade announced.

"See," Finch said triumphantly.

"Shut up," Scott mumbled. "Go on, Cade."

Cade turned to the girls first.

"When we arrived at the keep, the Codex started a timer," he said. "It said we had to take place in what it called a 'qualifying round.' And if this 'round' is anything like what we experienced when we arrived here, it doesn't sound like a walk in the park."

"Why didn't you tell us that before?" Grace said, crossing her arms.

"It didn't come up," Cade said, running a hand through his matted hair.

This was not good. Already they were suspicious of him, and he hadn't even got to the worst part yet. Now he turned to the others.

"Both Quintus and the Codex told me that to win the qualifying round, we're supposed to defend the keep from something. It's what the Romans had been doing before they got wiped out. If we don't replace them, we lose the game."

"The *game*?" Trix asked, her voice an octave higher than usual. "I thought you were *joking* before. What is it?"

"We don't know," Cade said. "All we know is that it's deadly. Fighting monsters. Mutants of some kind, maybe. We don't know for what . . . or for whom."

He gave an involuntary shudder, his mind drifting to the creatures the Romans had fought in the film.

"Told you it was a good idea to leave that place," Finch said, nodding to himself.

Cade held up a hand. This was it.

"Quintus told me something else," he said. "Something big."

The room fell silent, and Cade took a deep breath.

"He said if we don't take part, or we lose . . . planet Earth will be destroyed."

For a moment, nobody said anything. Then Finch let out an exaggerated laugh, slapping his knee with one hand.

"This kid tells you we're brought here by what . . . gods? And then you believe him?"

"The Codex confirmed it," Cade said, pointing at the floating drone.

"Who cares what it says," Finch said, still laughing. "It's all lies anyway."

"It knows more than you think," Cade said. "It's how I found this sword. It's how I confirmed where Quintus came from."

Finch rolled his eyes.

"So what, you're saying we should go play this game and get ourselves killed, because some dude who thinks he's a Roman and a flying robot told us that our entire planet will blow up if we don't? Do you know how ridiculous that sounds?"

"What do you think is going on out there?" Cade said, pointing down the passageway. "Have you forgotten what you've seen, heard—hell—even tasted?"

Finch looked away, shaking his head with pursed lips.

"What they said is hard to believe," Cade continued. "But then so is everything else. And everything else is *real.*"

"He has a point," Amber said, and Cade hadn't realized how much her support meant to him until that very moment.

"Screw the world, then," Finch snapped. "Even if it is true, I couldn't care less about anyone back home."

Cade groaned with exasperation, motioning to his surroundings.

"You want to live like this? Because Quintus left the keep a year ago, and this is where he's ended up."

"But he still left," Finch retorted, "and he knew what he was facing better than we do now. He'd clearly rather live out here than back at the keep. And he had weapons, armor, probably a whole bunch of other soldiers with him too. So what is it about that place that's making him hide out here?"

"Maybe he has the same attitude you have," Cade said, throwing up his hands. "Screw the world, right? Let's live in a dank hole and eat lizards."

"Sounds pretty good when the alternative is getting your guts ripped out by monsters, just because a robot told you to," Finch retorted.

"You mean like I almost did a few minutes ago?" Cade said. "It's not exactly much safer here. What happened to Quintus's friends, huh?"

"Maybe they stayed behind and died," Finch said.

The two glared at each other. After a few moments, Scott spoke.

"Look, I'm all for saving the world. But I don't think we have much of a chance without weapons."

Cade smiled. They were considering it at least.

"I agree," Amber said. "If we're going to fight, we need more than this axe."

Cade walked over to the wall, where his sword still sat, gathering dust. That was twice now he had left this room without it. Never again. Now, he slung it over his shoulder and drew the blade.

"If I can get everyone a sword like this one, would you fight?" he asked.

They paused, exchanging silent glasses.

"Maybe," Grace said.

"Yeah," Scott said, shuffling his feet. "We'd have a chance at least."

Amber nodded.

"Worse comes to worst we run away," Spex said. "See what happens. But we need everyone on board. Just a few of us won't stand a chance. I only survived the vipers last time by pure luck."

"Okay, only if the others agree." Scott nodded.

"How many more of you are there?" Grace asked.

"Five," Cade replied.

He had expected Amber to be pleased, but instead she looked conflicted, her eyes darting over their uniforms. The idea of being outnumbered by so many strangers likely worried her. Cade considered for a moment, and the trace of an idea began to take shape.

"Codex, bring up the map," Cade said.

This time it wasn't just Quintus who gasped when the map appeared beside the timer in the air.

02:10:42:21
02:10:42:20
02:10:42:19

"Told you the Codex knows a lot," Cade said, allowing himself a smirk.

He turned to Quintus and pointed at the spot where the keep was, then the timer. The legionary nodded, showing he understood what they meant. Cade then pointed to the others and himself in turn, before pointing at the keep once more. Quintus nodded again.

Now was the moment of truth. They could use a real warrior on their side. Cade pointed at Quintus and raised his eyebrows questioningly. Would he come with them? He pointed between Quintus and the others for added effect.

"What are you doing?" Finch said. "You look like an idiot."

"Shut up, Finch," Amber said.

Quintus looked at Cade for a moment, then drew a finger beneath his throat, pointing at the keep and the timer. He was telling them of the danger there. Now it was Cade's turn to nod. Then he shrugged his shoulders, as if to say they would go regardless. Then he pointed at Quintus again.

Again, the legionary paused. For a few agonizing seconds he stared at Cade, considering his new companion. Then he gave a final nod.

Cade whooped and clapped his shoulder.

"Well, if you want to stick around here, go ahead," Cade said to Finch. "We're going."

Then he turned back to the map.

"In the meantime, let's work out a way back to the *Witchcraft*. We don't have much time."

CHAPTER
36

I T SEEMED THAT THE SAUROPODS HAD BEEN FARING WELL WHEN they had left earlier, but when the group finally emerged from the temple complex, Cade was dismayed to see the remains of one of the youngsters. Lucky for them, the crocodogs were long gone, having stripped the beast to the bone in under an hour. Whatever remained had been picked almost clean by the piranha-like compies skittering about the place, leaving only a pile of bones and armored plating. Even the dead crocodog's corpse was gone, dragged away by some predator if not the other crocodogs themselves.

Now, only the pterosaurs remained, hunched over the sauropod skeleton like vultures and snapping the smaller bones between their powerful jaws.

"Ready?" Cade asked.

He didn't wait for a reply, instead walking across the open plaza, avoiding the many piles of dinosaur droppings that coated the ground. It seemed the predator attack had cleared out the place of larger herbivores, at least for now. Even the city's usual inhabitants were thin on the ground, and the few compies and pterosaurs he passed flitted away as soon as he neared them.

"Smells like a farm," Spex groaned, lifting a sullied boot. He'd stepped right in it.

"More like the can after Gobbler's dropped one in it," Scott said, holding his nose.

Cade hushed the boys, surprised at how relaxed they were. But then, they hadn't seen what he had. Not really.

The others hadn't been trapped up a tree by a T. rex's doppelganger, or been hunted by a pack of raptors like an animal. Every minute in the open was a risk.

And every risk brought the end of the world a little closer to reality. An end to his friends. His family.

They headed toward what turned out to be the smallest of the pyramids there, the same one that Cade had fought the raptors on. Cade could see the bloodied marks from where he had crawled the day before—far less than he thought there would be. It must have been shock, rather than blood loss, that had made him so weak.

As he walked, the wounds on his legs itched more than anything else, though after that morning's sprint, they throbbed when he put pressure on them. In a pinch he would be able to run again, though it wouldn't be easy.

Finally, they reached the pyramid, and it was a relief to step into the shade. The ground had been torn up by the raptors' talons near the base of the stairs, and Cade was shocked at the size of the footprints. Had he really fought such creatures? And won?

Well. With help from Quintus.

"There you are," Cade whispered, seeing the bag of swords just where he had left it. He'd had some irrational fear that the raptors had taken them, but of course they weren't that smart.

Kneeling with a wince, he fished inside and tugged out an oilcloth-wrapped sword for each of them, handing them out like candy.

"What are those?" Finch snapped.

"*Remnants identified as the swords named Nagamitsu, Kunitoshi,*" the Codex began. "*Tak—*"

Cade hushed it before going back in and giving each of them a scabbard too. Only Quintus refused the sword, preferring the gladius he had brought with him. In the light of day, Cade was again struck by the boy's gaunt figure, what with the stick-thin legs beneath him. A year in this place had taken a toll on him. Food was not so easy to come by.

"This is badass," Scott said, pulling off the cloth and admiring the blade. "Better than pickaxes."

"Keep quiet," Cade whispered. "This is where the raptors almost got me the other night. They could be waiting."

That shut them up.

Finch went to pick up the bag, still containing the remainder of the swords, but Scott got there first, slinging it over his shoulder and giving Cade a wink. Cade was glad. He had almost forgotten the way Finch had hoarded the weapons at the keep, such as they were, for himself and his two allies. Now he'd been lucky to get a sword at all.

Cade wished he hadn't had to arm Finch, but if it did come down to another confrontation with the raptors, he would need all the help he could get, wherever and whomever it came from. And even with a sword of his own, the power had shifted out of Finch's favor.

Trepidation filled Cade's head as he stared at the jungle's edge. Despite the hot midday sun, it was dark beneath the canopy. All his instincts were telling him to go back with Quintus. To take their time, talk it all out, make more of a plan.

But there was no time—the countdown was ticking away with every second. If the *Witchcraft* wouldn't start, they had a long walk ahead of them; perhaps too long. And if they missed the deadline, whatever opponents these so-called gods had in store for them would overrun the place. Which meant the world would end. His parents would die. His friends would die. The human race would die.

Everyone but the lost remnants left on this godforsaken planet.

"Come on," Cade said, hefting his sword and heading toward the jungle. "We've got a boat to catch."

His legs felt like he'd pulled every single muscle in them, but he managed well enough. Soon they were back in the jungle, surrounded by the whine of insects and the calls of the creatures from the canopy above.

It was a relief to get into the cover of the trees, however ominous the shaded interior felt. Even so, it seemed damper in the forest, and soon Cade was coated in sweat again.

He felt so dirty—his socks were crumbling with dried

blood in his boots, while dirt, sweat, soot, and more blood encrusted his face and arms. The first thing he was going to do when he got to the river was jump right in, wounds and river monsters be damned.

They walked through the charred remains of where Cade had set his fire—a vast swath of jungle where trees had been scorched black and the leaves burned to nothingness. The canopy above had been thinned, leaving patches of sunlight beaming through. Some of the vegetation, such that was left, was still smoking. Yet despite it all, green shoots were already emerging from the dark soil, reaching up for the light. Even in death, the cycle of life continued.

The group slowed as they walked through the ash-coated ground.

"If I'd done this back home, I'd be in so much trouble," Cade said as Spex trotted up beside him.

"You did this?" Spex whispered, impressed. "It took out a mile of the jungle."

Cade allowed himself half a smile.

"Well, it's not like any of the wildlife is endangered . . . right?"

Spex chuckled, and Cade didn't shush him, in part because they were nearing what he hoped was the right section of river. According to the Codex's map and his best guess as to where the *Witchcraft* was, they should have been right on top of it.

Even as he began to worry he had taken a wrong turn, he heard the rush of the river up ahead. He hurried forward, eager to get to the water, when a yelling figure jumped out in front of him. He fell backward, swiping blindly with his sword, but it was only Jim, brandishing the pickaxe above his head. Behind him, Gobbler poked his head around a tree trunk, his eyes wide with fear.

Cade felt his face flush with embarrassment.

"Holy . . . I didn't think I'd see *you* again," Jim said, moving to help Cade to his feet. He stared behind Cade, a grin slowly plastering across his face as he saw the new arrivals.

Finch cleared his throat as Jim bent to grip Cade's hand, as if expecting the boy to release it. But Jim ignored him and pulled Cade up.

"Nice sword."

"Thanks," Cade said, resisting the urge to return Jim's smile.

It seemed that Finch's influence over Jim was weakening, though Gobbler still embraced his old crony with enthusiasm. Cade wondered if Jim had done some soul-searching while Finch had been gone.

Cade wasn't one to hold a grudge, but it would be a while until he trusted Jim again. He hadn't been given the same choice as Jim had back at school, but he was sure he wouldn't have chosen as Jim did, had he been in Jim's shoes.

Still, with Jim being friendly and enough swords for everyone, the playing field was more than even. Between the humans at least. He suspected the playing field in the *real* game was stacked heavily against them.

Leaving Scott to introduce Quintus and the girls to the others, Cade hurried ahead to the boat. He found it pressed up against the beach and held there by a rusted anchor and a fraying rope. Beside it, he saw the broken remains of the

Chinese junk, which the anchor must have been salvaged from. It was exactly as Scott had described, with rotten rigging and sails, but also a rusted engine half-submerged at its rear.

Yoshi and Eric were huddled at the *Witchcraft*'s back end, up to their waists in the shallows. Both were covered in a layer of oily green gunk from their hands up to their shoulder blades, as if they had been reaching into the gas tank and scooping out the old, rotted fuel with their arms.

"All right, boys?" Cade said, filling his voice with as much bravado as he could muster. The trio would still need convincing to return to the keep, so best to put on a confident face. Eric and Yoshi turned, and Eric flashed him a rare smile.

"You made it," Eric said, wading ashore to embrace him.

"Whoa, whoa," Cade said, shoving him away. "I'm filthy enough as it is. How's it looking?"

"We've cleaned it out as best we can," Eric said, flicking some oil at Cade with a grin. "Yoshi almost climbed into the damned thing. He thinks it will run, with a bit of luck."

There was a large rusted canister propped on the deck of the Chinese ship that must have taken some strength to lift.

"Is that the diesel?" Cade asked.

"Damn right it is," Yoshi said, patting the can. "Plus three more like it on board. If this works, we'll be able to sail this thing for *weeks*."

Cade's heart sank. Somehow, he didn't think Yoshi was going to be impressed with his plan to just go back the way they had come.

"So, history boy," Eric said, slapping Cade's shoulder. "Any idea what this ship is?"

Cade turned to the Codex floating just behind him. It was strange how used to it he had become now.

"Watch this," he said, winking. This was a crucial moment. One that would make the Codex more credible in their eyes, and in turn its assertion that the world might be about to end.

"Codex, what is this ship?" he asked. "And feel free to give us a bit more detail this time."

The drone replied instantly.

"*Remnant identified as the* Sea Dragon. *It was owned by author, traveler, and adventurer Richard Halliburton. The ship was constructed when Halliburton challenged himself to sail across the Pacific Ocean on a Chinese junk, though equipped with a diesel engine in case they ran into trouble. Along with eight other crew members, the ship disappeared in 1939 during a typhoon, never to be seen again. Sightings of wreckage were rumored until as late as 1945, but all turned out to be hoaxes or false—*"

"All right, that's enough," Cade said, eyeing the timer.

02:09:58:38
02:09:58:37
02:09:58:36

As the Codex had been speaking, the others emerged from the jungle, shouting their greetings. Cade wasn't sure whether to quiet them. Would raptors attack them out in the open in such numbers? It was too late now anyway. They had to get out of there as soon as possible.

Eric waved and boarded the ship, leaving Cade and Yoshi together.

"Mystery solved," Yoshi said. "Maybe we can find out who Louis Le Prince was too."

Cade smiled.

"Or find out if I was right about those coins."

There was a shout from inside the *Witchcraft*'s cab, and the two turned to see Eric waving his arm through the front window.

"Moment of truth," he yelled. "Cross your fingers."

For a second there was silence, then a splutter as the engine turned over. Cade held his breath.

The splutter turned into a juddering roar, and now Cade joined in the cheers, wading into the water and whooping alongside Yoshi.

Finally, a victory.

Cade sank to his knees. It was blissfully cool on his skin, and he could practically feel the dirt dissolving from his face and body. Even his injured legs seemed to appreciate it, only stinging briefly before the cold water relieved them of the itching.

It was heavenly, and Cade let himself fall in before turning on his back and staring at the bright blue sky. He was going to have to convince the others to turn back soon enough. But not right now.

CHAPTER
37

THEY SAT INSIDE THE BOAT, PERCHED FACING ONE ANOTHER on the cushioned benches on either side. The removable padding had been thrown from the window already—the things were so rotted and covered in fungus that it was a wonder there was anything left of them.

Cade surveyed his potential allies, such as they were. Thirteen people, including him. Enough to defend an entire fort? Time would tell.

He had given each of them a sword, which had earned him some goodwill so far. Sufficient goodwill to get them to all sit and hear him out, while the boat remained anchored on shore. So he stood there, trying to look confident.

"By now, you will have all heard what the Codex, and Quintus, have told us. The world is at stake. The Romans have almost lost the game we've been brought here to play, and we're all that's left of the contenders. If we don't return to the keep, everyone we have ever loved will die. Our entire species, bar what survives on this planet, will die. I believe them."

He looked them each in the eye as he spoke, trying to convince them of his conviction. Most avoided his gaze. Only Amber returned it with any semblance of agreement, while others who met his eyes seemed filled with skepticism.

"Thanks to the arrival of Amber, Grace, Bea, and Trix— and our new swords—I think we have a fighting chance. What I'm asking you now is . . . will you come with me?"

He paused, perhaps somewhat dramatically. Spex was the first to speak.

"I don't think any of us can deny what we've seen here. It is entirely *possible* that the . . . people . . . who brought us here could destroy the earth if they wanted to. They have the technology. And it seems, given what they've made us do so far, that they might be willing to do it."

"Is there anyone here who doubts this?" Cade asked.

Finch raised his hand, joined by Gobbler, and after a hissed word from Finch, Jim followed suit. Yoshi reluctantly raised his own hand, as did Eric with an apologetic grimace. A moment later, Grace did the same. Trix, and then, after a nudge from her sister, Bea followed suit.

Damn. Eight against five.

And one of the five was Quintus. Did the others even think the Roman should have a vote?

"Well, then, let me try a different argument," Cade said. "That it's better to go to the keep *anyway*, even if losing the game has no consequence."

"How do you figure that?" Grace asked.

Cade had expected them to doubt the end of the world and had spent some time thinking on it. Now, it was time to see if it sounded as good in reality as it did in his head.

"Not all of you know this, but the girls and I were captured by some men out there in the jungle," Cade said. "Cruel, violent men, who I suspect planned to keep us as slaves. And there are loads of them. Maybe hundreds, hunting for people just like us."

"Are you serious?" Scott asked, looking at the girls.

Amber nodded grimly.

"We were lucky to escape," she said. "And after what happened, I wouldn't be surprised if they're specifically looking for us now. They seemed pretty angry."

"Well . . . damn," Yoshi said. "Do you have any idea who they are?"

"No," Cade said. "But whoever they are, they're bad news."

"It just keeps getting better," Eric said, rubbing tired eyes.

"And let's not forget the freaking dinosaurs," Cade said. "Scott, Finch, Spex, and I almost became dino-food today. I've had a grand total of three deadly encounters with the animals in as many days, and each time I survived by the skin of my teeth."

He yanked up his pants leg for dramatic effect, showing the shallow bite marks on his calf, each one a half circle, like that of a shark. It was the first time the others had seen them, and it looked far worse than it was. Bea looked a little paler, while Spex leaned forward, pushing his glasses up his nose in fascination.

"How long do you think we'd survive?" Cade asked. "A week? Two?"

"We could live on this," Finch muttered. "Anchor ourselves in the middle of the river."

"Could we?" Cade snapped. "What about the river monsters that live in these waters? Or the dinosaurs that can swim? I can tell you right now, raptors can."

Finch simply lifted his chin in defiance.

"That fruit we just ate," Cade said, pointing at the sacks of fruit that still remained on the boat. "Where did that come from? Do you see orchards of apple trees and fields of wheat out here?"

"We'd live off the dinosaurs," Finch said. "That Roman dude is doing okay."

"Quintus is a crack shot with a sling, unlike us, and he is certainly not okay," Cade said, trying and failing to keep his voice calm.

Noticing they were all looking at him, Quintus glanced up from the fig he had been devouring and smiled at them through the red pulp that coated his face. He popped the last of it in his mouth, groaning with pleasure. Bea edged away from him.

"Look at him, he's as skinny as a rake," Cade said, pointing at the boy's thin legs sticking out beneath the leather and red-cloth skirt he wore along with his tunic. "He spends his days holed up in a small room inside a crumbling temple, living off the vermin he can hit with his sling. He's slowly starving to death."

"Yeah, but he didn't go back to the keep," Finch said. "Because he knows it's more dangerous."

Cade bit back his reply. They had already covered this in the temple.

"But he *is* going back *now*," he replied, crossing his arms.

Finch opened his mouth, then closed it again.

Gotcha.

"At the keep, there's food enough to feed an entire legion, let alone the thirteen of us," Cade went on. "There's walls to protect us. Beds to sleep in, roofs to shelter us. Baths, toilets, clean water. More contenders could join us there, sent there by these 'gods' as Quintus calls them. And lastly . . ."

He paused, hoping to make his closing statement as impactful as possible.

"We might just find out what the *hell* is going on . . . and work out how to get home."

Cade let that sink in, hoping that they shared the same curiosity and desires he had. He could see the cogs turning in their heads, considering their options. It was working. They had to see reason. They just *had* to.

He saw Finch preparing to say something, but Cade cut him off.

"Or would you rather live out your existence starving to death in a dank hole, waiting to get captured or eaten, living with the knowledge that you might have doomed our world to destruction, and *still*, never knowing why you were brought here in the first place?"

That did it. In all honesty, Cade hadn't even been sure if it was the right decision before he'd made that speech. Somehow, he had convinced himself.

"I say we put it to a vote," Cade said. "Majority rules."

"Fine," Finch said, standing. "But the so-called Roman doesn't count."

The boy smiled at the others, and for a moment he almost looked friendly. Finch was guileful as a rattlesnake and twice as deadly.

"Everyone who wants to go to the keep, raise your hand. Simple as that."

He kept his arms crossed, looking each one in the eye, just as Cade had. It was a sly trick, to make them vote *for* Cade's plan. People who were unsure were far more likely to leave their hand down than raise it. It would feel less like a decision.

Then, to Cade's surprise, Amber stood too, staring down Finch with a cool gaze.

"Whatever happens, I'm going with Cade," she said, raising her hand.

Cade gave her a relieved smile. Another surprise followed, with timid Bea being the next to raise her hand. Now it was Trix's turn to be nudged by her sister. With all three of the other girls raising their hands, Grace sighed and followed their lead.

The girls weren't even contenders. They weren't even supposed to be a part of the game. Yet here they were, volunteering to fight. Cade's respect for them grew a great deal in that moment. They had more courage than half the boys on this boat. Maybe all of them, including him.

"I'm with you," Eric said. "I doubt that Earth is going to be destroyed, especially as this game seems to have been going on so long. But . . . I'd rather not risk it. And I think we've as much chance of dying out here as we do in the keep."

Six against six. Just one more!

But the remaining boys kept silent.

"I don't know," Yoshi said, his knee bobbing nervously. "It seems most people don't want to go with you . . . and I'm not sure enough to swing the vote."

"Yeah," Scott said simply.

Spex nodded silently. He avoided Cade's gaze, ashamed to be siding with Finch.

"Well, well, well," Finch said, rubbing his hands gleefully. "Even these bozos agree with me. Let's—"

"Hang on," Jim said.

The boy had been staring at his hands throughout, but Cade had barely paid attention to him, expecting him to vote with Finch. Jim looked up at Cade, and there was a gleam in his eye that Cade had never seen before.

"I'll go," he said.

"Seriously?" Gobbler growled, turning to Jim and pressing his face close. But Jim ignored him, even as Finch spun and fixed him with a glare of pure malice.

"I want to fight," he said. "I don't want to live this way."

He stood and went to sit opposite Finch and Gobbler.

"I've had enough," he said. "And if there's even a chance that winning this thing will let me go home, I'm going to take it."

"So," Cade said, the look of pure rage on Finch's face the only thing keeping a smile from his own. "Yoshi, if you would be so kind."

Yoshi jumped up and turned the key, muttering a prayer under his breath. But it seemed whatever god was watching over them was feeling generous, the key turning over and the engine roaring into life. The boat was soon juddering back into the river, while Spex took the initiative of pulling free the rope that was holding the cruiser to shore. And then, the Codex spoke.

"I'm sorry, Cade, but I must inform you that only contenders may take part in the qualifying round."

Its voice rang out through the cabin, the volume seemingly increased to be heard over the thunder of the engine. Cade felt his knees weaken. Just when he thought he had fixed everything, this world seemed to manage to pick it apart. But Amber was swift to reply.

"How does one become a contender?" she asked, holding up a hand to silence the panicked words starting on the others' lips.

"Volunteer," the Codex intoned.

"We volunteer," Amber said.

"Do you know what that even *means*?" Grace groaned.

"Please confirm: Amber Lin, Grace Jelani, Bea Prescott, and Trix Prescott volunteer to become contenders."

"You're signing your own death warrants," Finch warned, clearly still hoping to reverse the decision. "You'll die, just like us."

Amber didn't hesitate.

"I confirm," she said.

She turned, looking at the others.

"I confirm," Grace said, shaking her head in defeat.

"I confirm," Bea and Trix agreed after her.

"Confirmed," the Codex said.

Cade allowed himself to sit, groaning with relief at both

the comfort and the girls' decision. He had disliked Amber when they had first met. Now, he owed her more than he could rightly understand.

Finch sat down too, his face a picture of fury. His eyes were fixed on Jim, even as he avoided Cade's gaze. The betrayal had been absolute. Cade had always thought Finch's embarrassment would have amused him, but seeing the results only sent an icy chill down his spine.

Still, as the *Witchcraft* chugged back up the river and the jungle slipped by, Cade could not help but allow himself a brief moment to relish his change in fortune. Finally, things were going his way.

He could only hope it would last.

CHAPTER
38

CADE WATCHED THE JUNGLE'S EDGE GLIDE BY, SEARCHING FOR words that might break the grim quiet as the *Witchcraft* cruised upriver. Barely a word had been spoken since their vote, though anger still simmered.

The reality of their situation had dawned on them just a few minutes into the ride, made all the more obvious by the sinister timer, ticking incessantly down. Cade sat with Quintus in the back, and though they could not speak, the silence between them was not an awkward one. There was something about the legionary's presence that put Cade at ease.

It was slow going, moving against the river's flow. Yoshi was also wary of taxing the antique vessel any more than they had to, and so the *Witchcraft* chugged along at what felt like a snail's pace, stopping by the shore at times to prevent the old motor from overheating.

Still, Cade knew they would make it back with time to

spare. Already he could see the waterfall ahead and feel the mist it cast on his skin. Soon enough, they were passing into the stump-filled clearing and anchoring themselves on the plunge pool's bank. Cade looked over at the timer as the group leaped onto the land.

01:23:56:02
01:23:56:01
01:23:56:00

Not long to prepare, and it would be dark soon. They wouldn't get much done at night. Even if they could, they needed to balance that with being well rested for battle.

"What's the plan, then, oh great leader?" Scott said, giving Cade an exaggerated salute. "Perhaps you can rustle up some rocket launchers to go along with these swords?"

Leader?

"Not my leader," Finch muttered. He shoulder-banged Cade as he walked past.

Cade ignored him. Finch was a problem for later, but for now he needed him. Another fighter, however reluctant, could make all the difference.

But Eric wasn't having it.

"You can leave, you know," Eric said, stepping in front of Finch and nodding to the gloom of the forest edge.

Finch glowered, his hand straying to his sword, but Eric's looming presence made him think twice. He stalked off, and Gobbler scurried behind him.

The rest of them followed, picking their way through the

field of tree stumps and heading for the cave entrance at the bottom of the mountains. Behind them, the forest loomed high, and Cade was glad to be leaving it. It would be a relief to find a comfortable place to sleep once more. For a while, at least.

Cade saw Jim shaking his head. He was listening to Finch berate Gobbler, taking his anger out on him.

"Finch always was a coward," Jim said, nodding toward the pair. "But a vicious one. He only fights when he knows he can win. Kicks you when you're down, stabs you when you're not looking."

"You would know," Spex said, stony faced.

Jim couldn't meet his gaze.

"I'm sorry about that," he said. "You don't know how much I regret it. It keeps me up at night, thinking of what I've done."

"Oh yeah," Spex said, his words dripping with sarcasm. "I bet you lost sleep over it."

"If I could take it back, I would," Jim said, his voice almost a whisper.

Spex ignored him.

"So why'd you hang out with them?" Yoshi asked, the edge of accusation plain in his voice. "If you hate Finch so much."

"I was scared of him. Scared of what he'd do to me." Jim looked at his feet, ashamed.

"Guess I'm a coward too."

Cade saw Spex's expression change. Was that pity he saw? It was gone quickly, Spex preferring to jog ahead rather than continue the conversation. If Cade was struggling to forgive Jim, who had never done him a direct wrong, how hard would it be for Spex?

They passed into the shadow of the cave, walking down the black, echoing tunnel. Scott's voice drifted from the darkness.

"You never answered my question. Do we have a plan, or are we just waiting?"

Cade had spent the journey pondering that very issue.

"I'm assuming the attack will be coming from outside the walls, if the bone fields are any indication," he said, thinking aloud. "It's safe to say we'll be manning the ramparts, but all we'll be able to do with these swords is stab at anything climbing up. Plus, it's too wide for the thirteen of us to defend effectively. It's not going to be easy."

"Well, don't sugarcoat it," Scott groaned. "Tell us what you really think."

"Quintus has a sling," Cade said, hoping his next idea sounded as good as it did in his head. "And he's a crack shot with it. There's plenty of ammo for him in the armory, and slings are easy enough to make. Maybe he can teach us how to use them."

"I can't even throw a football," Spex moaned.

"We just need to manage a few volleys before they start climbing the walls," Cade said with as much confidence as he could muster. "If we even kill more than one of them, it'll be worth it."

"Whatever 'they' turns out to be," Amber muttered from the darkness.

Cade plowed on.

"Even if the slings don't work, we should drop rocks on them when they reach the walls," he said, remembering what he had read about siege warfare. "We should pile as many as we can on top of the ramparts."

It wasn't boiling oil, but it was better than nothing.

Finch's voice echoed back.

"That's it? Rocks? Great plan, genius."

Cade gritted his teeth, but ignored the jibe. He didn't have much else to work with.

Soon they emerged into the dusk light. The others trooped into the keep, but Cade had other ideas. He headed straight for the wall to inspect it, climbing up one of the two sets of stairs built near each end.

To his dismay, they were in worse shape than he remembered, the mortar crumbling beneath his feet. The top of the wall was not much better, with most of the crenulations missing to leave an uneven rampart that reached his waist. The platform's inner edge was a dangerous place to walk too, the stones so loose that they could come away and send someone tumbling down with them.

But Cade wasn't looking at the wall anymore. Because at the end of the canyon, a blue force field now stretched between the bone fields and the desert. And waiting on the other side was a horde of crouched figures, casting long shadows in the glow of the setting sun.

Vipers.

CHAPTER
39

THERE WERE AS MANY AS A HUNDRED OF THEM BY CADE'S guess, though he had little time to confirm it before it was too dark to count, the only source of light being the moons above and the soft glow of the force field. Now the thirteen stood on the wall, watching them in the gloom of night.

"A handful each," Scott murmured. "Well, two handfuls. Piece of cake, right?"

Cade didn't dignify that with a response. It was an insane number. True, some of them had defeated one before, and armed only with rocks or chains no less. But he knew they had used the dust to blind them like he had, or been helped along by the other boy kept in their section of the canyon. To face so many seemed an impossible task.

Now that he thought about it, their last challenge had been more of a puzzle to be solved than a battle to be won. Finding a weapon. Adapting the environment to create an advantage. Working together with others.

But this, this was . . . well, now that he thought about it, wasn't it the same? Hell, there was even the wall serving as the ledge, with them above and the monsters below.

It was just on a larger scale, with far more at stake. Now they had swords. And they were working together, more or less. So what was he missing? Adapting to the environment had to be more than just finding some rocks to drop on them. There had to be something else he could do.

"Not too late to get back on the boat," Finch called.

"Not too late to shut the hell up," Amber snapped back.

Cade ignored them. They had just under two days to prepare, a good portion of which would likely be spent eating, drinking, and sleeping.

"All right, guys, we won't get much done tonight," Cade said. "Let's get some food in us and sleep. We'll have to figure this out tomorrow."

"You think I'm going to bed with all those things over there?" Gobbler asked. "What's to say that invisible wall thing comes down and they slaughter us in our sleep? We should leave a watch or something."

Right now, Cade just wanted to sleep. He doubted that whoever their strange overlords were would set all this up only to kill them while they slumbered. If he trusted anything in this world, it was that the entities that had brought them here wanted them to play the game as it was meant to be played.

"Are you volunteering?" Cade asked. "It's awful dark out here."

Gobbler scratched the back of his head.

"Well, uh. Maybe for the first few hours. Finch'll keep me company, right, Finch?"

Finch rolled his eyes but assented with a curt nod. He was losing friends. He couldn't lose his last ally.

"Three hours, then," Cade said. "Anyone else?"

"I'll do it," Yoshi said. "And I don't need someone to baby-sit me."

Cade looked to the others, but already they were drifting toward the stairs, eager to get some shut-eye. All of them were dead on their feet. Only Quintus remained alert, staring out at the vipers with grim intensity.

"Fine," Cade sighed. "Wake me up when you're done, Yoshi."

Six hours' sleep. It would have to do.

Leaving Finch and Gobbler to their vigil, the rest of them trooped down to ground level and lit the torches there, taking two with them. They made their way to the quarters on the third floor of the keep, as they had done before. This time, Cade found himself with all the boys in one of the two rooms up there.

The opposite room was where the girls had set up camp—nobody wanted to sleep alone among the bunk beds or the doorless rooms downstairs. Of course, the door to the commander's room had to be left unlocked so those on watch could get in and wake them, but it was a comfort nonetheless.

Nine boys were far too many to fit in one bed though, so

Spex declared he would bring one of the three-tiered bunk beds up to the room, with Jim trying to make amends by volunteering to help.

Quintus was already curled up in the corner, having made a makeshift bed from the cushions in the room and looking more comfortable than he'd been in a long time. That left Cade, Eric, Scott, and Yoshi to share the main bed, since Gobbler and Finch were outside on watch.

Before they all crammed into it, Yoshi stopped Cade in his tracks and looked at the Codex following him.

"Who is Louis Le Prince?" Yoshi asked.

"Louis Le Prince invented the first film camera and projector. He disappeared mysteriously on a train with his prototype in the year 1890."

The pair of them exchanged a grin. A day ago, that would have been a revelation. Now it was just interesting.

Cade wondered if Louis had marched off and died with the legion or been left behind and eventually abandoned the keep like Quintus had.

He could hardly imagine what it would be like for a Victorian-era man to appear among a bunch of Romans upon another planet. Not to mention using his camera-projector to film them battling monstrosities.

He had to hand it to the gods. They had good taste in history.

That done, the pair squeezed into bed beside Eric and Scott. It was a tight fit, and Cade found himself hanging off the side of the bed. He sat up to see if there was more room on the other side.

"What else can that thing tell us?" Yoshi asked, stifling a yawn. Then he froze, his eyes widening.

"Codex, how can we get back home?"

"Contenders may return to their home planets when they reach the top of the leaderboard."

"Damn," Yoshi breathed. "A way back, then."

"Can we *see* this leaderboard?" Cade asked. "And what is it?"

"Action prohibited. Contenders must complete qualifying round to access leaderboard functions."

Cade thumped the bed.

"Just when you think you're getting somewhere," he moaned. "Why does it have to be so reticent?"

"Yeah, reticent little pest," said Scott, who clearly didn't know what reticent meant.

Cade couldn't help but smile.

"They probably don't tell us to give us another reason to play the damned game," Eric said. "Sounds like we'll have to survive tomorrow if we want to find out why we're here."

"Yeah, well, if it'd told us all this in the first place, we probably wouldn't have left here," Yoshi argued. "If they wanted us to stay and fight, they have a funny way of showing it."

Eric held up a hand.

"Maybe they wanted us to go into the caldera," he said. "There is a reason they created it."

Cade lay back down with a groan, sick of the whole debate.

"Pointless trying to work out what they want," he muttered. "It's all madness anyway. Why should their reasoning be any different?"

Somewhere far below, they could hear Jim cursing, and the

sound of wood thudding against stone. Clearly the bunk beds were not easy to manhandle up the steep steps.

They lay there for a minute, staring at the ceiling.

"Someone's got to put out the torch," Cade whispered.

"Not it," Eric said.

"Not it," Scott said quickly.

The only sound from Yoshi was a deep snore.

"Dammit," Cade said.

CHAPTER
40

CADE DRIFTED INTO CONSCIOUSNESS. THE SUN WAS FILTERING through the ragged curtains, filling the room with a honeyed glow. For a moment he basked in it, allowing himself a moment to enjoy the comfort of half sleep.

He sat up with a start, nearly hitting his head on the Codex floating above him. Nobody had come to wake him. Had Yoshi stayed out there all night? Cade stretched and rubbed the sleep from his eyes before stumbling over to the curtain and staring out at the wall. There was nobody there.

So much for the watch. Not that he had been particularly worried about it anyway. If their mysterious overlords wanted them dead so soon, they would never have put together this elaborate game. Still, it seemed strange for Yoshi to abandon his post. Unless . . . Finch and Gobbler hadn't woken him up either?

He scanned the beds. Spex and Jim had given up on bringing the bunk bed up, instead laying the straw-stuffed mattresses out on the floor. Spex and Gobbler had somehow managed to fall asleep with their faces pressed together, much to Cade's amusement. No sign of Finch, nor of Yoshi.

Curiosity and concern intermingled, enough to drive Cade from the warmth of the window into the upper floor's main chamber, the creak of the bedroom door eliciting groans from the others. He let them sleep, padding past the enormous stone table and to the bedroom door in the opposite wall.

Within, he saw Amber draped over the edge of the bed, her head hanging upside down, mouth lolling open. He was about to chuckle when he remembered that both Yoshi and Finch were missing—there were only the girls in there. And if they weren't on the wall . . . something was wrong.

Fighting growing panic, Cade hurried down the stairs to the ground floor. He saw it then, crusted on the floor in a spatter pattern that spoke of violence. Blood.

"Guys," Cade yelled. "Help! Help!"

When his eyes adjusted to the light of the window openings, he saw more blood smears. As if something had been dragged toward the stairs of the baths.

Cade's hand strayed for a sword that was not there—they were piled up in the bedroom. Above, he could hear movement and shouts of concern as the others came to join him, but he didn't wait. He jumped down the stairs, running into the gloomy cavern with his hands balled into fists.

He saw him then. Trussed up like a turkey, blood pooled on the stone beside his head. Yoshi.

Even now, the boy struggled against his bonds, groaning

through the gag that had been wrapped across his mouth. His eyes were wide, though whether with anger or fear it was hard to tell. Cade hurried over and tugged frantically at the tight knots.

With a sinking heart, Cade began to piece together what had happened. Finch was gone, and that probably meant the *Witchcraft* was too. He must have attacked Yoshi in the night, stolen the keys to the boat, and left.

Finally, the knotted rags came free. Yoshi yanked the gag from his mouth and spat out the wadded cloth that had been stuffed in there. Then he unleashed a tirade of curses that continued long after the other boys had turned up on the scene, their swords drawn, faces pale with fear. There was no sign of the girls—they must have slept through Cade's shouts.

When Yoshi was done, he took a deep breath and dabbed at the cut at the back of his head with the cloth he had spat out. He winced, but the cloth came away dry. It seemed the bleeding had stopped.

"Are you okay?" Spex asked, kneeling beside him.

"I'm all right," Yoshi groaned. "Head wounds, man. They bleed a lot."

"What happened?"

"He jumped me," Yoshi said. "Finch, after him and Gobbler came to get me. I woke up down here."

Cade swallowed. Whatever chance they had of leaving was now gone ... unless they planned on hiking through the dinosaur-infested jungle. The silver lining was that he wouldn't need to convince the others to stay anymore. But that was little consolation. In truth, he barely knew if he himself would have stayed, in the face of such overwhelming odds.

Now it seemed they would win, or die trying.

"Did you know about this, Gobbler?" Cade asked.

He turned, only to see the boy staring at the floor with glazed eyes.

"He left me . . . ," was all Gobbler said.

"I guess that answers that question," Yoshi said as Spex helped him to his feet.

"Scott, Spex, Jim, stay here," Cade said. "Eric, with me."

He took Gobbler's sword from the boy's nerveless fingers and hurried up the stairs, motioning for Quintus to stay. The soldier wordlessly stood guard by the steps, gladius in hand.

It took them five heart-pounding minutes to get through the tunnel and into the field of stumps, but Cade already knew in his heart the yacht would be gone. His suspicions were confirmed as soon as they emerged into daylight.

The plunge pool of the waterfall was glaringly empty.

CHAPTER
41

THEY TRUDGED TO THE WATER'S EDGE, AS IF BY SOME MIRACLE they would find the *Witchcraft* still there, hidden in the weeds. But all that remained was the wooden stake and the end of the attached rope that Finch had sliced through after pulling in the anchor. He must have left in a hurry. Cade sighed deeply and sat down on a stump. He wasn't sure how to feel.

Doubtless, Finch wouldn't last long on his own. But this meant one less fighter. No escape route if they lost or were forced to run. And a crushing blow to their morale.

There were footsteps behind them, and Cade turned to see that Yoshi had followed. The boy shook his head, then winced and touched his wound.

"It doesn't change anything," he said as if reading Cade's mind.

Cade grunted and lowered his head, sweat from the hot

sun above trickling down his cheeks. Eric sat beside him and squeezed his shoulder.

For a moment the three of them were silent. It was almost peaceful there in the dull roar of the waterfall, letting the cool mist from the crashing foam of the plunge pool coat them like morning dew.

Yoshi cleared his throat, and Cade turned to look at him. He had a sly smile upon his face.

"What's up?" Cade asked.

"I just realized. This sword," Yoshi said, "it's a Muramasa blade. Do you know what that means?"

"No," Cade said.

"Muramasa was a great swordsmith, second only to Masamune. But his swords were said to be cursed—once drawn, the blade must be bloodied before it may return to its scabbard, or the owner will be driven mad."

Yoshi looked him in the eye, and Cade realized that in some strange way, his friend was trying to cheer him up.

"Tomorrow, I plan to bloody it plenty."

Cade grinned and nodded despite himself. He would save telling Yoshi about the Honjo Masamune until after the battle—he had a feeling Yoshi would ask to trade for it. He'd become attached to the sword—it had saved his life more than once after all. Plus, he'd rather not have a cursed blade.

Eric stood, holding his own blade up. It was enormous, so long that with his height, he was probably the only one of them who could wield it, other than Grace perhaps.

"Who made this one?"

Yoshi looked closely at its base and shrugged.

"It's not a name I recognize."

Cade thought for a moment, then called out to the Codex over his shoulder.

01:08:23:15
01:08:23:14
01:08:23:13

"Codex, tell us about this sword. In detail, please."

The drone replied in its dull voice.

"Remnant identified as the Hotarumaru, forged by Kunitoshi Rai in 1297 CE. It is known colloquially as the Firefly sword, so named for a legend that tells the story of its owner, the leader of the Aso clan who damaged the sword in battle. That night, he dreamed of fireflies settling on the sword and awoke to find it had magically repaired itself. The sword went missing in 1945."

"Badass," Eric said, swiping the blade low against the ground and cutting the head of a flower clean off.

Cade grinned at the look of jealousy on Yoshi's face.

"How do you know so much about swords?" Eric asked.

"My mom is an arts dealer," Yoshi said. "Specializing in Japanese antiques. Swords are some of the pieces in highest demand."

He turned to Cade.

"Plus, I signed up for kendo lessons, hoping to find some marks to sell my fake swords to. You wanna find people obsessed with Japanese swords, go to the source, right?"

Cade's eyes lit up.

"You learned how to sword fight?" he asked.

"Well, yeah," Yoshi said, shrugging. "Only for a few months. Made my mom happy, so I stuck with it longer than I had to. Then I got caught, and she sent me away."

"Why didn't you tell us this before?" Cade demanded. "Don't you see, you can train us how to fight!"

Yoshi smiled and shook his head.

"Fighting a trained opponent with another blade isn't the same as fighting a monster."

"But—"

Cade stopped, realizing the truth of Yoshi's words.

"Well, at least you can teach us how to hold it right," he said. "Teach us how to strike, how to parry."

"I mean, I'm an amateur at best, but . . ."

Yoshi thought for a moment, then nodded.

"All right, then." Cade grinned. "That's what we'll do today."

"Good," Yoshi said, standing. "I'll go prep."

He strode off, though to prepare what, Cade had no idea.

"Don't you think it's a coincidence that he knows how to use a sword?" Eric said, breaking his long silence. "It's not exactly a common skill set."

Cade realized Eric was right. He furrowed his brows.

"Then we've got you, almost an *expert* on Rome. Spex with his general knowledge. Now Yoshi with his sword skills."

"And you?" Cade asked, raising his eyebrows.

"I guess we'll find out," Eric said. "Maybe for my size—I was a linebacker after all. But don't you think it's strange?"

Cade sighed.

"I think we *were* chosen for a reason," he said. "Maybe all of us know something useful."

"So, they got us sent to the school?" Eric asked, twisting his hands. "You think they have that much power? That they went to all that trouble?"

Cade stared at his hands, thinking back on his false conviction. Was it possible that these "gods" had planted the laptops?

"Maybe," was all Cade could say. "I *am* innocent."

He paused.

"Could they have done it to you?"

For a moment, Eric didn't reply. He stared into the rushing water of the waterfall.

"I know the rumors at school," Eric said. "That I'm a murderer. The truth is . . . I am."

Cade was speechless. Somehow, in getting to know the boy, he had convinced himself it was just a rumor. It seemed impossible a killer would be at school with them.

"I killed my best friend," he said, and to Cade's surprise, the boy's eyes were shiny with tears. "I never spoke at school because . . . I didn't want to make friends. I didn't deserve them."

"What happened?" Cade asked as gently as he could.

"We were celebrating winning the playoffs," Eric said. "Best season of my life."

Cade nodded, even as Eric's voice cracked with emotion.

"We went out drinking. Stole a keg from my older brother, threw a rager in a friend's house . . ."

Eric paused, then let out a long, shuddering breath.

"I made a choice. To drive. I don't remember making it. I only remember leaving the party and waking up in the hospital. But it was me in the driver's seat. And my best friend in the morgue."

They remained silent for a while longer, a lone tear trickling down Eric's face. Clearly, he had wanted to tell someone about it for quite some time.

"After that, I started drinking more," Eric said. "Lashing out, letting my rage get the better of me. My parents thought I needed a change."

Cade put an arm around Eric's shoulders. Together they stared out at the waterfall, letting the mist cover them like a cool balm. There was so much to do, and they would need to start soon. But there was time for this.

There was time.

CHAPTER
42

Yoshi had been busy. He had wandered around the tree stumps, collecting smaller pieces of lumber that the Romans must have discarded. Now, he had cobbled together several of these logs into two makeshift mannequins, held up and together by stakes in the ground and a rat's nest of loose twine he had taken from the storage room.

Quintus was off preparing his slinging lesson, but the rest of them lined up beside the waterfall, watching as Yoshi paced back and forth in front of them. He held his sword loosely in his hand, looking at them as he rubbed his chin.

"Today, I will not teach you to block any attacks," Yoshi said, half to himself and half to them.

"Why not?" Gobbler whined.

"I haven't been trained in how to block a rabid dog or a . . ." He flashed Amber a grin. "What did you call them? Piranha-chimps?"

"I think that was Cade's description," Amber laughed.

"Isn't that what they look like?" Cade groaned. "Tell me that's not accurate."

Amber nodded grudgingly.

"They don't look like 'vipers' though."

"That's because—" Cade began, but Yoshi stopped him with a raised hand.

"What I *will* teach you is how to hold a blade," Yoshi continued after taking a moment to gather his thoughts. "And how to swing it."

He turned to the side and held up his sword so they could see his grip.

"See how the hands don't touch each other," Yoshi said. "But instead the dominant hand holds the upper half of the handle, while the weaker hand holds the bottom. Your thumbs must never be on top of the hilt—only on the sides."

The group followed his example, extending the swords in front of them. Scott gave his blade a flourish as he did so, and Cade stepped away, wary of losing an eye. Yoshi caught his expression and grinned.

"Spread out," Yoshi called. "Let's not do the vipers' job for them."

They did so, and Yoshi now held the blade up, so that the sword was outstretched in front of him at 45 degrees, the point just below head height, his arms almost fully extended.

"You must keep some distance from your opponent," Yoshi said. "Our reach is our advantage. A viper must come close enough to touch you, while we can strike before they do—the farther away the beast is kept, the harder its work will be."

Again they followed his lead, and now the blade felt far heavier in Cade's hand. He was sweating already.

"Now, the first strike, and the simplest. It's called *men*."

Yoshi lifted the blade above his head and chopped down, stepping forward as he did so.

"Don't hesitate in your blow. Commit, or don't do it. There's no in-between," Yoshi said. "Step forward as you strike; close the distance with both the blade and your body, while keeping out of their range."

In unison, the group moved forward, bringing their blades down. Scott swung his so hard, it buried itself in the dirt. He chuckled and shuffled his feet as they looked at him.

"I'm more used to a baseball bat, you know?"

Yoshi had them repeat the move several times, adjusting their grips and how far they stepped. In particular, they all seemed to have trouble with how far back they swung the sword above their head before striking, and stopping the swing before their swords reached the ground. They were quick learners, and Yoshi was a good teacher. Soon, even Scott had the hang of it.

"Now, the diagonal downward cut," Yoshi said. "We call it *kesa-giri*, or monk's robe."

He stopped at their puzzled expressions.

"Because the cut follows the line of a monk's robe, down and across the chest," Yoshi explained, demonstrating the cut with his last syllable. "I would advise that you use this move when you can, instead of the *men* cut. It is less likely to trap your sword, or break it, in the skull."

Together, they followed his lead. It was much like the previous cut, but with a slight angle to it, entering where Cade envisioned the viper's shoulder might be and exiting toward the opposite hip. It was hard to do; even though the vipers were as large as humans, they were often hunched over or crouched, meaning that they had to aim lower than a swordsman typically would.

Yoshi nodded with approval as most of them got it right the first time, though he made them alternate between going top left to bottom right and vice versa. This time, it was Eric who was slower on the uptake, finding it hard to maneuver his far-longer sword. Cade caught Grace eyeing the Hotarumaru blade jealously. Of all the group, she was the only other one who might be able to wield it, matching Eric's considerable height and strength.

"Okay, say you've committed to your *men* or *kesa-giri* cut," Yoshi said. "And say you've missed, or only injured the beast. What do you do? Spex, please demonstrate."

Spex immediately stepped forward, cutting down, stopping his blade a foot from the ground. Swiftly, he raised the blade once more for a second attempt.

"See how he's left open while he raises the blade," Yoshi said, smiling. "This is when we do the *kiriage*, the diagonal upward cut. It is the hardest cut for a beginner, especially when recovering from a downward cut."

Yoshi imitated Spex, slicing down with a powerful grunt. But instead of stopping the blade, he allowed it to swing down and past him before he reversed his blade and swept it up, following the same path he had swung down on. Then his blade was reversed and positioned in the air once more, just as he had started.

"In the same time it took Spex to cut once and ready himself for a second strike, I completed two. Now you try."

This technique took the longest to master. Cade struggled to reverse his grip, for to do so, he had to cross his arms at the bottom of the downward swing. Still, they eventually managed it, though Cade could hardly imagine himself doing it in battle with a snarling viper in front of him.

Finally Yoshi taught them the simple *do*, a horizontal slice that could be reversed, much in the same way as the *kiriage*. When they were finished, Yoshi said, "That's the teaching part done. Any more, and it will be too much to remember. I only hope it's enough."

"Thank you, Yoshi," Cade said, and there were a chorus of mumbled thanks. "Let's practice a bit more, then Quintus will teach us how to sling stones, and we'll be done for the day. The rest of the preparations can be made tomorrow."

"You know," Gobbler said, "maybe we should focus on the sword stuff, have the girls learn the stone slinging."

There was a moment of silence.

"Are you kidding me?" Amber demanded, rounding on Gobbler. "Why?"

"Well, we're stronger, right?" Gobbler said.

Grace cleared her throat, crossing her muscled arms.

Gobbler hesitated. "Um, maybe not her."

Cade shook his head in disgust, unsure if this was misplaced chivalry or downright sexism.

"Gobbler, we'll need every—"

But Amber cut him off with a glare.

"All right, then," she said. "Let's see who's stronger."

Gobbler laughed.

"What, you wanna arm wrestle?"

Amber shook her head, a sly grin on her face. She strode forward to stand next to Yoshi, her blade in hand.

"Everyone hold your sword out straight," she said, extending her arm, the weapon's tip pointed directly in front of her.

The girls immediately did so, and Cade had a sneaking suspicion that they had done this before, with their hockey sticks. Regardless, the boys followed their example. Gobbler was the last to obey, a bead of sweat trickling down his forehead.

"First one to drop is *weakest*," she said, holding the blade unwaveringly ahead of her. "They'll tire fastest. Give up earliest, swing less. Right, Yoshi?"

Yoshi was grinning.

"That's right, Amber," he said.

He wasn't taking part in the game, and now he strode forward, tapping swords up and down the line with his own when they began to droop.

Cade looked over to Gobbler. His arm had the most meat on it, and Cade had seen him use his weight to his advantage before, barreling forward to crush other kids against the wall or floor. But now, it worked against him.

They stood there in the blazing sun for another few minutes. Cade's body ached all over, more because of the beatings it had taken than the exercise, but his month of hard workouts had prepared him well. He was proud to see that he was faring better than most.

In contrast, Gobbler was now soaked with perspiration,

shaking his head to rid his nose of the droplets that hung there. His arm shook and shook. Finally, his face beet red, eyes bloodshot with effort, he let it fall.

"Fancy that," Amber said, turning to point her sword at him. "Maybe we should have *you* on sling-stone duty. Or you could be the water boy, bring us drinks when the *real* fighters get parched."

"You've made your point," Gobbler growled.

One by one, more swords dropped. It seemed to Cade most of the boys had only been waiting for Gobbler to go first, letting their arms fall with relieved groans. The girls, on the other hand, were still going strong. Soon it was only Cade, Eric, and the girls left.

Bea went next, and Cade saw a flash of annoyance on Amber's face. Then Eric let out a long groan and dropped his sword. Cade's arm had almost lost all feeling, and slowly, ever so slowly, his sword tip drooped to the ground.

Grace and Trix dropped theirs moments later, leaving Amber undefeated, a grin on her face. To make her point, she swished it twice through the air before burying it in the ground.

"We play hockey," she said. "Every evening and most weekends. So don't talk to me about strength."

Grace leaned over to Cade.

"You don't poke mama bear," she whispered.

Cade grinned at Amber. Mama bear indeed.

CHAPTER
43

THE LAST OF THE AFTERNOON HAD BEEN SPENT TAKING TURNS chopping at the wooden targets that Yoshi had made. It was a satisfying exercise, if a tiring one. Yoshi had explained that the vipers' bodies would be far softer and easier to cut, but it was good to practice with a target to aim for, rather than swinging at the air.

Buoyed by their apparent success, their jubilance was cut short as Quintus led them to the wall. Now they surveyed the killing fields, the bone-littered canyon of flat, muddy earth, bordered by two curving cliffs. It was as long as four football field and half as wide. At the very end, the great glowing barrier remained, sealing it from the desert. And behind it, a hundred monstrous beasts sat patiently, watching with eyes like black pits.

Beside him, Cade could hear Spex whispering under his breath.

"As I walk through the valley of the shadow of death . . ."

"Psalms?" Cade asked, thinking back to the long stints in chapel at his old school.

"Coolio, 'Gangsta's Paradise.'" Spex grinned at him. "What can I say? I like old-school rap."

"Oh, right." Cade grinned back.

Still, the valley of the shadow of death was an apt description. The bones of a thousand different creatures must have been scattered throughout, and if the vipers were not still waiting at the canyon's end, Cade might well have gone to inspect them to see what form of enemy they would face. But there was no need now—he knew what was coming. In less than two days, at least a hundred of the things would be unleashed on them.

Whatever those things were. It was all still a mystery. Not prehistoric creatures from history. Then what? Mutants? Mythical creatures? Demons? It was strange, but at times his desire to understand the truth of this strange world distracted him from his desire to save his own planet. With each clue he had unraveled, the mystery of this place only seemed to get deeper. But now was not the time for such contemplations.

The monsters sat patiently, staring at them through the translucent force field. Cade was sure they were unintelligent, savage creatures, but he still felt a twinge of worry that his crew would be giving away their strategy by practicing here. It was too late now though. The sun was already making its way toward the horizon.

There was another mystery, one made all the more obvious as he looked at the timer.

01:01:47:51
01:01:47:50
01:01:47:49

It seemed to Cade that the days were passing in close to twenty-four-hour increments.

The coincidence of that seemed extraordinary to him. Although, so did everything else. Was it possible that this world had been designed to mirror Earth? Were the "gods" truly that powerful?

On his other side, Quintus cleared his throat, stirring Cade from his thoughts. The boy mounted the parapet, balancing there so they could all see. It was Quintus's job to demonstrate— Cade had already explained the basic principles of slinging for him, having read about them in his own studies of Roman warfare.

Luckily for the contenders, the storeroom had held plenty of rope, though it was somewhat ragged and moldy. Quintus had gone to the trouble of making a sling for each of them. And that was not all he had been up to while they were sword training.

Out in the valley, Quintus had created three piles of bones, marking out distances, though how far or for what purpose they served, Cade had no clue. Atop of each, he had placed what looked to be a viper's skull—eerily similar to human skulls but with jaws full of needle teeth, and wide, gaping eye sockets.

The legionary took up his sling and placed one of the lead weights from the storeroom into the leather pouch at its center. It was a weapon so old, it predated archery, its earliest instances used by Paleolithic shepherds to ward off hungry wolves. The same weapon David had used to kill Goliath. Simple. Deadly.

Cade looked at the sling. A rope with a leather strap in the center, a finger loop on one end and a plain knot on the other. Quintus let the weapon dangle, his finger in the loop, the knotted end clutched in his palm. Then he whipped it in a circle around his head, releasing the rope at the apex of his throw. The rope unfurled, hurling the lead bullet, then snapped taut as it caught on his finger. The projectile moved so fast that Cade couldn't see it, then he saw a tuft of earth burst, the stone skipping along the ground halfway down the canyon. It looked like it had missed the second closest bone pile by a hair's breadth.

Swiftly, Quintus caught the loose end, dropped another weight into the leather and repeated the movement. There was a veritable thrum as the bullet tore through the air. This time, it cracked home, smashing into the very nearest pile. A direct hit.

The viper skull shattered, needle teeth flying like splinters. The legionary whooped, throwing his hands in the air. He turned to the others, who clapped with amazement.

"Holy cow," Jim shouted. "These things can do some damage!"

But Quintus wasn't done. Now he dropped a third stone in, a look of grim determination on his face. He whipped the sling around his head and let out a grunt of exertion, sending the projectile high into the air. Cade lost track of the small black dot, but it was clear where it hit when the force field flickered, a crackle rippling from the impact site at its center.

Cade gaped at the sight. He had heard that slingers could throw their stones even farther than archers could shoot their arrows, and now he saw the proof of it. Quintus had thrown it the length of the canyon, as far as four football fields, end to end.

The young legionary bowed amid the whoops and cheers from the others, then gestured at Cade to try himself.

"Really," Cade asked. "Me first?"

Quintus simply stared at him expectantly, and Cade sighed. All along the parapet, Quintus had laid out the boxes of lead bullets, and now Cade bent to pick one up. It was heavier than he had expected, and as he held it in his palm, it looked to him like a black grape–sized football.

Cade placed it into the leather cradle in the center of his rope and put his finger through the loop, clutching the other loose end in his hand. He tried to remember how Quintus had set it up. It had surprised him how little the soldier had swirled the weapon above his head, only letting the rope helicopter once before releasing it on the second go-round, lurching his body forward like a baseball pitcher.

"Go on," Yoshi called out. "It's getting dark."

Cade tried. He really did. But when he went to throw, he released too early, the bullet catapulting off to the side, only to plop on the ground, barely halfway to the first marker. It had gone about as fast and far as if he'd thrown it by hand.

Quintus scratched his head, then motioned for Cade to try again. It was going to be a long evening.

CHAPTER
44

Q UINTUS DRILLED THEM HARD, BARKING OUT "*IACITE*," THE
Latin word for "throw" every ten seconds. It was their
job to keep up, while maintaining a barrage that, if inaccurate,
would still land somewhere near each of the three bone-pile
markers, the farthest of which was just over halfway down the
canyon.

To Gobbler's chagrin, the girls were faring better than
most of the boys, their hand-eye coordination honed from
years of intensive hockey practice.

It had almost reached nightfall by the time all of them
could consistently reach the final pile of bones, though the
viper skull remained conspicuously intact.

Cade had finally realized what the markers were for—
estimates for how far the vipers would travel every ten seconds as they charged through the canyon. Which meant that
they would likely be at the wall in less than a minute—giving

the defenders three throws each before the monsters were directly below them.

As the evening wore on, Cade began to think that it hardly seemed worth the practice, but Quintus seemed pleased enough with their progress, slapping them on their backs and grinning widely. He supposed three throws from twelve slingers meant thirty-six chances to kill or injure the vipers. If every one hit, that was a third of their enemies gone. Of course, that was an optimistic estimate.

As the last light of the sun disappeared, the red moon was already high in the sky, its smaller white counterpart combining with the rusty glow to produce a light akin to the last moments of sunset. Only then did Quintus stop the exercise, gesturing for them that he was done for the night.

The others staggered down the steps amid groans of exhaustion, some massaging aching shoulders. Cade only hoped they would not be aching tomorrow afternoon when the timer reached zero. They needed to be at their fittest. Fortunately, they would have some time to rest tomorrow, with their only task being to carry stones to the tops of the walls. And then, in the early evening . . . they would fight.

Cade stayed upon the walls, taking one final look at the future battlefield. How many others had stood in this exact same place over the centuries, preparing to do battle? Had they felt as ill-prepared as he did?

There was something the others seemed to have forgotten, but Cade could not shake it from his thoughts. This would not be their final battle. Victory here meant only that they would have joined the game. And judging from the bones below, it was a game that would get far more deadly as time went by.

Was taking part in this game just delaying the inevitable, prolonging their agony? Quintus had been here over a year, yet even that amount of time in this place seemed unimaginable.

Cade was sure that Quintus had never fought in the game. Only guarded the wall until the timer started and then run away. Cade wanted to know what the young legionary had heard from the other Romans, the ones who had been there before Quintus and the rest of the Ninth Legion had appeared in the desert.

Some hint, or clue, even if he drew pictures in the dirt, or Cade's half-remembered Latin allowed some understanding through.

Cade turned, only to see that Quintus had not joined the others in the keep. Instead, he was hurrying for the tunnel, clutching his sword and sling. That was strange. What could he want out there in the dark?

There was a pit in Cade's stomach as the answer swam unbidden to Cade's mind. Quintus had finally seen for himself what they were up against. And now, he had decided to return to the jungle. Cade could hardly blame him. The legionary had done more than enough for them. And yet, Cade felt his feet moving, taking him down the stairs and after Quintus.

He picked up his pace as he entered the tunnel, only to see that Quintus was already much of the way down. Cade might have shouted, but of course Quintus would not hear him. Instead, Cade broke into a jog, forcing his aching, injured legs to move.

If anything, he wanted to thank Quintus and send him on his way. No hard feelings, no guilt. It was the least he could do.

By the time Cade exited the tunnel and into the meadow of tree stumps, Quintus was nowhere to be seen. Cade scanned the trees, searching for the boy's retreating figure. It was quiet, a stark contrast to the orchestra of animals that he usually heard at night. Here, on the edge of the enormous trees, the only sound was the soft susurration of the breeze, and the gentlest buzz of insects.

Thinking he was too late, Cade turned to return to the keep. Only then did he see him, just out of the corner of his eye. The flash of Quintus's pale, naked ass as he waded into the plunge pool of the waterfall.

This was no good-bye. Quintus was skinny-dipping.

"Oh for heaven's sake," came a voice from behind Cade.

He turned to find Amber glaring at him. She held what looked like a scavenged curtain from the keep, folded like a towel over her arm.

"Had the same idea as I did, did you?" she demanded.

"Uh-umm . . . ," Cade stuttered.

"Well, come on," she said. "But keep your eyes and hands to yourself."

She strode off toward the waterfall, leaving a bewildered Cade to look after her. Quintus was nowhere to be seen, lost in the mist. Clearly, she wanted to wash off the sweat of the day, and not in the company of almost naked teenage boys.

Now that she mentioned it, a dip in the chill waters of the pool seemed like heaven. He might not have thought of it, especially given the size of the fish he had seen in the waters of the river, but Quintus seemed to feel safe enough in the plunge pool. And he had lived in this world for a good while.

So Cade followed Amber down to the water, trailing behind her with his hands in his pockets. To his surprise, Amber leaped into the water fully dressed, knee-high socks and all. Only then did she remove her clothing, throwing each item on the bank, treading water all the while.

"What?" Amber said as Cade eyed her wet garments. "They were filthy; might as well give everything a wash at the same time."

Cade dithered by the bank a moment longer, but one raised eyebrow from Amber had him jumping in. It was numbingly cold, even after the day's sun. For a moment he let himself sink, his boots thumping on the rocky bottom. Then he pushed off and emerged with a great gush of breath, still acclimating to the temperature.

It was a relief, really, to have the cool water seep over him and wash away the accumulated sweat from the day. And this water seemed far clearer and cleaner than the silty river water Cade had taken a brief dip in yesterday, though not so clear that Cade felt embarrassed to take off his own clothes and throw them on the bank.

For a moment, Cade and Amber looked at each other across the water, obscured by the heavy mist that accompanied the billowing roar of the waterfall beyond them. In the dim light of the red moon, the water was dark, too dark to see anything below the neck. Even so, it was a charged moment. They could die tomorrow. It could be their last night together, and here they were, alone.

Well, not quite alone. They could both see a naked Quintus crouched on the far bank, quite unashamed as his pale buttocks mooned them from across the dark water. Nothing like a good mooning to take the romance out of a moment. That and the Codex, floating in silent watchfulness above him.

Still, Amber swam closer, as it was hard to speak over the roar of the waterfall.

"Shame about the *Witchcraft*," Amber said, first to break the silence. "That Finch seemed a proper git. Did you know him long?"

Cade grimaced at the reminder of their lost vessel.

"I knew him for six months, and he was even worse before," he said.

Amber peered at him for a moment, then furrowed her brows.

"You're not like the others," she said.

Cade shrugged.

"I thought so too at first . . . but we're not so different. Not where it matters. They're good guys, for the most part. Good guys who made some bad choices."

She smiled at him.

"I guess you're right. But what I really meant to ask is . . . why did your parents send you to that new school?"

Cade hesitated.

"Was that too personal? Don't answer, it's fine," Amber said, and for the first time, he saw her blush from cheek to cheek.

It was endearing, and he hadn't realized just how intimidating she'd seemed until now. She seemed so fearless . . . so certain.

"No, it's okay," Cade said, sighing. "My old school found a dozen laptops under my bed in my dorm. Thought I'd stolen them, but it wasn't me."

"Laptops?" Amber asked. "Where have I heard that before?"

Cade laughed.

"I keep forgetting where . . . or I guess I mean *when*, you come from. Laptops are portable computers."

"You fit a dozen computers under your bed? Must have been a big bed." Amber said.

"They're a bit smaller than your time," Cade chuckled. "Man, I wish I had my phone to show you. It would blow your mind."

"I think I've had my mind blown enough over the past few days," Amber groaned, splashing some water on her face. "I keep thinking I'm going to wake up. But I never do."

Cade nodded, and for a while they stayed silent, just enjoying the night air.

"You know as much as I do now. Any thoughts on what this place is?"

Amber considered for a moment, her face pale in the moonlight as she trod water.

"Have you seen anyone, or anything, beyond your time?" Amber asked.

"I mean, the Codex and the force fields are pretty advanced, but I don't know if they're from our future."

"What if they are?" Amber said. "What if these so-called gods are people from the future? People who discovered time travel, and use it for . . . this? For fun?"

Cade stared at her.

"That's messed up."

"Do you have a different theory?"

"I'd like to believe people are better than that."

Amber laughed.

"Quintus's people weren't better than that—they had gladiators. Why wouldn't the people of our future?"

"Because I believe in progress," Cade said, though his words lacked conviction. "We get better. Not worse."

"Tell that to the people who died in the Second World War," Amber said. "Or the first, for that matter."

Cade had no reply. She was right. Of course she was right. But he didn't want to believe it.

He could only nod in agreement. There wasn't much else to say.

"Turn around," Amber said suddenly.

Cade did so, and he heard the splash of Amber clambering out onto the bank.

"None of this matters if we don't win tomorrow," Amber called. "Let's just hope swords and stones are enough."

After counting to ten, Cade turned slowly, only to see her striding off, wrapped in her curtain towel.

She was right. The mystery of why they were here could wait. There was a battle to be won.

CHAPTER
45

LEFT ALONE IN THE PLUNGE POOL, CADE PADDLED CLOSER TO the waterfall. Soon, he was lost in the cool mist. It was peaceful there, the empty dark of the water beneath him and the white fog above.

Something tugged on his leg. Before he could react, Cade was pulled under, a silent scream of bubbles pouring from his mouth. He kicked out, panicking, and the grip released him. Cade clawed his way upward, choking on the dark liquid. Frantic, he burst from the water . . . only to find Quintus laughing hysterically beside him.

"You little shit!" Cade yelled.

Quintus laughed on, and as Cade's heartbeat slowed to normal, he offered a reluctant grin. Once he'd calmed down, the legionary beckoned Cade to follow him.

Together, they splashed to the other side of the plunge pool, where Quintus stopped to crouch on the round rocks at the bottom of the shallows.

"Wish I could speak to you," Cade said, finding his own rock to squat on. "I bet there's a whole lot you could tell us about how this all works."

Quintus's eyes were closed; his toes wiggled beneath the water. Cade didn't mind not being heard. It felt good to unload his worries.

"These overlords. Or gods. And the Strategos, whoever he is. They've given us the resources we need. Scattered the jungle with weapons and tools. It doesn't make sense. It's like they want us to win and lose at the same time."

He scratched an insect bite behind his ear and thought out the problem.

"We need more. Guns. Armor. Codex, show me the map again."

00:21:22:34
00:21:22:33
00:21:22:32

The drone hovered closer and projected the bird's-eye view of the area, glowing in the gloom, and Cade zoomed in to the keep with a pinch of his fingers. To his dismay, he could only find a dozen or so dots in and around the keep, those that represented the projector and themselves.

All the others were much farther away, and as he explored them, few suggested that significantly better weapons could be found there.

He stared at the moonlit tree line, contemplating whether they could justify heading out on foot to explore the closest of the blue dots. A cluster of them, that they might make it there and back from, before the timer ended, if they set out in the morning.

The Codex told him they were Roman ships dating back to 36 BC, lost by Emperor Octavian in a storm. But he was sure the Romans would have stripped them of anything useful by now. All they might get were scraps, things the Romans had overlooked. It wasn't worth the risk.

No, they would have to make use of what they had here. Not that there was much. They only had two things from anything close to modern day, the projector and the *Witchcraft*, but now the latter was gone and the former would only be useful in battle if they planned on dropping it on the vipers' heads.

An idea came unbidden to Cade's mind. The diesel fuel in the *Witchcraft* could have been used to make Molotov cocktails. Fuel poured into the amphorae with flaming cloths attached, thrown onto the creatures as they massed at the base of the wall below.

Hell, they could have just poured the fuel straight onto the vipers from the barrels themselves and dropped a burning torch to light it. It might have been a game changer.

He cursed Finch under his breath, but it was no use crying over spilled milk. The *Witchcraft* was gone.

There was something else that Cade could use though. Hindsight. His modern mind, and a machine with access to all earthbound knowledge hovering in front of him. He considered that for a moment and found himself drawing a blank. It wasn't like he could make a gun or a computer out here.

The bow had revolutionized warfare for thousands of

years, evolving from the short bow to the recurve bow to the longbow. But he wouldn't even know where to start. Finding and shaping the right wood, manufacturing the strings, making the arrows. A daunting task for one with the luxury of time. An impossible one without it.

Perhaps if he put aside Iron Age weaponry and looked forward to the industrial age. To gunpowder. But then, they didn't have enough time to make it, or the right ingredients.

Cade heard a scratching sound and was bemused to find Quintus had pried something from beneath the water with his gladius. A flat rock. Quintus continued prodding at it. Befuddled, Cade ignored him and turned back to his musing.

What was Quintus's equivalent? The Romans had used something called Greek fire, a form of napalm that would burn even on the surface of the oceans in naval warfare. But that recipe had been lost, and even if the Codex knew it, it likely contained ingredients they didn't have access to. It was theorized that the substance was made from quicklime, sulfur and bat guano to name but a few potential ingredients. The mystery had fascinated his father for years.

No, Cade was left with things that even a caveman would be better at making: spears. No better than their swords. And he knew from disastrous attempts during his childhood camping trips that a sharpened stick was not the same as a javelin.

Bereft of tools and infrastructure, their modern know-how was reduced to that of a small child. It was useless.

Oblivious to Cade's gloomy thoughts, Quintus let out a yelp of triumph.

Curious, Cade looked closer. The rock had been pried in

two. Only it wasn't a rock at all, but a mollusk of some kind. It looked much like an oyster, only far larger.

So this is where all those shells from the trash pile came from.

Quintus sawed his gladius into the fleshy gray oval that was the creature living within, then slurped half into his mouth. He caught Cade's eye and proffered him the remaining morsel. Cade contemplated it, his mind and belly at odds with each other. It looked like a dinosaur had blown its nose onto a pickled lung.

And then he saw it. The solution to all their problems. Sitting there in the palm of the legionary's hand.

"Quintus, you're a genius," Cade said.

He snatched the remains of the mollusk and swallowed it down triumphantly. It tasted as bad as it looked, but Cade knew he needed his strength.

There was work to do.

CHAPTER
46

00:01:57:09
00:01:57:08
00:01:57:07

"You've cracked, haven't you?" Scott said, shaking his head.

Cade grinned and ignored him. He pushed more wood into the makeshift kiln he had made, a large, simple tube made of clay and straw, with an air hole in its base. Inside, the coals glowed almost white, and flames roared as they flared from the tube's top. The heat was immense, but still Cade lowered his face and blew into the fiery maelstrom.

"The others are wondering what you're up to," Scott said, scratching the stubble sprouting on his chin.

"I'll explain later," Cade said. "Just keep looking for rocks."

Scott sighed and strode off, muttering under his breath. Cade busied himself with thrusting more wood into the kiln, glad that he had built it in the shadow of the keep. The shade provided some small comfort in the oppressive heat of the day.

He had barely slept, spending much of the night taking

clay from the banks of the plunge pool and carrying it by hand to the relative shelter of the keep and its walls, where the breeze would not disturb his efforts and the materials he needed were close at hand. A single gust of wind at the wrong moment could ruin everything he had planned.

The wood added, Cade looked over his shoulder to survey the work that had been done that morning. At the top of the wall, dozens of rocks ranging from the size of a bowling ball to an exercise ball had been piled upon the battlements.

The problem had turned out not to be carrying the rocks up, but finding any. They had salvaged some of the rubble that had fallen from the structure, but the mountainside lacked boulders of a suitable size. Most of those in the plunge pool were too large, and even a smaller one they'd found there had required the efforts of almost all of them, a lot of cursing, and several bruised fingers to hoist it to the top of the walls.

Of all the others, only Yoshi had avoided most of the back-breaking labor, setting himself up beside the well and sharpening each of the swords with a large flat pebble he had found. Quintus's gladius was no longer a rusted stabbing weapon, but instead a sharp, shining blade. When the legionary had seen it, he'd expressed his joy by hugging Yoshi so hard, the boy needed to slap Quintus's back for him to let go.

Cade watched Bea hurry past, another amphora full of water balanced on her head. Cade knew that outside, they would be sloshing it along the base of the wall, where earlier they had dug a rough trench, having lined the inside with leaves to help it retain water. Even the shy girl was resentful, but to the group's credit, none had questioned him until now.

Backbreaking work, and with no reasoning as to why. But Cade hadn't had time to explain—it had taken him most of the night to gather the materials, and now the process needed to start immediately.

The flames now burning themselves down, Cade laid out the dozen clay bowls he had taken from the dormitory in the keep. Nearby, some of the substance he had prepared earlier sat in a forlorn pile. He only wished he had more.

The fire burned on, and Cade wanted to help the others; pull his weight. But this was too important. Instead, he crouched on his haunches and watched the flames.

When the ashes within the kiln had cooled, Cade carefully scooped out its precious contents, trying to keep the burned shells intact and away from the gray ashes they rested upon. For that was what he was doing.

Burning every shell he could find, snail, egg, or mollusk, until they were crumbling white fragments. He was careful to wipe the sweat from his fingers before touching them; he had to do it all barehanded. As he did so, he kept a strip of cloth wrapped around his face, and wiped his fingers on his uniform at regular intervals. Still, the tips of his fingers were red and raw by the time he was done.

Finally, he was ready. Each bowl was filled to the brim with the shells' burned remains, and now he carefully crushed them to dust using a blunt piece of firewood. Soon, he was left with bowlfuls of chalky powder. He covered each with a second bowl, keeping the contents safe from the breeze. It had all taken the best part of the night and morning, and the afternoon sun was at its zenith. He crouched there, beside his precious cargo.

"All right, you've got to tell us what all this is about," Amber said.

Cade turned to see the rest of the group trailing after her, each one soaked in sweat, their hair plastered across their foreheads. He forced a smile, hoping that they would understand.

"What you see here is quicklime, or calcium oxide," Cade said, pointing at the bowls. "Burned shells, crushed to a powder. It's the key ingredient in concrete—I think that's what they used to make mortar for the walls, unless they found a source of limestone nearby."

The others stared at him blankly. Cade plowed on.

"Quicklime reacts violently with moisture," he said. "So much so that it's been used as a weapon for centuries. If inhaled, it'll scorch your lungs and throat. Get it in your eyes, you'll be blinded as they boil in their sockets. Wet skin, and it'll fry you."

Jim gave a low whistle.

"Chemical warfare," Grace breathed.

"An ancient form of it, yes," Cade said. "And what with vipers having such big eyes . . . well, I thought it was a good idea."

He smiled.

"That's why you've been having us wet the base of the wall," Amber said. "So it burns their skin when it's wet too."

"That's right. They've been drying out in the desert this whole time, so it was the only way," Cade said. "And there's no stopping it once it starts, so don't get any on you. Water only makes it worse. Obviously."

Eric strode over and clapped Cade on the back.

"You're a genius," he said.

Cade shrugged, trying not to grin.

"I just hope it works," he said. "I confirmed all this with the Codex; it even told me how to make the kiln . . . it knows a lot. But if it didn't burn properly, or the powder reacts with the moisture from the air before the battle, it might not work perfectly, if at all."

"Whatever, man," Jim said. "You're a hero in my book."

Cade stood and looked over at the Codex. He had sent it away from him, for the incessant countdown had made him nervous. But he already knew how long they had left. Less than two hours to go.

Not nearly enough time for all he had planned.

"Is Quintus here?" Cade asked. "You should all get some more practice with the slinging. We've got enough boulders up top, and the foot of the wall must be good and wet by now."

"Yeah," Scott said. "He's up there."

Cade glanced up, only to see the legionary staring out at the glowing barrier. As he watched, the boy lifted a sling and swung it once, whipping it over his head. Even from where he stood, Cade heard the thrum in the air and the distinct crack as it made contact with the force field. Beyond, he heard a series of screeches from the vipers, disturbed by the noise.

"All right, you've got about two hours to practice," Cade said. "Take these bowls up to the wall while you're at it. Carefully!"

They groaned and did as he asked, but Cade took Amber aside before she could join them.

"Do you need the practice?" Cade asked. "How good are you with slinging?"

Amber smiled and crossed her arms.

"Better than you," she said.

"Okay, then you're with me," Cade said, glancing at his pile of leftover firewood. "I've got another idea."

CHAPTER
47

THERE WAS NOTHING MORE TO BE DONE. OR AT LEAST, NO time left to do it. Now they stood along the battlements, surveying the battlefield.

The vipers were massed against the force field, staring silently with their inky black eyes, mouths hanging open as they panted in the heat. If they were dehydrated or suffering from heatstroke, they did not show it. Instead, they squatted on their haunches like brown toads, near-motionless. Waiting, just like Cade was.

It was as if they knew what was about to come. What instinct had driven them here? When he had first appeared on this planet, it had all made sense—carnivorous hunger prompting them to attack him as they waited on the ledge. As they massed in the dry heat, it seemed something else was controlling them, keeping them in place. Pheromones, perhaps, or some form of mind control. He wouldn't put anything past the so-called gods.

Not that any of that mattered now. They were here; that was all he needed to know. Ahead of him, the Codex floated above the bone fields, its timer ticking down.

00:00:01:11

00:00:01:10

00:00:01:09

One minute to go. Cade pulled back his hood so as not to block his field of view, then looked up and down the ramparts, making sure everyone was in position. Gobbler, Jim, Scott, and Eric protected the left flank, while Quintus, Yoshi, and Spex protected the middle.

Amber, Grace, Trix, and Bea were on the right flank, while Cade paced back and forth along the center, ready to shore up wherever help was needed. As the one responsible for their being here, it was his job to stand where he could direct them all. Even if it meant being where the fighting would be thickest.

With Amber and Quintus closest to him, he felt a little better, but the hilt of his sword was slippery with sweat in his hands. He had pocketed some of the ashes from the fire, and now he rubbed it between his palms until they were gritty and dry once more.

00:00:00:05

00:00:00:04

00:00:00:03

"Get ready," Cade shouted.

As if they heard him, the vipers finally began to stir, their

fish-egg eyes swiveling in their sockets as the barrier flickered out of existence. Then, as one . . . they charged.

Their speed was extraordinary, the lithe bodies leaping
and loping across the bone-strewn ground. Scores of them, so
many that it looked like a muddy wave flowing over the black
earth. Quintus's sling stone was already in the air, disappearing into the masses and leaving a single broken corpse behind.

A second slug followed the first, but Cade forced himself
to look away from Quintus's movements. He couldn't afford
to be distracted if he was to direct the others.

"Come on," he whispered, his sword in his left hand, sling
in the other.

The frontrunners reached the farthest marker, knocking
the piled bones askew.

"Throw," Cade yelled, twirling his sling above his head.

Twelve lead sling stones whipped through the air, too fast
and small to follow. Cade didn't see the impact, only a single
sprawled body left in the horde's wake and two injured strag-
glers limping behind it. A second, more ragged volley followed
the first, for now they were throwing at will. It was hard to
miss with so many targets, and the dull smack of lead on flesh
was accompanied by yowls of anger.

Cade had imagined the slingers being a game changer, but
already the frontrunners had reached the halfway mark
between the desert and the wall. But there was a surprise waiting for them, and now their screeches of pain began in
earnest.

He and Amber had left dozens of sharpened stakes in the
wet earth, the tips fire hardened in his kiln and buried at ran-

dom. Even as he watched, the closest viper reared back, yanking a sliver of wood from the ground with its impaled hand. Its motions were mimicked up and down the line, but still more passed through the field of spikes unhindered, breaking up the stampede and turning the single wave into a staggered flow of monsters.

Two more salvos followed before the first of them reached the shadows of the walls, a half dozen of the fastest that had escaped their stake field. There, Cade and Amber had left far larger stakes, packed close enough that they were almost like a second wall. These were not so effective. Most of the vipers just maneuvered around the loosely spaced wall, while others yanked them out and trampled over them. Still, it bought the defenders precious seconds. Many vipers were limping behind, and the death count was close to a dozen.

The sling stone attack continued, but the slowing of the creatures came with its own disadvantages—the vipers were now scattered along the canyon, far harder to hit than the roiling crowd they had formed earlier.

And despite the group's efforts, the first of the creatures had arrived at the wall's base, crawling through the wet trench with hisses of apparent pleasure. Clearly, their time spent in the heat had not been pleasant for them, buying Cade a few more precious seconds as the monsters slithered around in the trenches like pigs in mud.

But whatever instinct was driving the monsters to attack soon outweighed the pleasures of the trench, and now the first of the monsters dug its claws into the wall, just beneath Cade, squalling encouragement to those around it.

More followed, and the vipers wasted no time in climbing. Cade could do nothing but watch as their claws hooked deep into the crumbling mortar, giving them ample purchase as they scrabbled upward.

"Throw, then ready swords," Cade bellowed, hurling a final stone at an injured viper below. To his surprise, it struck home, and even over the yowling of the attackers, he heard the beast's collarbone break with an audible snap.

Letting the rope fall from his fingers, he gripped his sword two handed and stared at the scattered vipers climbing the length of the walls.

"Not yet," he whispered, looking at the boulders resting on the parapet in front of him.

His strategy of slowing the vipers was working against him, for half the vipers were straggling, picking their way through the minefield of stakes. He needed them massed for his next move. Even so, there were plenty gathered beneath the wall, with more joining every second. It would have to be enough.

The first viper, a scarred creature with snaggled teeth, was directly below. The monster gained a foot each time it leaped and backslid, frantic to get at him. Cade took one more look at it, quelling the nausea that swirled in his stomach. He could smell its animal stench and see its needle teeth glistening. It was time.

"Rocks," he bellowed, tipping a beach ball–sized boulder over the rampart.

It tumbled down, dislodging mortar on its way, before connecting with the lead viper and knocking it into the crowd.

The stone thudded on top of it with a crackle of breaking bones. All along the wall, similar scenes were taking place as the others pushed theirs down. But still the vipers climbed, if anything more frantic in their desire to get at the human flesh above.

Cade had hoped to be methodical with the rocks, but now the entire breadth of the wall was being swarmed by the monstrosities. He pushed down another stone, and another, barely looking as he frantically tipped those that remained over the top.

Only a few were as effective as the first, but these still made their mark. With each falling viper, those behind it cascaded in turn. But some clung doggedly on, enduring the rocks that loosened their teeth and bloodied their taut-skinned faces.

Soon there was no rubble left. By now, most of the vipers had edged their way across the bone fields, until almost all who remained were massed beneath them.

Cade forced a grim smile and raised a clenched fist. Along the wall, the others waited for his signal, tugging the lids from their bowls. Cade did the same, waiting to tip it forward. He peered over the edge, and the black globes of eyes fixated hungrily on him. He could hear the gurgle of their breathing now. Still he kept his arm outstretched.

"Almost," he whispered to himself. "Almost."

The first viper's claw hooked over the wall, and it warbled a long, triumphant howl. Cade dropped his fist and flung the bowl into the empty space.

White powder billowed like smoke. It had seemed a pitiful amount in the bowls, but once it hit the air it turned into a dust plume that drifted wide and settled on the crowds below, if not as far or as thickly as Cade had hoped.

There was little time to see the results though, for a howling beast was dragging itself over the edge. Cade took his sword and stabbed down, the blade grating as it slipped through its nasal passage and deep into its throat.

Blood sprayed, hot and caustic. He watched the viper fall, taking others with it. But the wall was wide on either side of him, and now others were cresting the top. Cade chopped down, his blade clanging on the rampart as it severed a reaching claw.

The beast jerked away, and Cade spun as another mounted the parapet behind him. He swung in a wide arc, slicing through its shoulder and deep into its chest. It tipped over, and Cade almost lost his blade, managing to yank it free with a grunt.

Beside him, Amber yelled in anger as a body tumbled from the wall, hitting the churned ground beneath with a wet slap. Her sword went with it, trapped in the beast's skull, but Amber was swift to heft her axe from the ground beside her and chop down at her next opponent.

The others were holding their own too, though he could barely snatch more than a glance before stabbing down at another viper vaulting the parapet. It was then that he heard the squealing, so loud it hurt his ears. He risked a glimpse over the wall, ignoring a third viper scrambling up on his right.

Beneath, he saw the creatures below pawing at their eyes, their long tongues roaming their dust-encrusted faces. Others were choking and dry heaving, the caustic powder deep in their throats and lungs.

Not all had been incapacitated though, especially those who were farthest back. Fortunately, many of these specimens were the ones who had lingered, the injured and the cowardly. But still the horde climbed, even as their very bodies sizzled. Blinded and breathless, the sightless specimens continued by touch and sound alone.

Cade pivoted and stabbed at the newly arrived viper on his right, but the creature skittered out of reach. He heard the scrape of claws behind him, but he dared not turn his back. Sandwiched between two opponents, he could only charge forward, skewering the viper through the chest. He was rewarded with a rake across his forearms for his trouble, a parting gift from the dying creature.

The pain of it almost made him drop the sword, but he gritted his teeth and kicked the corpse from his blade.

He turned, only to see two more vipers dragging themselves up behind the first. Beyond, Amber was in a worse situation, forced back to the precarious edge of the inner rampart as vipers surrounded her.

Already?

Cade's heart fell, realization hitting him like a punch to the gut.

The walls had fallen.

CHAPTER
48

"RETREAT!" CADE YELLED, TURNING AND RUNNING FOR Quintus. "Back to the keep!"

The defenders sprinted for the nearest stairways, and Cade grabbed the legionary by the arm. Four corpses lay beside the boy, and Cade had to pull hard before Quintus allowed himself to be dragged away. He screamed hoarsely at the monsters, still stabbing his gladius as more of them crested the wall.

Hearts pounding, they leaped down the steps two at a time until they reached the ground below. Behind, the creatures yowled in triumph . . . and the sky suddenly darkened. Cade collapsed as a weight fell onto his back. Claws raked deep, then Quintus's blade swung from above and Eric's strong hand dragged him over the cobbles. In shock, Cade could only scrabble backward until Eric hurled him bodily through the open doorway of the keep.

But not all had made it so easily. Still more vipers leaped from above, collapsing the knees of the retreating defenders. Spex fell beneath a duo of leaping beasts, but Jim dragged him up after two swift chops of his sword, throwing the injured boy's arm over his shoulder.

Close by, Amber decapitated another that had the meat of Bea's shoulders in its teeth. She shoved the girl on, and Cade could see the monsters closing on the two retreating pairs, with the others not far ahead of them.

Cade struggled to his feet, shouting, but Eric placed a hand on Cade's chest. For the briefest of moments, their eyes met, and Cade saw the intent in his friend's eyes. Then he pushed, and Cade sprawled on his back, Eric sprinting back into the court-yard filled with vipers.

Eric charged toward the pursuing monsters, roaring a challenge, and now the flood changed direction, abandoning their pursuit of the injured defenders for the approaching foe. Cade tried to follow but was blocked as the survivors stumbled through the doorway, saved by the distraction.

He could only watch as the boy was surrounded, vipers swarming him. Eric's blade rose and fell, ignoring the swiping claws and snapping teeth that latched onto his limbs. Despite his great strength, he collapsed to his knees and disappeared beneath the swarm.

"Eric!" Cade screamed, watching as the creatures piled on top of him. Then his view was blocked, the others shoving the heavy projector across the entrance.

The windows had been barricaded with benches, beds, and tables, but the doorway had been left clear for their retreat.

Now the survivors shored up the makeshift barrier of the projector with benches and tables, until the way was piled high with wood.

It was not a moment too soon. On the other side, the beasts scratched and clawed, but Cade sated his fury by plunging his sword between the gaps in the barricade. He relished the satisfying resistance of flesh with each jab, until the creatures backed away, screeching their hatred. Soon Cade was stabbing at empty air, cursing bitterly in the gloom.

The survivors stood in silence, adjusting to the darkness. The interior was ill lit, the only source of light from four crackling torches ensconced in the walls of the atrium. Only then did Cade see the two boys, lying next to each other beside the entrance. And the blood pooling between them.

Spex and Jim.

He rushed over, ripping at their clothing to staunch the wounds. But already he could see it was too late. There were deep claw punctures in Jim's chest. Too deep. Still, he smiled at Cade, even as his eyes began to glaze over.

"I saved him," Jim spluttered, blood staining his teeth.

Spex pulled himself up and turned to the injured boy, desperately trying to stem the flow of blood. Cade didn't have the heart to tell Spex it was too late. Instead, he knelt beside them, barely cognizant of the others gathered behind him.

"Yes, you did, Jim," Spex said softly. "You saved me."

Jim's eyelashes fluttered, his breath rattling in his throat. Cade went to take his hand, but before he could, he saw Spex's bloodied fingers close over Jim's. Jim stared blindly above, clutching Spex's hand like a lifeline.

Spex held onto Jim, even after the boy's arm fell limp. Moments later, Jim passed, a peaceful smile on his face. Cade choked, and closed Jim's eyes with a trembling hand. Then, almost as if by some unheard signal, the creatures outside began to howl.

Cade wiped away bitter tears, turning his mind to the task at hand. It wasn't over yet—not by a long shot.

"Whoever's not wounded, go check the other barricades," Cade said, unable to take his eyes from Jim's face.

He heard the patter of feet, the others rushing at his order. When he finally pulled himself away, leaving Spex beside the body, he saw only Bea was there, tightening a bandage around her injured shoulder.

"Is it bad?" Cade asked, shrugging his arm free of his shirt to bare his own wounded back.

Bea kneeled beside him and peered at his wound, then inspected both his wrists where the claws had raked them earlier.

"Not too deep," the girl said, "but they got you good. Here, let me wash them."

Cade gritted his teeth as the girl poured water over his wounds, then again as a swathe of cloth was pressed over them and tied in place around his back and wrists.

"You're pretty good at that," Cade said.

"I did a first aid course back at school," Bea said. "Never thought I'd have to use it so soon."

"Lucky us," Cade said.

In dribs and drabs, the others returned, the barricades secure for now.

To Cade's surprise, everyone was wounded, just not so badly that they had felt they needed to stay behind. Spex's back had been raked terribly, and Yoshi had sustained a bite to his thigh—a red ring of uneven punctures that Bea dabbed at with a cloth. Most had lacerations on their wrists and arms. None had escaped entirely unscathed, and Bea had taken on the role of medic, bandaging them and leaving Cade to stare at the moving shadows through the gaps of their makeshift stockade.

He shrugged his shirt back on and stood, swaying a little. It hurt, but he was still in the fight.

The crash of vipers attacking the window barricades in the barracks sounded, and Trix and Grace rushed to repulse them. The sound of battered wood was replaced with yowls of pain. Soon enough, the noise stopped.

For a moment the world was quiet, and Cade could hear only the patter of claws on the cobbles outside.

He took a deep breath, waiting for the next attack. Then the baying of the monsters outside began once more, rising louder and louder. It seemed they were keeping their distance for now.

The survivors looked at one another, but none dared to say a word.

They were trapped.

CHAPTER
49

THEY MUST HAVE KILLED THIRTY VIPERS IN ALL AND INJURED many more. But as the hisses from outside continued, Cade felt little triumph. There was no telling how long the monsters would remain there, and they were in a far worse position than before. Still, he used the time to recover his faculties and plan their next move.

He drank long and deep and scarfed down the fruit they had gathered earlier from the mountaintop. They had planned for this retreat, preparing the bandages, water, and food earlier. But there was only enough for a few days. If it came to a prolonged siege, they would starve eventually.

It seemed obvious now. But there just hadn't been time to predict what might happen; the retreat to the keep had seemed a last resort. How could he have known?

Now he sat in silence with the remaining defenders, hoping the creatures would give up. It was hot inside, made worse by the crackling torches. With the barricades blocking the windows and doors, their only other light source was the moonlight that filtered through the gaps.

They had dragged Jim farther into the atrium and covered him with the sackcloths from the barracks. It was a poor resting place for the courageous boy, but far better than what was transpiring outside. In the minutes that followed, they could hear the beasts feasting on Eric's remains and see their heads jerking over the prone body through the barricade's cracks.

It was going to be a long night . . . if they lasted that long. Only Scott, Amber, and Quintus were with him. Grace and Yoshi protected the barracks and storeroom barricades respectively, with the twins Bea and Trix on the second floor, and Spex and Gobbler manning the windows up top.

It was the second and third floors where the barricades were weakest, with the wooden bed and table in each room laid across their openings. Despite this, Cade hoped the creatures would have a harder time breaking in while clinging to the sides of the building.

Earlier they had heard the scrabbling of claws along the walls, and the screeches of anger as the defenders above stabbed at the vipers trying to get in. Ten minutes later and the beasts had quieted, their vocalizations reduced to a low murmur. It was almost as if they were talking, but Cade thought it was more an expression of emotion than anything else. It certainly sounded angry.

"You think they'll leave?" Scott whispered, breaking the quiet. "Maybe they'll head for the jungle. Let the dinosaurs have 'em."

"There's something drawing them to this place," Cade said, shaking his head. "And we're an obvious food source. They won't give up so easy."

"Do we have to kill all of them?" Amber asked.

He turned to the Codex and looked at it expectantly.

"Victory conditions are determined by the Strategos," it intoned. *"The Strategos's judgment is final."*

"There's that damn word again," Scott muttered.

"If they run away, we win," Cade said, speaking with far more confidence than he felt. "So let's give them such a hard time, they do."

Amber sighed. "I think—"

But Cade didn't get to hear what Amber thought. There was a crash from above, followed by a garbled shout from Gobbler. More yells followed, and Cade made out a single word.

"Help!"

Cade ran, his back flaring with pain as he jumped up the stairs. Footsteps smacked behind him, but he didn't look back. Already he could hear screams.

"Hold on!" he yelled, charging past the second floor, where the twins stayed in place, defending the windows from vipers that were suddenly on the attack.

He burst into the main chamber above, and took in the scene in one frantic glance.

The vipers had come in through the roof. Shattered tiles lay across the floor, while viper after viper poured in from a jagged hole above. Spex stood on the table beneath, swinging his sword and bleeding from a dozen wounds.

More vipers poured in from the two chambers on either side, the barricades broken. Gobbler's body lay in one of the doorways, a bloody, ragged parody of its former self. Vipers surrounded him, clogging up the entryway. They looked up at Cade with bloodied faces before turning back to gorge once more.

"My god," Cade breathed.

Vipers circled the table, ignoring Cade. They could smell Spex's blood, snorting through their piggish nostrils. Even as Cade watched, one leaped onto Spex's back. Yelling, Spex pulled it off and stabbed down, twisting his blade through its skull. Another leaped, skittering along the table as it slashed his leg.

He fell to one knee, groaning like a wounded bull. The vipers edged closer, sensing victory.

Cade raised his sword, but Spex held up a hand. He gave Cade a grim smile.

"Go below, Cade," he said, staggering to his feet. "Win this."

Cade forced down the hot rage inside him and gave him a single nod.

"Come on!" Spex roared, charging.

He barreled through the vipers and leaped from the table, landing among the creatures massed on Gobbler's body. He swung his blade like a baseball bat, cleaving left and right.

Vipers fell beneath his sword, distracted by the flesh at their feet. But it was not long before they swarmed. Claws tore Spex's body, and teeth closed around his neck, yet still he fought on, screaming with anger.

Then Cade was dragged away, down the stairs. Amber and Quintus had followed him.

"Trix, Bea, follow us," Amber yelled, helping Quintus pull Cade to the second floor.

"Let me go!" Cade yelled.

"Don't let him die for nothing," Amber hissed, manhandling him to the next set of stairs.

Above, Spex's cries grew weaker, and Cade could hardly think of what to do. The barracks had a stone ceiling, but it was no more than a thin barrier between the viper-filled chambers on the upper floors. The vipers would break through that eventually, attack from above. It was the same for the storage room.

That left them one option.

"On me," Cade yelled, running down the stairs. "Everyone on me!"

Spex went silent, and the screeches of triumph above told him they had seconds to spare.

"Hurry," Cade cried as Grace and Yoshi sprinted into the atrium. Already the entrance's barricade was shaking, and a clawed fist erupted through splintering wood. The entire horde would be pouring in any second. Sixty or more of the murderous, savage creatures.

"Follow me," he snarled, snatching a torch from the wall. He had never felt such rage.

He hastened for the broad staircase at the very end of the chamber, the others following at a run. Howls echoed behind him as he sprinted down the stairs, almost falling in his hurry but catching himself at the bottom, his heart thundering in his chest, breath coming thick and fast.

Thinking quickly, he lit the torches on either side of the stairway, giving them two pools of light to see in. The panting survivors arranged themselves in a row on either side of him, listening to the sounds above. The top of the stairs was dark, but Cade could hear the vipers there, gathering their courage to charge.

"We take as many of them as we can," Cade said. "Don't take a step back. If they surround us, we're finished."

The defenders pressed in, standing a foot apart in a ring around the stairwell.

Just eight of us. Have we really lost so many?

Behind them, Cade could hear the rush of water of the underground river. He turned, looking to the dark, flowing water, the bathing pool, and the latrines behind it. Too open. The stairwell was where they would fight.

Cade took a deep breath, and the Codex floated beside him, its implacable, silent gaze fixed on all of them.

"I hope your goddamned Strategos is watching," he growled.

He hurled his torch up the steps, revealing the massed creatures above. Their bodies were covered in burns, many of them milky-eyed from the quicklime, others breathing hoarsely. Some even skittered back from the flames, fearful.

But behind, more creatures pressed in, shoving the frontrunners down. A larger, scarred specimen leaped forward, stamping at the torch with its claw. The flame sputtered and died, leaving the viper crouched in the shadows. It threw back its head and caterwauled in triumph.

At that, they came in a howling, screeching wave.

Too fast.

The horde tumbled down the stairs in a frantic scramble, tripping over one another and crashing at the bottom in a tangle of limbs. Cade swung once, twice, barely seeing what he was hitting as he chopped over and over into the massed bodies.

Corpses littered the stairwell as the other defenders closed in, casting red ribbons of blood as the swords rose and fell. The injured vipers clambered back and were trampled in turn by those behind them. On the vipers came, crawling over their own dead, and Cade screamed his hatred, stabbing, kicking, and spitting with wild abandon.

He never saw it coming. One leaped from the stairs above, grappling him to the floor. Its face split open, mouth gaping wide as it went for his head. Cade craned back, even as the needle points lunged for him.

Amber's axehead darted between them, the teeth clashing on the steel. The stench of carrion made him gag, the viper's saliva dripping as its fangs scraped across his nose. Then a boot kicked the viper's head aside, and Amber lifted Cade to his feet. Quintus finished the stunned creature with a stab through the chest.

Dazed, Cade staggered forward and rejoined the battle. Still the monsters charged, choking the stairwell in a mass of red-brown bodies. But these were the injured and the blind, those that had been too slow to join the first wave. They were more hesitant, reluctant to get in range of the jabbing, slicing blades.

With fewer coming over the veritable wall of corpses, the defenders finished off the wounded, stabbing down before they could crawl back to their brethren. Cade stared at the creatures above. There were as many as thirty there, but none looked so confident as they had before.

They were on the brink. He could sense it.

"We take the fight to them," Cade called hoarsely. "With me. Now!"

They charged, leaping over the bodies, clambering one-handed toward the monsters above. Cade was the first up, and he stabbed his sword like a spear, sending the creatures scrabbling back. He staggered to his feet, only to be slammed down to his knees as a viper leaped onto his shoulders. He threw it off, but not before a claw sliced him across the forehead. Half-blinded by blood, Cade fought on, cutting the beast from shoulder to sternum and pushing it off his blade with a bellow of anger.

Then Amber and Quintus were beside him, their swinging blades punching through flesh and bone. The vipers scrambled back, and now even those at the top of the stairwell backed away. Cade staggered toward them, and the second torch arced over his head, landing among them.

"How do you like that?" Grace yelled.

The monsters hissed with fear, backing away from the light.

"Come on!" Cade shouted.

He staggered onward, slipping in the pooling blood. Scott and Yoshi overtook him, yelling wordlessly. The world was a haze of pain and exhaustion, but Cade forced himself to keep going. Amber lifted him by the collar, keeping him on his feet. Leaning against each other like drunk sailors, they limped up the final steps.

But when they reached the top, there were no vipers to greet them. Only bloodied claw prints on the ground, and the sound of receding screeches outside.

Cade fell to his knees, letting his sword clatter to the floor. And then, out of the gloom behind him, the Codex spoke.

"*Congratulations,*" it said. "*You have won.*"

CHAPTER
50

CADE STARED AT THE CEILING, LYING ON THE MAKESHIFT BED of the commander's room. It was the only one that had survived the battle, and now he was sprawled on the musty, straw-filled mattress, waiting for the feeling of relief to come. Only, it never did.

It was hours later now, with the early sun blushing the horizon. The room was cast in darkness, and both Gobbler's and Spex's blood still stained the floor in the doorway. The dead vipers had been hurled out the window. Their corpses would be burned later.

He grieved for his companions. He had felt guilt before—when he'd accidentally offended someone or had lied to his parents. This was different. People had died because of him.

Because he'd *chosen* to believe the Codex. Because he convinced them to fight. Convinced them to die for a cause they didn't even know was real or not. Of the six schoolboys who had fought alongside him, now only two remained. Four dead, and it was all his fault. Some small comfort was that the girls had escaped unscathed . . . though that was a loose definition of the word. He was glad of that.

The others were outside, burying their friends. They'd chosen to do it on the mountaintop, but Cade hadn't had the strength for the climb, blood loss and exhaustion having taken their toll. So they'd left him to rest, and Quintus on the wall, watching in case the retreating vipers returned.

Cade doubted they'd be back. He and the others had won. The Codex had said so.

He stared at the drone now as it hovered silently in the center of the room. It had saved him plenty of times, yet he hated it. Even if it was just a tool. Was it his tool . . . or theirs?

"Codex," Cade croaked. "Come here."

The drone zoomed over, hovering just beside his head. He scooted back, sitting up with his back against the wall. For a moment, he felt a twinge of guilt for asking it questions while the others weren't there. They had just as much right to hear this as he did. But he couldn't wait.

Now that they had won, the Codex would answer his questions. It had said so.

"I want to know why we're here," he said.

Silence.

The Codex seemed to observe him.

"Answer prohibited."

Cade stared at it in disbelief.

"Are you kidding me?" he said, stabbing his finger at the bloodied floor. "After everything we've done?"

The Codex turned away from him, pointing toward the darkness of the corner.

Cade growled under his breath.

"How dare you?" he yelled, ignoring the pain in his hoarse throat. "You two-faced—"

"My my," came a voice. "You *do* have a temper. Forgive my little joke."

Cade stared. There was a figure there, standing in the gloom. Even as he watched, he could see the faintest blue glow surrounding it. A projection from the Codex.

"Show yourself," Cade growled.

The figure stepped out from the shadows, and Cade's eyes widened in disbelief.

A little girl. Complete in a pinafore dress, with chocolate ringlets surrounding cherubic, blushing cheeks. She skipped toward him, and Cade scrambled back in horror. Somewhere behind her innocent blue eyes lay something else.

Something . . . wrong.

She curtsied primly, her eyes never leaving his face.

"Don't worry, Cade," she said, smiling sweetly. "I wouldn't hurt you. After all, we're going to have such *fun* together."

She frowned at Cade's expression, then pouted, sticking out her bottom lip in a parody of sulking.

"You don't like it?" she asked, patting her hair and curt-sying. As she did so, her brown tresses changed to Goldilocks blond.

"I made her just for you. She's supposed to put you at ease."

"Who are you?" Cade managed. Whatever this apparition

was, it was doing just the opposite. His heart was pounding, mouth so dry he could hardly speak.

The girl sat on the edge of the bed, kicking her heels. She wore dainty little slippers with buckles on the tops.

"The first men I brought here called me Abaddon," she sighed, almost nostalgically. "They called this place Abaddon too. But I've had many names."

Abaddon turned her head and smiled at him. Or he supposed, *their* head. It helped to remember that it was not a little girl speaking to him at all.

"But I suppose that's not what you really mean," Abaddon said.

Cade found his voice.

"You're damned right it's not," he whispered.

Abaddon clapped the girl's hands and gave a tinkling laugh. They crawled onto the bed, but the mattress didn't move beneath the girl's weight. It gave Cade some courage, knowing the being wasn't really there.

"It's been a while since I could talk in such terms," Abaddon giggled. "The Roman contenders were getting *so* boring. Gods this and gods that. Worship is a tedious thing. This is better."

Cade lifted his chin and met Abaddon's gaze.

"Tell me," he said.

The girl's smile widened. Abaddon laid the girl's hand upon his, and Cade's hairs stood on end as a static fuzz settled on his skin.

"We were the first," Abaddon said. "The first life, seven billion years ago, formed in the primordial soup of the universe. Before your little planet was even dreamed of, my species transcended mortality. Transcended sustenance, transcended *need*. I am older than your sun. Can you imagine such a thing?"

Cade shook his head, even as understanding cascaded over him. It was an ancient, alien thing. He could almost see it behind those wide eyes. As if those billions of years had chipped away at its soul to leave a withered husk in its place. There was no kindness there.

"Of course, immortality has its price," Abaddon said. "Without death, we and others like us might have spread like a virus across the universe. Eaten it away, left it empty. There was only one solution. Will you guess what it was, Cade?"

He had no answer.

"We made ourselves, and the universe, barren. Infertile. No children for us, nor rivaled life to infect or supplant us. A terrible price to pay, foisted on us by our foolish leaders. And then we lived on. Drifting through time."

"What then?" Cade demanded. "What does that have to do with any of this?"

The facade of innocence disappeared in an instant.

"Patience, child," Abaddon snapped, the angelic face twisting in a rictus of anger. "You asked who I am, and so I answer. Remember your place, or I shall erase your very atoms from existence."

Cade fell silent, and the girl's expression switched back to its friendly mask. Cade sensed it then. Abaddon was unhinged.

"Death is a sweet release. Or at least many of us thought so. We killed ourselves, to end the endlessness. It was an epidemic, culling our species over the millennia. Boredom is a terrible thing. It destroys the mind."

It was macabre to hear a child speaking in such a way. Cade felt sick.

"Five billion years ago, the last of us met. Twenty-one. All that remained of our great species, once numbering in the billions. All that remained of life. Something had to change."

Now they were getting somewhere. Despite himself, Cade leaned forward.

"It was decided we *would* have children. Of a sort. Each of us was given permission to seed a single planet with life. To watch it grow, nurture it. Something to give us purpose. To entertain."

Abaddon sat back and tossed the girl's ringlets.

"Don't you see?" they laughed. "I made you. The Romans were right, in a way. I *am* your god."

Cade's head spun with the horror of it.

"But that wasn't enough. Does a man not bore of watching the ants? And does he not desire the spirit of competition among his peers?"

Abaddon smiled sweetly, and now Cade could see the insanity in the ancient being's eyes.

"So we made this world. Took specimens from our respective planets and gave them each a piece of it. The Romans called this world *Acies*, and named the other members of my species the *pantheon*. Quite apt, don't you think?"

"And how did the Romans get here?" Cade demanded. "How is Quintus here? Can you control time itself?"

Abaddon giggled.

"No, silly goose. I have gathered countless specimens from your planet since life first formed upon it. Some of them are brought here immediately, as I did with you and your friends. Others we keep . . . how might you understand it? On ice?"

Cade didn't understand. Abaddon gave him a sympathetic smile and spoke slowly, as if to a child.

"Those girls you found, I have kept them frozen for decades, only to release them a few days ago. I had expected to watch them get eaten, so it was *such fun* to see you run into them."

The little girl paused and Abaddon clapped her little hands.

"*Bravo*, by the way. A fine trick, convincing them to join you. I'm not sure you would have won otherwise."

"So you don't move people back and forth in time," Cade said, trying to understand. "You just . . . store them and wait . . . until you want to put them in the game?"

"I forget how clever you humans have become," Abaddon said, letting out a soft sigh. "Indeed. I like to leave little surprises from my collection in the caldera for my contenders. People. Tools. Artifacts. Whatever I want, be it useful to them or not. Think of this place as my garden, for me to populate and decorate as I wish. It adds an interesting component to the game, don't you think?"

Cade thought back to the Olmec head and the Mayan city. Interesting . . . well, that was one word for it.

"The animals you encountered in the jungle are just a few of the menagerie I keep at my disposal—the earth has given me many children to play with over the mega-annums. And of course, more recently, I have had plenty of humans to call upon too."

Abaddon peered out the window as if to make the girl examine Quintus standing guard on the wall.

"Your friend, Quintus, had been on ice for almost a thousand years before the older Romans summoned his legion from where I had stored them. The Romans have been my contenders for the longest of times."

Abaddon paused, a bemused smile on their face.

"Of course, they're almost all dead now. That's why I brought you to replace them."

But Cade was still trying to understand the last thing Abaddon had said.

"Wait, these Romans . . . summoned Quintus and the Ninth Legion?" Cade asked. "You mean they asked you to . . . unfreeze them? Why?"

"For the game, of course. *The* game. Life is conflict, you see, and this place is a celebration of it. But you've made me get ahead of myself. Naughty boy."

Abaddon made the girl wag a dainty finger at him.

"It's a simple game, really. We have a leaderboard, and each planet's representatives, or contenders as I call them, must fight one another to move their planet up and down it. Fall low enough on the leaderboard and your world is destroyed— we developed weapons capable of doing so before your planet even existed."

Cade closed his eyes, letting the truth of it sink in. This was madness. Madness.

"And if we top it?" Cade breathed.

"Move to the top, and we might send the current contenders back home. Of course, you're far off from that—you're almost at the bottom!"

Abaddon giggled.

"But let's save the rules of the game for our next little chat."

Cade felt sick. The horror of the situation was suffocating.

"And the vipers?" Cade asked, choking back the nausea. "Were they from a rival planet?"

"Oh, you *are* a curious one," Abaddon said, clapping their hands gleefully. "I chose my new contenders well. But then, I know I have. I've been watching you for a long time."

Cade stared at the little girl. How much did Abaddon know about him? About the others?

Abaddon's expression changed, and then they sighed wistfully.

"No, the vipers are what's left of the creatures from my first planet, before they fell too low on the leaderboard and I was forced to wipe the life from it. My previous experiment was a failure, but I kept some of the specimens to play with."

"You seeded another planet? Before Earth?" Cade asked.

"You know it as Mars. Earth is my second attempt."

Cade could hardly believe what he was hearing. It was like some sick joke.

"I thought I'd design a qualifying round, just for fun. Test your mettle. You haven't played the *real* game yet. My fellow members and I are eager to put my new contenders to the test."

"Fun?" Cade spat. "Nothing about this game is fun. My friends died in front of my eyes."

Abaddon blinked innocently at him.

"But you do want to go home, don't you?"

Cade had never felt so angry. Abaddon had chosen their avatar well. To them, Cade was nothing but a spoiled child's plaything. A toy to be tossed aside when something better came along.

"You're a monster," he said.

Abaddon laughed.

"Does a farmer care if his cattle see him so?"

"We're not cattle," Cade said, pressing his palm against his chest. "We're thinking, feeling beings."

"Your intellect is to mine as yours is to a plant," Abaddon replied, the sweet smile on the girl's face belying the cruelty behind it. "Conversing with you is like playing chess with an amoeba. You are less than cattle to me. Less than bacteria. Thinking beings? You don't know what a thinking being is."

"So it's all relative, right?" Cade asked bitterly.

"Good," Abaddon said, smiling prettily at him. "You understand."

Cade glared at them, speechless with rage. He had never known such anger. There was nothing he could do about this. Abaddon held all the cards. Could kill him with a click of the little girl's fingers. He was at Abaddon's mercy, and it seemed the alien had none to spare.

The girl jumped off the bed.

"It's time," Abaddon said in a singsong voice, pirouetting like a ballerina.

"Time for what?" Cade asked.

"To play, of course," Abaddon said.

A timer appeared above the girl's head, slowly counting down. Then, just like that, Abaddon was no longer there. Cade was alone in the room, staring into the gloom. The Codex floated up to Cade's face.

"Rest well, Cade," came Abaddon's voice. "The game is just beginning."

ACKNOWLEDGMENTS

There have been a great many people who I owe a debt of gratitude for their contribution to the creation and publication of *The Chosen*.

I would like to thank my UK agent, Juliet Mushens, for all her hard work, teaming up with many amazing publishers around the world. She has been my guiding light throughout the entire process and my life would not be the same without her.

Thank you to the publishing teams at Feiwel and Friends and Hodder Childrens for helping bring a beautiful book to as many readers as possible. They have done fantastic work and have stuck with me from start to finish. In particular, I would like to thank:

Jean Feiwel, Emily Settle, Liz Szabla, Patrick Collins, Kim Waymer, Melinda Ackell, Alexei Esikoff, Julia Gardiner, Mariel Dawson, Kathleen Breitenfeld, Katie Quinn, Morgan Dubin, Katie Halata, Emma Goldhawk, Naomi Greenwood, Samantha Swinnerton, Sarah Lambert, Tig Wallace, Michelle Brackenborough, Naomi Berwin, Sarah Jeffcoate, Ruth Girmatsion, and Nic Goode.

I would like to thank my friends and family for their ongoing support, guidance, and patience. Vic James, Sasha Alsberg, Dominic Wong, Michael Miller, Brook Aspden, as well as Liege, Jay, Sindri, and Raj Matharu, you guys rock.

Finally, thank you, the readers, for all you have done. Your comments, reviews messages, and encouragement have meant the world to me. It is ultimately you that made me a success, and you that keep me writing. I will be forever astonished, honored and grateful for your support.

Thank you.

TARAN MATHARU

GOFISH

TARAN MATHARU

©Sally Felton

What did you want to be when you grew up?
Definitely an author. Although, for a brief while, I also wanted to be an archaeologist—I grew up living near the Natural History Museum in London and it's still one of my favorite places in the world.

When did you realize you wanted to be a writer?
I think it was when I first started reading. In fact, it was probably even earlier than that, as I used to listen to books on tape before I went to sleep. I loved stories and wanted to tell my own. In fact, I started writing my first book at the age of nine.

What's your most embarrassing childhood memory?
Someone stole my trousers when I went swimming with my classmates. I had to walk back to school for twenty minutes in the middle of the day, with nothing but a towel wrapped around my waist.

What's your favorite childhood memory?
I once spent two weeks in the Amazon. I fished for piranha, swam in alligator-infested water, hung out with the local tribes,

and ate grubs for breakfast. It was a fantastic adventure and some of my experiences there are reflected in my writing.

As a young person, who did you look up to most?
I had a great deal of respect for my English teacher, a kind, good-humored man with a deep passion for literature. He once wrote on a piece of homework I did, "You are going to be a serious writer." It was inspiring.

What was your favorite thing about school?
Hanging out with friends, for sure. My favorite subjects were English and history.

What were your hobbies as a kid? What are your hobbies now?
I spent a lot of my childhood reading, writing, and playing video games. When I visited my family in Brazil, I would also go horseback riding in the countryside. These days, I still like to do all of those things, but I have also taken up fishing and travel.

Did you play sports as a kid?
I used to play rugby as a winger and I was a champion swimmer at the age of thirteen.

What was your first job, and what was your worst job?
My first job was probably my worst job, too. My employers didn't have much for me to do as I was doing unpaid work experience, so they found some incredibly old accounting files in a dusty drawer that hadn't been touched in years. They left a huge stack of files on my desk and told me to copy all of it onto a spreadsheet, on the off chance they might need to access them on a computer. The numbers were so small, I had to

use a magnifying glass to read them. I did this for two months, and I doubt they ever used the final spreadsheet. Worst. Job. Ever.

How did you celebrate publishing your first book?
My publicist sent me some champagne, so I popped that open and had a party with my family and close friends.

Where do you write your books?
I have an office where I live, but I use it more for doing boring administrative work like taxes and accounting. I wish I could say I write in my office, but I often find myself writing in bed. It's a bad habit and one I plan on breaking.

What did it feel like to become a Wattpad sensation? How did your interactions with users on Wattpad affect your experience writing *The Novice*?
It was surreal. I was backpacking in Australia at the time with very little access to the Internet, so I almost didn't realize how successful the book had become until I returned home. The feedback and encouragement from my readers was wonderful and it helped me write at a furious pace. I wrote the first half of *The Novice* in one month!

What was the best feedback you received from the Wattpad community?
Honestly, it was when people said I had inspired them to read more, or write their own books. I think reading and writing are so important, especially for young people.

What advice would you give to someone who is self-published, and looking to work with a traditional publisher?
It's important to remember that publishing is a business. Make sure you keep track of the size of your readership and how well

your book has been doing, so that publishers see you as a good proposition.

What challenges do you face in the writing process, and how do you overcome them?

I think motivation can be the hardest part of writing. Writing is such a solitary experience and often no one but you will read your work until it's finished. I would recommend sharing your writing with others, to get feedback and encouragement as you write.

What has been your favorite or most memorable experience with a fan?

There have been so many, it's quite hard to pick just one! Receiving messages from fans who have enjoyed and connected with my series is a daily occurrence, and it always makes my day. Some foreign fans say it helped them with their fluency in English. I have received messages from people who had given up on reading, but had their passion for it reignited after reading my books. Perhaps the most memorable message was from a man who was reading my book while his wife was having a difficult birth. He wasn't allowed in the emergency room and needed something to distract him. He told me the book had helped him get through one of the hardest moments of his life.

I absolutely love fan art and I tend to share it on my author social media if the artist lets me. There are also over forty-five fanfiction stories set in the Summoner universe on Wattpad, and I have read every single one of them! Something I find really cool is that there are several contributors to a Summoner wiki online, which I occasionally tweak and keep an eye on, myself. I feel really grateful to these guys. They take time out of their days to make my world more real. Meeting fans in person is my favorite thing; sometimes they even cosplay as Fletcher or Sylva when I meet them. One fan is making a board game to play with his friends, and others use my world for their D&D-style roleplaying adventures. Another fan is trying to build all of Hominum in Minecraft—a pretty tall order that I actually tried and gave up on, myself!

What is your favorite word?
My favorite word is *qi*, because it has won me many a game of Scrabble.

If you could live in any fictional world, what would it be?
I think it would probably be Harry Potter's world. But definitely after the events of the book series. . . . I wouldn't want to live in a world where Voldemort was still around!

Who is your favorite fictional character?
I think it has to be Spider-Man. He has a unique set of superpowers that really stand out, and he's very much an everyman who tries to do what's right.

What was your favorite book when you were a kid? Do you have a favorite book now?
For my favorite book as a kid, I'll cheat and name a series instead. It was the Redwall series by Brian Jacques, where anthropomorphic animals battle in an epic fantasy world. These days, I like to read more historical fiction. I love Wilbur Smith's *Birds of Prey*, a novel set in the seventeenth century about war and piracy along the wild coasts of Africa.

If you could travel in time, where would you go and what would you do?
I would probably be a bit of a tourist and watch all the major historical battles and events. More important, I would solve history's biggest mysteries, such as what happened to the Ninth Legion and who Jack the Ripper was. My book *The Chosen*

actually explores many of history's mysteries, especially those surrounding missing groups of people. It is this love for what we *don't* know about history that helped inspire that series.

What's the best advice you have ever received about writing?
To finish what you start. A completed novel is worth far more than an incomplete one.

What advice do you wish someone had given you when you were younger?
That writing is a viable career, if you take it seriously enough. I ended up studying business at university, which has helped me somewhat in my writing career, but I wish I had studied something I was passionate about instead, like creative writing.

Do you ever get writer's block? What do you do to get back on track?
Sometimes! I find there are a few tricks to start writing again.

1.   Set a daily target word count, so you have something to aim for.
2.   Make it public by telling your friends and family about the book, so you have the added pressure to finish it. It's kind of like telling your friends you're going to run a marathon.
3.   Find beta readers. It makes the experience more social and can be really encouraging! Joining writing groups or sharing on places like Wattpad are good ways of finding readers.
4.   Always make a start. Even on days you really don't feel like writing, tell yourself you'll just write one sentence. You will be surprised how often that one sentence will turn into an intense writing session.
5.   Don't edit—I know it sounds crazy, but you can really

get bogged down in the details and spend too much time tinkering. Do that later; finishing the book is more important.

6.   When you finish your writing session, stop midsentence. It's always easier to continue that way, allowing you to easily pick up where you left off the previous day. I also try to make a start on the next chapter when the writing juices are flowing. That way, I don't start my next session staring at a blank page.

7.   Plan ahead—sometimes you can write yourself into a corner and get stuck. Plotting the story can help avoid this trap.

8.   Have fun! If you find yourself becoming bored of your own story, you can trust that the readers will be, too. If this happens, change it up a bit. Add in an unexpected plot twist and see where it takes you.

What do you want readers to remember about your books?
I like to think my readers would learn something new, be it about survival techniques, prehistoric creatures that existed, or fascinating historical mysteries that as yet have no answer.

What would you do if you ever stopped writing?
I don't think that's possible. But I would probably try to start my own business.

If you were a superhero, what would your superpower be?
Immortality for sure. If you're immortal, you'll never die. Then I could save up and buy my superpowers like Batman.

What would your readers be most surprised to learn about you?

1.   I am originally half-Brazilian and half-Indian, but I was born and raised in London. I have visited both countries and I speak Portuguese very well.

2. I once saved my little sister from a rampaging hippo in Kenya. I picked her up and climbed up a wall before it reached us. I can still remember the sound of it snorting below us when we got to the top!

3. My first story was called "Wizswords," and I wrote it at nine years old. It was about a family of wizards and warriors who were in a constant battle with an evil witch called Widower. It also featured ant people who stood about an inch high and had an entire civilization of their own, riding bees, grasshoppers, and beetles and building their own tiny roads and houses.

4. I like to eat local foods when I travel. So far, I have eaten crocodile, kangaroo, llama, camel, alpaca, zebra, piranha, and firefly grub. Interestingly enough, I ate a piranha I caught myself, in the same water I had been swimming in a few minutes earlier!

THE FIRST BATTLE IS OVER,
BUT THE GAME IS JUST BEGINNING . . .

THE
CHALLENGER

CONTENDER—BOOK TWO

TARAN MATHARU
New York Times–Bestselling Author of the SUMMONER Series

KEEP READING FOR AN EXCERPT.

CHAPTER
1

THERE WAS BLOOD IN THE WATER. CADE HEAVED ON HIS FISH-
ing line, dismayed at the wriggling mass that churned
beneath the surface. His catch, a flat silver-bellied fish,
emerged half-eaten, flopping glassy-eyed to the shoreline of
the river.

It had been this way with every cast, the shoals of small
fish descending on any other that showed distress, stripping
flesh as it twisted on his line. Twice before, he had pulled in
little more than a skeleton, though even the scraps that hung
off the bone were worth keeping.

Still, the silver fish was prize enough for the hungry boy,
and there was no time for another cast. Beside him, Quintus
pointed at the sky, warning of the setting sun. Together, they
pushed their ragged haul into their wicker basket and stole
away into the undergrowth, keeping to the shadows.

It was a curse that the fish only began to rise at dusk,

when the insects descended. They whined about their heads, but Cade did not slap at them. By now, he could tell by their sound which insects would simply sup on the salty sweat on his skin, and which would sting him for the blood beneath. This time, there were few of the latter.

The boys caught sight of the waterfall not far along the river. It was always a risk, leaving the clearing beyond the keep. But their fruit-heavy diet was taking its toll. Cade's stomach churned at the sight of figs, and their attempts to trap the rodents that frequented the orchards on top of the mountain had not met with any success.

These same rodents were the reason for their unvaried meals, as they'd eaten up most of the ground vegetables the Romans had left behind. What was left, they had set aside, fenced off, and replanted for next season, painful as that had been. It amazed Cade how much food eight people could consume in such a short time, and now it was fruit, fruit, and more fruit.

Quintus caught his attention and spoke, giving him a thumbs-up at the same time.

"Good trip."

Cade smiled and nodded, still amazed at the boy's progress. Quintus's English had come along in leaps and bounds, and Cade had become used to his unique diction. Cade's Latin was returning too, swimming back from the recesses of his memory. In fact, all the contenders were practicing it, with Amber and the other girls already having studied it at school.

They'd had little to do in the two months since the battle. Two months of staring at the timer, waiting for the Codex to speak. No questions, cajoling, or even threats had succeeded in breaking its silence. It was the great weight that hung above them. That and the timer ticking down inexorably.

Relieved to be home, the pair hurried down the black tunnel that led them back to the keep. The fish stew they would have that night was one of the few things Cade had to look forward to. Yoshi had turned out to be an excellent cook, limited though he was by their paltry stock of ingredients.

"Any luck?" Amber called as they ducked out of the tunnel.

"Some," Cade said begrudgingly.

Amber sat alone, cross-legged upon the cobbles. The girl was prodding at their small communal fire, and Cade was again struck by how strange it seemed to see her in school uniform.

"Guys," Amber called. "They're back."

Cade set the basket down and grinned as the others emerged from the keep, their usual lethargy interrupted by the news of the fishermen's arrival.

"Wanna whip this up?" Cade asked Yoshi, seeing his friend rub his hands together at the sight of the wicker basket.

"You have no idea," Yoshi muttered. "Hand it over."

Without waiting for a response, the boy lifted each fish one by one, grimacing at the sorry state of the first pair; they were mostly skin and bone. Grace shook her head at the sight, but laid a hand on Yoshi's shoulder as the boy dropped them back in with disappointment.

"The bones are still good for a broth," Grace said. "My mum makes one that'll blow your socks off." She wrinkled her nose. "Shame we don't have any chili."

Yoshi nodded mournfully, but Scott rolled his eyes.

"I'd eat a week-old hot dog out of a wrestler's jockstrap if it meant an end to all these figs," he said. "Cook it however you want, just leave some for me."

"Gross," Bea muttered, and Trix gave the boy a glare.

The twins looked sickly pale, and not just from Scott's joke. They had all lost weight over the past two months, but then the twins had been slight to start with. It was another source of worry for Cade, though none had broached it with them.

The only silver lining was that the contenders had all been given time to heal from their wounds. Perhaps too much time. Cade stared up at the light from the windows of the top floor of the keep, where the Codex and its glowing timer had settled since his conversation with Abaddon.

The timer had begun at three months. And now, they had a little more than one left, ticking away like a bomb. Far, far more than they had been given before the qualifying round.

It scared Cade, this extra time. Scared everyone. As if they were supposed to be preparing. As if somehow, it would make up for the halving of their numbers. Four schoolgirls, three delinquents, and . . . Quintus.

Thank the heavens for Quintus. It was he who knew how to replant the crops, how to protect against the vermin. How to grind the wheat in a bowl to make flour pancakes. He had even brought down a pterosaur with his sling, though the wily creatures now knew to stay away.

So here they sat in limbo, waiting. Though for what, they didn't know. Only that it would be cruel, and violent, with unimaginable consequences.

Such thoughts were ever present at the back of Cade's mind, but now they swirled to the forefront as he watched his friends around the fire. He knew them now. Cared about them. Their two months of healing had been more than merely physical.

He knew the joyride that landed Scott in jail had been a cry for attention following his mother's death. Knew Grace prayed every night to the small crucifix around her neck. He learned Bea and Trix had never spent a night away from their parents. That Yoshi's greatest frustration was the keep's lack of music, while Amber's was the lack of chocolate.

His frustration mounting, Cade's feet moved unbidden to the keep. They carried him up the stairs, and he tried to forget the pooled blood and bodies that had once littered the floors, the sight of which had turned a safe home into nothing more than a shelter from the wind and rain.

He walked on past the empty rooms, to the round table at the very top. To the ominous glow of the timer, and the Codex that was its source. He stood, his fists clenched, as the numbers flashed and changed.

$$36{:}22{:}58{:}26$$
$$36{:}22{:}58{:}25$$
$$36{:}22{:}58{:}24$$

"Is this fun for you?" Cade asked. "Watching us scratch out an existence here?"

His voice felt strange in the empty room. Like he was talking to himself.

"Some game master you are," Cade said, layering his words with as much contempt as he could muster. "I'm sure it will be great fun to watch us all be butchered when our four months are up. Fun for you, and your so-called pantheon."

The Codex's lens stared back, silent and implacable. Cade plowed on.

"I bet they'll be super impressed with the eight half-starved teenagers you offer up as a challenge."

Something moved within the floating drone, so minutely it was almost imperceptible. A gear, twitching. A circuit sparking.

"I hate to think of all those remnants you left in the jungle. So carefully curated, selected from the very best of human history. Never to be used. Just to rust and rot once we're dead. We're the last, right? Nobody else will use them."

Nothing.

He tried again. "So this is Abaddon's swan song for Earth. Going out with a fizzle, not a bang. Eight trussed lambs, ready for the slaughter. I thought you would have something better planned."

Silence.

Cade tried not to let his frustration show. He turned, letting his anger dissolve into thoughts of fish stew.

Then . . . a voice.

"Do not presume to know my stratagem, foolish little child."

Cade's breath caught in his throat, his stomach twisting. Slowly, he turned, and jumped to see the Codex hovering before his face. The room, once bright with the timer's glow, now fell to darkness.

"Oh, come now, is this not what you wanted?" the voice said. "My attention? Be careful what you wish for, boy."

It was a deeper voice, rasping and cruel, not girlish like last time. But then, Abaddon's last form had been to put him at ease. That was no longer the intention.

"Call the others," Abaddon commanded. "It's time to play."

Don't miss the *New York Times*–
and *USA Today*–bestselling

SUMMONER

series

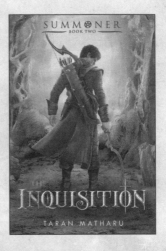